Seeking Sugar and Spice

Praise for Award-Winning, *Island of Miracles*

"A beautiful account of the love and healing support of community!"

Chandi Owen, Author

"I can already see the Hallmark Channel movie!"

Anne, Goodreads

Praise for Award-Winning, *Island of Promise*

"[Amy] draws you in to the lives of her characters…she paints the picture so eloquently it's almost like you are there.

Cindy, Amazon

"I love Amy Schisler's books. I cried tears of both sadness and joy while reading this. I read this book in a day!"

Mitzi Mead, Goodreads

Praise for *The Devil's Fortune*

"The Devil's Fortune is a beautifully written, atmospheric tale chock-full of adventure and secrets. It gripped me throughout and left me feeling satisfied in the end. Highly recommended!"

Carissa Ann Lynch, USA Today bestselling author of MY SISTER IS MISSING

"Schisler once again delivers on her unique ability to combine rich history with a brilliantly layered cast of characters. The lines of what was, what is, and what is yet to be are beautifully weaved within this tale of pirates, treasures, secrets, faith and love. Destiny awaits!"

Alexa Jacobs, Author & President, Maryland Romance Writers

Praise for Award-Winning, *Whispering Vines*

"The heartbreaking, endearing, charming, and romantic scenes will surely inveigle you to keep reading."

Serious Reading Book Review

"Schisler's writing is a verbal masterpiece of art."

Alexa Jacobs, Author & President of Maryland Romance Writers

Also Available by Amy Schisler

Novels

A Place to Call Home
Picture Me
Whispering Vines
Summer's Squall
The Devil's Fortune
The Good Wine

Chincoteague Island
Trilogy
Island of Miracles
Island of Promise
Island of Hope

Chincoteague Sunsets
Trilogy
Seeking Tranquility
Seeking Sugar and Spice

Buffalo River Series
*Desert Fire, Mountain
Rain*
Under the Summer Moon
Sapphires in Snow

Children's Books
Crabbing With Granddad
The Greatest Gift

Spiritual Books
A Devotional Alphabet
Meet the Saints from A-Z
Stations of the Cross
Meditations for Moms
(with Anne Kennedy,
Susan Anthony, Chandi
Owen, and Wendy Clark)

Seeking Sugar and Spice

By Amy Schisler

Copyright 2023 by Amy Schisler
Chesapeake Sunrise Publishing
Bozman, Maryland

Published by:
Chesapeake Sunrise Publishing
Amy Schisler
Bozman, MD
2023

Dedicated to my daughters who encourage me to follow
my dreams as I encourage them to follow theirs.

Prologue

"Aunt Meg, you can't do that. The entries aren't supposed to be tampered with once they're placed on the table."

"Hush, Ruth. I'm worried I didn't add enough of my secret ingredient, and I want to be sure this knocks the socks off the judges."

Meg tried to be inconspicuous as she tilted the flask toward the bowl of chili and poured in some more of her homemade whiskey. She hastily tucked it into her purse and jumped away from the table as the judges were led into the room.

Thirty minutes later, an argument broke out as the winners were announced for the forty-fifth annual Chincoteague Chili Cook-off to benefit the fire company.

"I've held this title for seventeen years," an older man cried out. "What do you mean Shelby Swann is the new champion?"

"That's my grandmother's prize-winning recipe. It won eight blue ribbons in the county fair back in Easton. Hers can't be better than this," a woman shouted from the back.

"What kind of experience do you judges have?" Meg, the woman with the flask, asked with indignation.

"My restaurant has been serving this for over twenty years. Locals and visitors alike tell me all the time that it's the best they've ever had."

Tucked into the corner of the room nearest to the exit, a man in a baseball cap and sunglasses stood surveying the chaos. The man's eyes twinkled behind the dark glasses. He pulled the cap farther down over his forehead and tugged at his wife's elbow.

"Let's go before things get out of hand. I've got a phone call to make to my manager."

"Oh no, not another one," his wife groaned as they made their way out onto the sidewalk.

"This is going to be the most fun yet. Imagine it, a friendly competition pitting neighbor against neighbor, the best cooks in the town vying for the top spot. Every small town in America will want to participate. This will put small towns and their restaurants on the map. It will be like *Diners, Drive-ins, and Dives*, only better."

"Just what the world needs. One more cooking show and one more chance for people with knives in their hands and fire at their fingertips to try to kill each other over a prize."

"Not just any prize," he said with a smile. "The winner will get yearlong advertising on all my shows plus a brand-new kitchen makeover to allow them to make their meals better than ever."

"And how are you going to choose the small town for the pilot?"

"I don't have to choose. You've already done it for me. Thank you, my love, for insisting on a weekend away on this quaint island." He leaned over and kissed her on the cheek while simultaneously pulling his phone from his pocket.

"Great," she muttered as he immediately started spouting off his ideas to his manager, using language he didn't dare use with her.

I was really enjoying this little island. I hope he doesn't destroy its charm and sense of community in the short time he'll take the island by storm. Not even a hurricane could cause the damage that a 'friendly competition' can create.

Famed celebrity chef and television entrepreneur, Gideon Randall, has announced a new reality show with a surprising twist. *Neighbor vs. Neighbor* will pit the restaurants, eateries, and bakeries of one small town against each other in a bid to see which establishment has the best chef and the tastiest food. The cooking competition will bring together professional chefs and hometown cooks, both culinary-educated and self-taught, to showcase all the cooking talent the town has to offer. Stay tuned for more details and the premier date.

TV Guide, May 10

Chapter One

"Can they do this?" Holly took off her apron and tossed it onto the freshly cleaned counter before reaching for her coffee cup. The lunch rush had just ended at the Sand and Sugar Café, and Holly wasn't happy with the letter that had been delivered during the busiest time of the day.

Diane put down the letter after reading it through twice. "I guess they can," she said. "I don't remember them ever doing this before, not in the thirty years I owned this place." She accepted the coffee that Holly offered. "Thanks, Holly. I'm so glad to see you're still making the good stuff."

Holly laughed. "I thought that was conditional on your sale of the business." She led her mentor to a table and sat down.

"It would've been if I could've made it legally binding," Diane said.

"Don't worry. I know that everyone comes here for our coffee because they know just how good it is." Holly tucked a stray hair behind her ear and exhaled. She gestured toward the letter lying on the counter. "So, about this demand."

"Maybe it's good news," Diane offered. "Maybe the council or the chamber has money it wants to spend on the local restaurants."

Holly frowned. "I suppose it could be good news. In my experience, though, a command appearance in front of some branch of government typically does not bode well."

Diane shrugged. "Don't worry until you have something to worry about, then let God worry for you."

"I sure wish I had your faith, Diane. For most of my life, it's been the things I didn't know I had to worry about that always came around to bite me." She tasted a bitterness in her mouth that didn't come from the coffee.

Diane reached over and covered Holly's hand with her own. "Don't blame yourself. It's his loss."

Holly looked away and blinked. *I will not do this again,* she willed herself before turning back to Diane and forcing a smile.

"I know. I keep telling myself that, but it's my loss, too. I spent two years of my life preparing for what I thought was a certain future. How could I have wasted all that time and never have known that he wasn't invested at all? He talked the talk, but when it came down to it, he couldn't walk the walk."

Diane patted Holly's hand. "Not all men can. But most men do. Give yourself some time to grieve, pamper yourself, then take a deep breath and let your heart open itself up again. The right one is out there, and he won't make demands on you or put you between the proverbial rock and hard place."

"Humph," Holly snorted. "We'll see. In the meantime, speaking of demands, I guess I need to get myself cleaned up and ready to face the town council for this mandatory emergency meeting. Whatever they have to tell us, I hope it's not going to be something else that knocks the wind out of me."

"Whatever it is, you'll handle it. I have faith in you," Diane told her as both women stood.

Holly leaned over and hugged Diane. "Thanks. I'm glad somebody does."

"Lots of people do. It's going to be fine. No worrying." Diane smiled and waved goodbye. "I've got to go. I'm babysitting this afternoon and evening so Christy and Jared can pick up Molly from boarding school."

"I guess it's that time of year. I can't wait to ask Molly how she liked school."

Diane laughed. "Molly loves school. She loves anything that increases the knowledge in that incredible brain of hers."

Holly shook her head and smiled. "I can't imagine having all those smarts at such a young age. Or having a sister or brother with that kind of brain capacity. I give Christy a lot of credit for raising Molly after their parents passed away."

"Christy has done a remarkable job. Now with Jared as part of their family, Molly has another scientific genius and father figure to help guide her."

Holly sighed as she thought about how happy Christy and Jared were. Diane must have recognized the look.

"Your time will come, Holly. Just be patient."

Holly shrugged. "I have no choice but to be patient, I suppose. At least I have this place to keep me busy. Have a good afternoon, Diane. I'll let you know what happens at the meeting."

Holly let out a long breath as she watched the former donut shop owner head out the door. Some days, Holly loved owning her own business. Other days, she wondered why she ever thought this was a good idea.

***

"No. No way. I'm not going. Do they have any idea the effect a three o'clock meeting will have on the dinner rush? They can't demand I show up just a few hours before my restaurant opens without any regard for my business. They didn't even say what the meeting is about. They didn't even spell the name of the restaurant correctly."

Lorenzo tossed the letter into a nearby trash can before walking to the stove and picking up a long wooden spoon from a simmering pot. He sniffed the spoon and winced before adding a heavy dose of oregano to the sauce.

"Well, we all told you nobody would know what Speziato means and people would get it wrong."

Lorenzo shot Antonia an annoyed look. "It's 2023. They can't look it up on Google Translate? It says right there, 'spicy'."

Antonia sighed. " Back to the meeting. I understand, Lorenzo, but you have to go. It says it's mandatory." "As Lorenzo's front-of-house manager at Speziato, as well as his baby sister, Antonia knew there was only so much sway she had when his mind was made up. Nevertheless, she tried to keep up with him as he breezed from one station to another, smelling, tasting, spicing up, and dressing down.

"You call this creamy?" He barked at one of his sous chefs. "The special is seafood fettucine in a cream sauce, not a bowl of milk."

He looked at the already-plated salads. "Who made these salads? Did you even look at the lettuce? Is lettuce supposed to be this color?"

As he headed to the walk-in, he stopped abruptly, and Antonia banged into his backside. "Antonia!" He snapped. "Would you stop following me around? I have a kitchen to run, and my employees are doing everything in their power to ruin my recipes and my reputation."

"I'm sorry, Lorenzo, but please hear me out."

He stood, crossing his arms, and looked at Antonia, wondering why he ever hired her to begin with. Yes, she had experience. Yes, she knew and appreciated his family's reputation. She knew everything there was to know about good Italian cuisine. Still, she was only nineteen and not even finished college. He never should have taken her on as his protégée.

"What is it? Talk fast. I don't have all afternoon to waste on meetings of any kind despite what the town council thinks."

Antonia took a deep breath. "I know you don't think it's important, but the letter said that the meeting's agenda affects every restaurant in town. What if they're going to pass some crazy law that affects the way you do things? Do you know there's a law in the state of Florida that says restaurants can be fined for breaking or chipping more than three dishes per day? And in St. Cloud, Minnesota, it's illegal to eat hamburgers on Sundays. In North Dakota, beer and pretzels are not legally allowed to be served together. And in Indiana, you're not allowed to go to the movies or ride a public streetcar within four hours of eating garlic."

"What? I'd never be allowed to go to the theater again."

Antonia smiled. She'd baited him into that one.

"Are you putting me on?" Lorenzo asked.

"Actually, I'm not. That's a real law. And who knows what the council is cooking up with this meeting. No pun intended."

Lorenzo rolled his eyes. "Oh, for Heaven's sake. I'll go. But you'd better make sure this place doesn't burn down while I'm gone. Nobody in the kitchen is competent enough to be left alone."

"And yet you handpicked every one of them," she said with narrowed eyes and puckered lips.

"Be good, little sister, or I'm sending you back to Baltimore." He pulled on her ponytail like he used to when they were young. "I'll be back. Don't do anything I wouldn't do."

"You never know how to have any fun, Lorenzo," she called after him.

What did she know? She was a kid. Fun was overrated and led to nothing but heartache.

***

The public meeting room for the Chincoteague City Council was standing room only and as hot as the summer sand. Holly fanned herself in the back of the room as she waited for the council to begin. She looked around the room and recognized all but one face. She thought he was the person who had been hired for her former job as the manager of a local seafood restaurant, though they hadn't yet met.

It looked like every restaurant had sent a representative, either the owner or manager or longtime staff member. She wondered what new stipulation the council was going to impose and how her almost non-existent bank account would weather it. She knew that buying the donut shop in January and then spending the next several months updating it and turning it into a three-meal café would take a hit on her finances. She just didn't realize how hard that hit would be. If it wasn't a good summer on the island, she'd have to give up her tiny house, at the very least.

The president of the council banged her gavel to bring everyone to order, and a hush fell over the room. Just before the president opened her mouth to speak, the door slammed open, and a disheveled newcomer bounded in. His face turned red as he realized he was both late and the object of all eyes in the room.

"Sorry," he said before shuffling to an empty wall space in the back.

Holly didn't know him, but judging by the white coat he wore, he was a chef. He was tall and slender with dark brown hair and thick eyebrows that accentuated rather than overpowered his features. He was about thirty, give or take, and she wondered how long he'd been here and where he worked. She was pretty sure she knew every chef on the island.

Then it dawned on her. A new Italian place had recently opened on the opposite end of the island where a few new businesses were beginning to crop up. That had been quite the controversy when the land was sold for commercial use. It was believed that the restaurant and the other businesses there were going to have an uphill climb with the locals, but she'd heard good things about the food and atmosphere in the new establishment. Maybe it was going to get the town's support after all.

She turned her attention back to the front of the room where the president was talking about the past summer and how visitors had returned in big numbers, but not as big as they'd all hoped.

"This brings me to why I've gathered you all here this afternoon," Loretta Chandler told them, carefully moving her gaze around the room to make eye contact with every person there. "We've been given an opportunity to promote our wonderful island here to a lot of people. The whole country, in fact. Maybe the world."

She paused, and Holly's interest piqued. She could use an opportunity to promote the café.

"Gideon Randall is bringing his new show, *Neighbor vs. Neighbor,* to the island." Loretta grinned broadly, obviously expecting much enthusiasm, perhaps even a round of applause.

On the contrary, Holly didn't think the room could get any quieter. The place became so devoid of sound, she could hear the person next to her swallow and a fly hit the window several feet away. Finally, someone spoke.

"You mean he's bringing the whole production here? For some kind of competition reality show?" Dawn, owner of Seaside Grill, asked in the way one would carefully ask a young child to repeat herself.

"Yes, that's exactly what I mean," Loretta confirmed.

In the space of a millisecond, the room erupted with chatter. Holly's mind raced. What would this mean for a little café like hers that specialized in coffee, donuts, and croissant sandwiches? She tentatively raised her hand.

"Um, I may be in the minority, but I've never heard of this show. How does the competition work? I mean, first, do we all have to participate? And if so, would my place be going against someone like, say, Ropewalk?"

Again, the room got quiet, or almost quiet as a few people whispered amongst themselves.

"Well," Loretta said. "I'm not sure how it will work as it's a new show. But yes, in order for the production deal to go through, everyone has to participate."

A roar went up as people pelted the president with questions. "What about our regular customers? Who's going to take care of them while we do this?" "Will we get paid?" "What's the prize at the end?" "How can a sandwich shop go against a seafood restaurant?"

Loretta banged her gavel. "I don't have all the answers. I'm sorry. But Gideon wants to Zoom with us—all of us—to explain the details."

"When?" someone asked.

"Two days from now. This same time."

Holly looked around the room. There was a mixture of expressions on the faces of her colleagues. Some people looked to be in shock, unable to close their gaping mouths, while others had furrowed brows and twisted mouths as though they couldn't quite understand what the president was talking about. Holly's gaze stopped on the newcomer who looked…completely irritated.

His eyes were narrowed, and his mouth was set in such a straight, tight line that his lips were invisible. He shook his head and appeared to be taking deep breaths through his nose. Either that, or he was enormously good at holding his breath.

Holly turned her attention back to Loretta who was thanking everyone for coming and saying she would see them all on Thursday. The Council stood and exited through a door behind their long, dark table, while everyone else looked at one another in bewilderment.

They slowly left the room in small clusters, each talking amongst themselves about the possibilities this could lead to, both good and bad. Holly left alone and walked back to the café wondering what they were getting themselves into.

***

"This is awesome!" Antonia said. "Really awesome. I mean, it's Gideon Randall, and that means everyone will watch it. It would put Speziato on everyone's list. Oh my gosh, Dad will flip."

"Slow down," Lorenzo told her as he carefully sliced mushrooms, his own enthusiasm completely on hold. "First, we'd have to win."

"We'd win," his sister assured him. "It's in our blood. Four generations of Italian restaurants, all with award-winning menus. Who else can say that?"

"We don't know the rules. Our expertise might not mean anything."

Lorenzo was trying to stay calm and rational rather than let his chef's temper take control. While he held his sister's belief that their food was the best anywhere, he'd seen one or two episodes of these reality shows—not that he'd ever actually sat down and watched one of his own choosing—and they seemed to be more about drama than cooking. He wasn't sure this would be good for them.

Antonia continued to prattle on, talking about strengths and skills and technical knowledge, but Lorenzo tuned her out. He concentrated on the mushrooms, taking slow, even breaths as he made each slice. His Uncle Dom was always calm, always rational. He was a man of prayer who rarely let anything worry him. Even his battle with cancer, a battle he very nearly lost, was fought with dignity and strength underlined by faith. What would he do in this situation?

"What do you think?" Antonia pulled him from his thoughts with a nudge.

"About what?"

She made a throaty noise of irritation. "About everything I just said. We have every advantage, don't you think?"

"What about education? Some of these other chefs went to culinary school."

"And where are they now?" She used her fingers to enumerate. "Working for someone else, cooking a set menu, not living the dream. Look at you. You were practically born in a kitchen."

"*You* were practically born in a kitchen. The doctor warned Mamma that twins usually come early, but would she listen?"

Antonia sighed. "You're missing the point." She jabbed him with her finger. "You were in the kitchen from birth. You were raised with a knife in one hand and a wooden spoon in the other. Dad taught you everything he knew, and you can cook circles around him even without the schooling he had. And that's because you never needed it. You're the real chef in the family. While Dad cooks the recipes handed down from his parents and grandparents, you make them something special, something unique. You have the kind of skills that can't be taught in a classroom."

Lorenzo smiled. "Trying to butter me up?"

"No," she said emphatically. "I'm trying to tell you that we can win this thing. You can win this thing. I know you can, and so do you."

It wasn't anything he'd ever thought of before, pitting his food against another's. He was a chef, and a darn good one, but he didn't cook to be the best or win prizes. He cooked because he loved it. And that was the problem. Would this competition change the way he looked at what he did? How much of himself would he be allowed to showcase, and did he want to showcase any of himself to the world? He didn't want his life under a microscope. He had secrets he didn't want to get out. He was an imposter with no formal training and even less confidence, and he was afraid that soon, the whole world would know it.

***

"Well, I think it's exciting," Dina said as she popped one of Holly's Island Delight pastries into her mouth. The friend group was gathered at Christy's house for their weekly get-together. "The whole world will be watching our little island for something other than ponies swimming across the channel."

"Hey, watch it," Taylor said. "Those ponies are what makes our island unique! Plus they're the loves of my life, besides Nick, of course." She finished her glass of wine, and Holly reached for the bottle on the coffee table between them.

"It's not the whole world," Holly corrected Dina as she poured all of them another glass of wine.

"No more for me," Christy said, holding her hand over her glass. "One is plenty for Sally." She looked down at the baby at her breast. "The experts say it's an old wives' tale that alcohol gets into my milk, but I'm still taking it easy."

"As you should," Tori said. "I've seen my share of over-indulgence, and I think you're smart to play it safe."

Tori would know, Holly thought. Tori had been an EMT on the island since she was sixteen.

"I'll take Christy's," Dina said. "It was a rough day at the bank."

"It's always a rough day at the bank," Tori said. "You need a new job."

"I love my job," Dina protested.

Holly rolled her eyes. "Anyway, it's not the whole world. It's a national show."

"Until Hulu picks it up," Tori said.

Holly let her head fall back on the sofa cushion. "Ugh. I don't want to think about that."

"Why?" Dina asked, reaching for a croissant sandwich.

"What if I'm a complete failure?" She looked around the room at her best friends. "I can't compete with trained chefs. I have a degree in hospitality and a small talent for using someone else's recipes and making them taste good."

"Taste better," Christy corrected. "Even Diane admits it. Somehow, you work your own kind of magic into the dough and batter to come out with a pastry that tastes like a little bite of Heaven."

"And look how you've taken Diane's original donut recipes and expanded on them." Tori said. "She had so many unique flavors, but you've managed to add even more. Plus, you added recipes of your own, not just croissants and other pastries. Your savory sandwiches are the talk of the island."

"I wouldn't go that far," Holly said.

"I would," Taylor argued, waving a sandwich in the air. "Nobody knows more about the sandwiches and pastries on the island than my husband, and he's all but quit going to any place but yours."

"Yeah, but that's sandwiches. I don't know how to cook anything other than pastries or how to construct any meals other than sandwiches, chips, and a pickle. Just because I managed a restaurant and then decided to jump into owning one doesn't mean I know what I'm doing. If I wasn't so broke, I'd have a real pastry chef working for me."

"You don't need one," Christy said. "Believe me. You know how to cook, bake, and create plates of great food. Just because you don't have the training doesn't mean you don't have the skill. In fact," she said as she rose slowly, keeping her sleeping daughter as still as possible. "I think this competition is going to challenge you in so many positive ways that your cooking is going to flourish. Just wait and see. And go ahead and pour me half a glass while I tuck this little one into her crib."

Holly looked at the others. "What do you think? Is she just being nice?"

"She's right," Taylor said, licking her fingers.

"One-hundred percent," agreed Dina, plopping the last piece of her sandwich into her mouth.

Holly took a deep breath and let it out. "I hope you're all right, but I'm really nervous about what we're going to hear tomorrow."

"Don't be," a new voice chimed in as Christy's sister, Molly, entered. "Cooking and baking are just science. You just have to know the proper way to balance everything to achieve the best results." Molly swept in, grabbed the last pastry on the plate, and headed for the stairs. "And you've got a secret weapon," she said.

"What's that?" Holly yelled as the precocious twelve-year-old disappeared.

"Me," Molly called back.

Holly raised a brow and looked around the room. "Well, that sure cleared things up, didn't it?"

I was raised by my grandparents. They ran this great restaurant at 56th and 8th in New York. [Robby smiles at the memory.] It was a posh neighborhood. Most of their regulars frequented Carnegie Hall and stayed at the Plaza. I loved the place, but I hated living in the city. Don't get me wrong, I love going back and seeing the sites and visiting friends and family, but I wanted to raise a family somewhere they could run free and enjoy the outdoors and not have to worry about all the city stuff. We came here on vacation once, right after Bev and I got married, and I knew this was where I wanted to raise our kids. We talked about it, and after a couple years, I got hired at JR's. [Video of the inside and outside of the restaurant plays while Robby continues to talk.] I went to CIA, you know, the Culinary Institute of America, and I know what I'm doing in the kitchen. I don't own JR's, but I love it and try to make JR and the rest of the staff proud.

Chapter Two

The room was abuzz as everyone waited for the famous chef to appear on the large monitor. Lorenzo stood in the back and cracked his knuckles. He noticed a few faces that weren't there two days prior and wondered who they were. It occurred to him that he spent so much time at the restaurant, he knew very few people on the island. On the occasions he spoke to diners—and he tried to do that nightly—he didn't know the locals from the tourists. He thought of the vibrant community his family was a part of back in Little Italy, Baltimore, and wondered if he should be more involved in his own community.

When the screen danced to life, a hush fell over the room. Lorenzo pulled out his phone and opened his notes app. He almost wished he'd sent Antonia instead. She was much better at sorting through information and determining what was important to note. On the other hand, he reminded himself, this was a great opportunity to get to know his peers.

"Good afternoon, chefs, bakers, and restaurateurs! I hope you're all excited about our show coming to your island," Gideon said in his Scottish American accent.

A few people shouted enthusiastically, while others nodded, and some remained stoic. Lorenzo was among the latter. Even if he was going to get to know his peers, he still wasn't feeling enthusiastic about the competition.

"We've developed a great program that will showcase your island and your talents. Are you ready to hear about it?"

Shouts went up around the room, but Lorenzo remained unmoved. He wanted details before he allowed any reaction.

"I can't tell you the fine details of the show because it would ruin the element of surprise and take out all the fun, but I've looked at what each of you does in your eateries, and I can assure you that everyone will have an advantage at one time or another. You'll be able to rely both on what you know and experiment with some new techniques and creations." He took a long drink of water before continuing.

"Now, as far as the rules. Every business that cooks or bakes must participate, or we won't do the show. Period. You're competing individually, but the overall goal is to highlight your town and your local businesses. You must choose one chef or cook to represent your business. You can't tag team or try to switch up once the taping begins. The chef can be at any level of education or experience. The competition will take place over the course of two weeks—twelve days of competition, one day of rest, and an extra day in case of anything unforeseen—and will take up to ten hours each day from beginning to end." He raised his hands as protests began and told them to wait a 'bleeping' minute. "I get that you're a summer resort island. While we're filming the show, other members of my crew will interview your staff and visitors and use the footage in the show. That will get you lots of publicity leading up to and during the airing; and to help you out even more, I will provide your establishments with a guest chef, one of my apprentices, for the week."

Lorenzo frowned. An apprentice chef in his restaurant? That would not do. He'd put in a call to his family. Someone would have to come down and help him out. Maybe one of his older siblings, Marissa or Adrian. They both had kids, but the kids were getting older. Lorenzo bet his sister would love two weeks away from home. Or she and Adrian could switch off half-way.

"We'll do this the last two weeks of June. You'll be back at work well before the island's carnival and the famous pony penning."

"But that's only a month from now," an attractive blond said, her eyes wide with terror. Lorenzo didn't know her though he knew most, if not all, of the others, at least by sight.

Gideon threw out one of the many expletives he was known to drop into almost every sentence. "Come on, people. Don't you think I know what I'm doing?" Another expletive fell from his lips.

"Everything will be in place by then. I've already talked to the city council. We've got the timeline in place for the kitchen installments to begin next week."

"Kitchen installments?" asked Bob, who owned Prime Rib and Rockfish and had welcomed Lorenzo to the island when Speziato first opened.

Gideon rolled his eyes and rhetorically asked Bob what kind of 'bleeping' idiot he thought he was. "We're having temporary cooking stations installed in the community center. Just like you see on my other shows. You'll have everything you need to make your dishes—ovens, stovetops, top-of-the-line countertop appliances, brand-name kitchen tools, the works." As he talked about the setup, another string of words Lorenzo was very familiar with rolled off Gideon's tongue. It was a language many chefs employed on crazy, busy nights when nothing was going right.

"Can we see it ahead of time?" asked Anna from Uno Taco Dos Tequilas. Lorenzo liked her food and thought of her as one of his primary opponents, though in truth, all the restaurants on the island were quite good.

Gideon answered with a quick and decisive no before asking for more questions.

"Are only restaurants allowed?" asked a voice from the back of the room, near where Lorenzo was standing. He turned to see a nice-looking brunette, about forty, whom he recognized but didn't know from where.

"Ah, interesting question. You must be either Cynthia Wu or Kayla Middleton."

She nodded at the monitor. "Yes, sir, I'm Kayla. You know who I am?"

Lorenzo recalled the name and the delightful welcome basket Kayla had sent to the restaurant on its opening day with a note that wished him luck with his new business.

"I know of you," Gideon said. "I asked for a ledger of all the eating establishments and chefs in town, and your business was on the list. Catering, right?"

"Yes, that's correct. I have a business license and health department approval, but I operate out of my home. My husband and our boys help with orders, deliveries, and events, but I do most of the cooking."

"I've already run it past my producer and attorney. We want you on board. By the stated rules, you'll have to be on board. Along with Cynthia, a local TikTok chef."

"Now, hold on," protested a man unknown to Lorenzo. "This is for restaurants, not caterers or internet cooks."

Gideon asked the man who he was.

"Walt Stevenson of Dockside Family Style Restaurant."

Gideon took a moment to consult his notes. "Ah, yes, I see here that you also do catering out of your restaurant. Is that correct?" he asked.

"Well, yes, but we do the cooking in the—"

"Would you consider your own catering business up to the level of Kayla's?"

"You bet your—"

"Okay, then. It's fair. Kayla will participate as will Cynthia. Any other questions?"

"But Kayla published a cookbook a couple years ago. That makes her a—"

Gideon cut Walt off with a string of obscenities detailing how he could publish his own cookbook after the competition, but Kayla was in whether he liked it or not.

Lorenzo watched Walt scowl and turn away, but the rest of the group seemed fine with the entry of the two women, himself included.

"Now, about where you'll be staying while you're on the show—"

"Staying?"

"The whole time?"

"What's that about?"

As the room erupted with protests, Gideon waited them out patiently. When it was quiet, he said, "Come on, folks. Reality TV has been around long enough for you to know the basic rules. You'll be staying at Chincoteague Harbor, a small resort area on the island where you will each have your own."

"What do we get if we win?" asked Dawn, owner of Seaside Grill.

"Now, that's a good question," Gideon said. "The winner will receive $300,000 to spend his or her business. They will also receive a year's worth of free advertising during all my cooking shows for both the restaurant and the island."

"Wow," Walt said. "That's pretty awesome."

Gideon then went on to explain more about where they would be sequestered and for how long before laying out the basic rules for both on and off the set. There were a lot of rules, and Lorenzo was unhappy about most of them.

***

When the video call was over, the room filled with chatter. Lorenzo began walking to the door while sending a text to Antonia that he was on his way back to Speziato. Not paying attention to where he was going, he bumped into the blonde woman who had spoken earlier, causing him to drop his phone.

"I'm so sorry," he said as he instinctively bent to pick it up.

"Oh, I'm sorry," she said as she, too, bent to pick up his phone.

This led to a knock on the head for both.

"Ouch," they said, straightening and rubbing their foreheads.

The woman laughed. "Sorry, it's a little tight in here."

Lorenzo had the sudden thought that her eyes were the color of a male blue jay, not just blue, but brilliant blue, like none he'd ever seen before. He could almost picture them sprouting wings and taking flight.

What an absurd thought. What's wrong with you?

He shook his head and winced.

"Oh gosh," she said, taking his hand and leading him outside. "Did I hurt you? Are you okay?"

He looked down and saw her hand holding onto his and gently pulled away. "No—I mean, yes. I mean, I'm okay."

She frowned and pursed her lips. "Are you sure? My café is just across the street. I could get you some ice."

He slipped his phone into his pocket and looked across the street. "The donut shop?"

Her frown deepened. "Well, it used to be a donut shop. Now it's a café. We serve sandwiches, too."

"Oh, right," he said slowly. "Thanks, but I've got to get back to Speziato, my restaurant. I'm sorry to have bumped into you."

"No, I think I bumped into you, but if you're sure you're okay…"

"I'm sure. I grew up with a lot of brothers and sisters. I'm used to getting bumped into and knocked on the head. It was usually on purpose."

She laughed, and he smiled back, thinking he should start eating donuts more often.

"Well, all right then. I'm going to get back to work. I guess I'll see you at the competition." She motioned her head in the direction of the community center.

"Yeah," he felt himself grimacing. "I guess so."

"You don't seem too excited," she said.

"I'm not," he admitted. Then he realized what he had said and straightened up. "Not that I don't think I can win. I can. I will. I just don't have time for stupid games and reality shows."

Her smile vanished. "Yeah, well, I guess you're stuck, aren't you? It sounds like nobody has a choice. If one place backs out, the competition is over for everyone."

"And that's bad because…?"

Her jaw flexed, and her eyes went from blue jay-blue to high intensity fire-blue. "Well, some of us could benefit from the publicity."

"Yes, I suppose some of you could." *What the heck? Where had that come from? He was supposed to be getting to know his colleagues, not insulting them.*

Her eyes widened as she took a step back. "Well, I guess I'll see you there." She turned and walked into the street, stopping abruptly when a car screeched to a halt and the driver laid on its horn. She—Lorenzo realized he still didn't know her name—waved an apology to the driver and ran across the road and into the donut shop. Former donut shop. Sandwich shop.

Lorenzo shook his head. Instead of meeting another business owner, he almost got her killed. Great way to begin this ridiculous competition.

He managed to find his car though his mind was up in a tree somewhere, trying to locate a bird that had just flown away.

***

Holly stomped her way into the café. Her hands were shaking, and she didn't know if it was out of anger or because she was nearly hit by a car thanks to some jerk, already certain he was going to win because his cooking was so much better than hers and everyone else's. She grabbed her apron and slung the strings around her waist. She tied them tightly and let out a huff of air.

"That good a meeting?" Molly asked before pointing to the apron. "And you might want to loosen that. You're going to cause your cardiovascular system to constrict, which can eventually result in neurovascular compromise. That's kind of like your leg falling asleep, but worse. It's common in girls, mostly girls anyway, who suffer from rubber band constriction syndrome. You know, when they wear those silly wrist bands or even hair ties on their wrists that are too tight and—"

"Molly, I get it. Thanks." Holly undid the strings and retied them. "How were things while I was gone?"

"Everything was fine. Nick came in. He got a couple sandwiches, one for then and one for later. He said Taylor was going to be working all day on a landscaping job and then had a Saltwater Cowboy slash Cowgirl meeting later. I told him that eating two sandwiches in one day was not good for him and that he should consider one of your signature salads instead, but he laughed at me." Molly crossed her arms against her chest and twisted her mouth. Holly couldn't help but laugh.

"You can't teach an old dog new tricks."

"Technically, you can. You see, dogs actually get smarter as they get older—"

"Molly," Holly blew a stray hair away from her face and tilted her neck from side to side to loosen it.

"Thanks for helping. Would you mind going in the back and updating the inventory list? You remember how, right?"

"Sure, I can do that. I get the feeling you want me to be quiet and give you some space. It's fine. I'm used to that. My roommate used to hold her hand up like this." She demonstrated by holding her right hand in a halting position. "That meant that she needed me to shut up and get lost for a while."

"Molly, that's terrible."

Molly shrugged. "Nah, I get it. I can be a bit much. Besides, sixteen-year-olds have all these hormone imbalances, so she's got that going on. And I think she's upset that I got a better grade in nuclear physics than she did, but whatever. It's not like we're going to major in the same discipline when we get to Harvard, so it won't matter in the long run."

"Hey, Molly, where's Freddy?" Holly looked around but didn't see the other employee.

"He's in the back washing dishes. Come to think of it, he's been back there a while. I'll check on him."

"Molly, before you go, I have a question."

"Sure, what's up?"

"What does Speziato mean? I think it's Italian."

"Spicy. I looked it up when I was researching your competition. The owner's from Baltimore. A long line of chefs, if I remember right."

"Huh. Thanks."

"Sure thing," Molly said before bounding from the room.

Holly watched the little girl—*did that term even apply to Molly?*—go into the kitchen and wondered how Christy did it. Holly loved the girl, but her chatter and her intellect were on major steroids, and it could be overwhelming at times. But researching her competition was a good idea…

The bell over the door rang, and Holly smiled at the family of four. Research would have to wait.

"Feel free to sit anywhere. Looking for a late lunch or an afternoon pick-me-up?"

After letting them look over the sandwich menu, Holly took their order and went to the counter where Freddy was already putting together a sandwich.

"I heard one of them say Greek Isle sandwich, right?"

"Right. Thanks."

"No prob. How'd it go today?"

"Okay. A little thinner on the figs, Freddy. We don't want the sandwich to be too thick to eat. And make sure the feta is flattened between the slices of prosciutto."

"I got it. What did Gideon Randall say? About the competition?"

Holly told Freddy about the competition while she worked on a caprese croissant sandwich with mozzarella, sun-dried tomatoes, artichoke, arugula, and homemade basil pesto.

"So, we're going to have one of his apprentices in here while you compete? That's cool."

"Maybe, but don't get your hopes up because Diane is planning on covering for me. Besides, I'd rather be here. Nobody is happy that we won't be able to return to our normal lives until it's all over. I'm really upset about it. Especially since I'll probably be doing nothing but sitting by the hotel pool having a pity party after day one."

Freddy stopped and looked at her with his big, brown, puppy dog eyes. "Why would you say that Miss Holly? You're good at cooking and coming up with recipes. Look at these sandwiches." He waved his hand over their work as Holly began making a turkey BLT.

"I'm not that kind of good, Freddy."

"You are, and everyone knows it. My friends would love to trade places with me."

"That's because they all work outside all summer, and you're in the AC. By the time school starts, you'll be so sick of my food, you'll be jumping out of bed and ready to hit the books."

Freddy laughed. "I doubt that, and seriously, give yourself some credit. You've got a real chance at this thing, a real good chance."

She had a feeling not everyone felt that way, and she pictured a certain restaurant owner's face as she aggressively crushed a garlic clove under the blade of a large knife.

Just then, the door opened, and the bell signaled a customer. Holly looked up, and her stomach dropped. She wasn't sure if the butterflies in her gut were excitement or dread.

"Chad?"

"Hey there. I thought I'd come by to check in and see how you feel about the town's big news. Any idea how you're going to prepare?" He pulled out a stool at the counter and sat down like it was the most normal thing in the world. At one time, it had been.

"Not yet, Chad, we just found out this week, and besides, I'm not allowed to talk about it."

"Yeah, but you can at least tell me what you're thinking."

Why do you care? You made it abundantly clear that you didn't want to be part of my life.

"I can't, and to be honest, I'm pretty busy. I've missed most of the afternoon, and now I have to figure out how to run a restaurant when I have to be out of communication with everyone for two weeks."

"Wow. I hadn't heard that." Chad stood. "I'll let you work, but how about when you're done, you text me, and I'll walk you home? Maybe get some dinner?"

Perplexed, Holly stood and stared. A few weeks ago, she would have welcomed the offer, had even prayed for something like this to happen. Now, however, Chad was just part of her past.

"No, thanks, Chad. I'm sure you'll still have work to do at the marina. I'm surprised you were able to get away to come by just now."

He frowned, and his eyes clouded over. Had she hurt his feelings?

When was the last time you chose me over that stupid marina? Oh, yeah, never.

"I, uh, I thought you'd be happy to see me." He chewed on his lower lip, a habit she detested since it always left his lip chapped and broken. But it wasn't her problem anymore.

"It's nice to see you, Chad. Now, I've got work to do."

She hadn't meant for it to sound harsh. Harsh was hearing that he just didn't feel the same way anymore and thought she should move on after two years of planning a life together. She'd cried for days. Now, however, all she wanted was for him to leave so she could figure out what needed to be done to ensure that she would still have a business by the time this whole show ended.

***

Antonia was waiting at the door when Lorenzo returned to the restaurant.

"Well, what was he like? Was he nice or was he scary like on his shows? Does he really cuss like a sailor? When's this all taking place? What are the rules? How many restaurants are competing? What's—"

Lorenzo put up his hand to cut her off. "Antonia, enough. I've got a kitchen to run and a staff to manage, and I'm getting a headache."

He tried to brush past her, but she stepped into his path.

"Whoa. I get nothing? You're not going to share anything you found out?"

"Not now," he said in a tone that was meant to convey his irritation with the whole thing. As any younger sister would, though, Antonia persisted.

"Come on." She followed him to the kitchen. "Was it that bad? Will the show be terrible? Was he a horrible person?"

Lorenzo stopped, closed his eyes, and took a very long breath. He counted to ten before releasing it. Without opening his eyes, he said, "I will talk when I'm ready to talk. I need to process this, chew on it for a while." He opened his eyes and looked at her. "And I do have a restaurant to run, especially since my manager seems to be too busy playing twenty questions, or in this case, one hundred questions." He leveled his gaze on her and locked his jaw.

"Sheesh," she said turning and walking away. "And I thought Dad was a pain to work for."

Lorenzo turned and walked to the stove. He turned on the burner, doused a pan with a heavy-handed pour of olive oil, and while the oil heated up, dispensed himself a heavy-handed pour of wine.

***

Several hours later, Lorenzo was wiping down counters, turning off burners, and considering taking the time to sharpen his knives. He recognized that he was putting off going home and spending a restless night thinking about the competition. He was new to town and had no choice but to compete. He could not be the one to dash everyone else's dreams. And he certainly didn't want to get on Gideon Randall's bad side.

He walked out of the kitchen into the empty dining room and dropped into a chair at one of the two-tops by the window. He straightened the napkin at one setting and lifted the knife from the other, inspecting it for spots. He set it back down and stared out over the channel.

His sister was right that he had grown up in the kitchen in his parents' restaurant. He had spent his entire life learning how to cook the most tantalizing Italian food. He knew everything there was to know about managing a business, choosing the best ingredients, putting together a menu, and creating just the right atmosphere. He was an expert on charming his customers, plating dishes, and even pairing wines—his Aunt Marta had convinced him to get his sommelier's certification to enhance his hands-on education, and he was glad he did.

There was no reason to think that he couldn't do just as well as, if not better than, his competitors, except…

Lorenzo blew out his breath and put his elbows on the table. He bent his head down and held it in his hands. He knew he was good at what he did. Very good. Even without a culinary education, he knew he could outcook almost anybody. But could he stack up to the standards of the most famous chef in the world? Would he look like an idiot on national television? Would he become the laughingstock of the island and his neighborhood back in Baltimore? Would he embarrass his family, make his father ashamed? Maybe he wouldn't even pass the required mental health test they all had to undergo before taping began. He was feeling anything but mentally stable as these questions bounced around his brain.

And then there was the biggest question of all. Would she hear about it and find a way to tune in? Would it remind her that he wasn't good enough for her? Would the biggest reason he left Maryland see him on television and be reassured that she had made the right decision in leaving him behind?

Would his unwillingness to change be his downfall—again?

***

Holly closed and locked the door to her little beach house. She hung her purse by the front door and tossed her keys into a dish on the small table in the postage stamp entryway. A timed lamp glowed softly in the corner of the TV room, giving her just enough light to take off her work shoes and toss them into the closet.

Rather than head into the bathroom to get ready for bed, Holly slumped into the oversized armchair that was too big for the room but too comfortable to get rid of. An orange tabby cat sprang into her lap and purred as she stroked him from his head to the end of his raised tail.

"Hello, Tang," she whispered to her nearly lifelong companion. Holly had adopted the abandoned kitten when she was eight years old, almost eighteen years ago, and she knew their days together were numbered. "What have you been doing all day to keep yourself entertained? Did you eat everything in your bowl?"

The cat curled up in Holly's lap and closed his eyes, his purring continuing as he drifted to sleep, just about the only thing he did these days. The thought of losing him brought tears to her eyes, and she blinked them away.

"Want to hear about my day?" she asked quietly. "We eked out another day, so we can keep the lights on, thank Heaven. Molly's back at work, and as talkative as she is, she's a heck of a worker. I went to that meeting I told you about. Gideon Randall held nothing back about his expectations for this competition, which I'll probably lose in round one, by the way, if I pass the mental health exam, which is questionable right now." She sighed loudly, and Tang—short for Tangerine—shifted in her lap.

"Oh, and I almost died." She swallowed as she recalled her terror at almost being hit by a car and how she kept herself calm through sheer will alone. Tang didn't seem to understand the importance of her words and slept peacefully, still purring, without a care in his little world. Holly continued to stroke his fur and tried to keep the other part of that scenario out of her mind. Despite her resolve to forget about the man she'd bumped heads with, her mind conjured his face.

"He was such a jerk," she told Tang. "Acting like he was already the foregone winner and implying that my café wasn't any real competition." She made a noise of irritation. "Well, I'm sure he's right, but still. He's never even been inside. How does he know anything about my abilities? Just because he owns a restaurant with a fancy Italian name doesn't mean anything." She grunted in annoyance again. She wanted to be angry with the man, but she knew this wasn't about him. It was about the promise she had made.

When her grandmother's attorney had informed Holly that she'd been bequeathed $25,000, all she could think of was how she would rather give back every penny of the money just to have her grandmother back by her side. When she'd signed the deed to the donut shop, she knew it was her chance to finally live up to the ideal her grandmother had of her. Now, she had a real chance to do what Grammy had always believed she could—to prove to the world she could be a success despite her lack of confidence.

But if that was the case, why was she so convinced she had already failed?

I'm Jane, a fifty-five-year-old divorcee. I worked at the Chincoteague Deli for thirty-seven years before Covid shut us down. I started when I was just fifteen. I was a busgirl then moved up to waitress, and then I became the head cook. It's not really what I thought I'd be doing with my life, but it's where I ended up, and I'm okay with that. [Jane smiles confidently.] After it closed, I started working at Captain Morgan's Seafood, and I have to say, I love it there. [Video of the restaurant plays while Jane talks.] I love the customers and the summer crowds and the staff. I just hope I can hold my own against the rest of the cooks on the island. I'm going to give it my best.

Chapter Three

"Three more specials needed, two tagliatelle, and one penne with vodka sauce." Jamie called out to the other chefs. "Let's get moving, everyone."

Lorenzo smiled. His instinct that Jamie would be the perfect addition to the kitchen was right on. The guy was a brilliant chef with a good head on his shoulders who led with the right balance of command and comradery. He made Lorenzo's dual role of head chef and owner run much smoother than it would have otherwise.

With pans sizzling, pots boiling, and fryers popping, the kitchen swelled with the symphonic sounds of fine food being fashioned and formed. Not merely cooked but created—something Lorenzo learned from his parents. A good chef isn't just a cook, he or she is an artist.

"It's a full house tonight," Antonia said as she rushed into the kitchen. "We're going to need more salads and desserts prepped."

Lorenzo caught glimpses of his sister running in and out of the walk-in, giving instructions to the prep cooks, and checking in with the wait staff. Bringing her with him was a complete pain most days, but it was also a stroke of genius. Sure, she was young, but no younger than he was when he and his father began planning his future and talking about opening a second restaurant in a location far enough away from home that Lorenzo could establish himself as a restaurateur apart from his family's stellar reputation. Of course, Grace Somers had been the catalyst that finally sent him off on his own, but Lorenzo didn't like giving her that much credit.

He flipped a Tuscan style filet mignon and scanned the kitchen. He was pleased. Everything was humming along with finesse and just the right amount of fervor, an orchestra fined-tuned in rhythm and harmony. Until a loud crash interrupted its smooth cadence. Lorenzo spun around, looking for the cause of the disruption. His eyes widened.

"I'm so sorry," one of his young waitresses said as she tried to salvage the meals that were strewn across the floor among broken plates and spilled sauces. "I'm really, really sorry."

Worse than the loss of food was the look on her face. She was bright red, and Lorenzo could see the welling of tears in her eyes. She was just about beyond the verge of losing all composure, exacerbated by the fact that they had a full house and limited staff. Lorenzo motioned to Jamie to monitor the dishes he was creating and hastily moved toward Jenny.

"I'm so—"

"Enough," Lorenzo commanded. "It happens. Tell the chefs what you need. Let the bussers clean this up while you go into the back and pull yourself together. You have other tables and customers to appease. Tell them what happened. They will forgive you if you own up to it, especially when you tell them that you will bring them a round of drinks on the house." After she nodded and wiped her knees as she stood, she looked at him with gratitude.

"I'm not being fired?"

Lorenzo shook his head. "Not if you go out there and tell the truth. Never lie. Never tell a table that the kitchen did something wrong when it was your fault. Never put blame on anyone else if you make a mistake, forget to put in an order, or," he smiled and nodded toward the mess on the ground, "when you drop a tray of food. That, I will not tolerate."

Jenny nodded vigorously and turned toward the other chefs.

"And Jenny," Lorenzo said, making her halt and look back at him. "This is good prep for you. If you think waitressing is stressful, just wait until the day you begin your residency. Meals can be remade, patients can't." He gave her a smile that let her know that she could handle this, and she smiled back.

"Thanks, Lorenzo. I needed that reminder."

"Okay, show's over," he yelled. "Everyone back to work. We've got extra meals to make."

By the time Lorenzo looked back down, the bussers had gotten the whole mess cleared up, and the kitchen was once again humming as it should be. He'd learned long ago that when the head chef loses his cool, it puts everyone on edge, raises the tension to an unworkable level, and contributes to a bad night all the way around—from poorly cooked food to a floundering wait staff and unhappy customers. He was terse, critical, and demanding, but he always tried to remain calm in a perceived crisis.

Lorenzo was certain that this was one of the many lessons that would propel him to victory in the upcoming competition.

***

"Nice place," Tori remarked to Holly as the hostess led them to their seats.

"It is," Holly said. "It smells wonderful in here, too." She wasn't great at identifying ingredients through smell, but she was getting better. Molly had been working with her on how to tell one spice from another, scientifically speaking, of course. She could detect the garlic easily, as well as the seafood. Distinguishing between baking spices was something she was quite good at, but she had work to do on the savory ones. She worried that her lack of experience using a wider range of ingredients was going to hurt her. She was also worried that she didn't know her competition well enough. She smiled at the hostess as she took her seat, still wondering how she could up her game.

"Holly? Don't you think so?"

"I'm sorry," Holly said, giving her head a little shake. "I was thinking about the show. What did you say?"

"I said, the menu looks great. It's a far cry from a pizza place."

Holly opened the menu and scanned the entrees. She felt her stomach drop like on a roller coaster. The meals sounded incredible—polenta with mushrooms and sausage, risotto alla Milanese, fritto misto with local seafood, ragù alla Bolognese, and at least ten other quintessentially Italian concoctions.

"Let's try the arancini for an appetizer," Tori suggested. "It sounds so good. Listen, 'a ball of rice stuffed with sausage and cheese, coated in breadcrumbs, and deep fried to perfection'."

Before Holly could answer, their waitress was at the table, and no introductions were necessary.

"Holly? Tori? Hey guys! Welcome to Speziato. What would you like to drink?"

"Jenny, you're working here?" Tori asked Taylor's younger sister.

Jenny nodded. "Just started this week. I needed to work someplace where I could make good money. Once I graduate in May, the cost of my education will skyrocket."

"Have you decided where you'll go to medical school?" Holly asked, trying to take her mind off the menu in front of her.

"I'd like to go to Hopkins if they'll take me."

"They'll take you," Tori assured her. "You graduated valedictorian. It's a no-brainer."

"Maybe for college, but not med school. It's a whole other world. So, Holly, are you excited about the competition?"

Holly held her breath to keep from sighing out loud. All anyone wanted to talk about was the competition.

"I'm, uh, looking forward to it," she forced herself to say with a fake smile, hoping her best friend's sister wouldn't notice her insincerity.

"It's going to be exciting," Jenny said. "Lorenzo is an amazing chef. I'm having a hard time giving an answer when customers ask for recommendations. Everything on the menu is to die for, from what I've sampled. Speaking of which, how about your drink order?"

Tori jumped in. "We want an order of arancini to start. What wine goes well with that?"

"I'll have to ask. One glass each or a bottle?"

"One each," said Tori. "We'll have a different wine with dinner. I've been told that the selection here is unbelievable."

Jenny nodded enthusiastically. "I'm not a big wine person myself, but the customers who do know wine rave over them. There's this one label that comes from an Italian vineyard owned by someone in Lorenzo's family that people just go nuts over. Mostly red, so I'll see how one of those pairs with your dinner choices. Should I put this in for now?"

"Yes, please," Holly managed to say. "Thanks, Jenny."

"You okay?" Tori asked after Jenny disappeared into a sea of servers, bussers, and customers being seated.

Holly shrugged. "Just worried. How can I compete with this?" She waved her hand over the menu.

Tori reached for her friend's hand. "Who says you have to compete with this? If you ask me, this cooking show isn't about competing with others, even if it is called *Neighbor vs. Neighbor*. It's about competing with yourself."

Holly scrunched her brow and looked at Tori. "What do you mean?"

"Look," Tori said, sitting back in her chair. "You can't compete with this. Plain and simple. But the chef from this place probably can't compete with your specialty donuts or your amazing croissants. Nobody can compete with Jane at Captain Morgan's when it comes to fresh, homemade pies, and who can beat Dawn's secret crab imperial recipe? Everyone is good at cooking within their specialties, but you're all going to be challenged to step out of your comfort zones, and some are just going to be better at it than others. And why is that? Not because of training or cooking skills or knowing the right temperature for cooking a piece of steak. Those who shine in this thing are going to do so because they know who they are in here." She placed a fist over her heart.

"Whoever wins this is going to do so not by being the best chef but by being confident in themselves. They aren't going to crack under pressure. They're going to think things through and proceed methodically, making sure they don't make mistakes. If they're faced with having to cook something they don't know how to make, they're going to think about what they do know how to make and figure out how to transfer their skill and knowledge with the familiar recipe onto the one in front of them. You can do that. You're always calm under pressure. You're never afraid to try something new, in the kitchen and in life. You aren't afraid to experiment. You are exactly the kind of person who really shines on these shows."

When Tori finished, Holly sat in her chair, blinked, and felt dumbfounded. While she was letting everything Tori said wash over her, Jenny returned with their wine. They asked for some more time to look over the menu, and Jenny went to check on their appetizer. Holly took a long sip of the wine and licked her lips before speaking.

"How do you know all that? I mean, are you just trying to build me up, or do you have some hidden insight into these things?"

Tori laughed and set down her glass. "Winter is pretty slow around the station. The guys and I have a lot of time on our hands, and one thing we all like to do is eat. Well, cook and eat, but we're amateurs. That translates into watching lots and lots of cooking shows. And I'm telling you, it's not about the cooking. It's all about the mindset."

Holly took another drink of wine while she pondered Tori's advice. Maybe she was thinking about this all wrong. Maybe she was good enough to compete alongside the others. Still, it couldn't hurt to see just how good the competition was. She picked up her menu and began looking over the offerings with a new outlook on the show.

***

Like his father taught him, Lorenzo always took the time to get out of the kitchen and speak to his customers. His father, Paul, insisted that a good chef had to connect with those who were eating what he cooked. He also said that before walking around and speaking to everyone, it was important to stand back and watch. Was anyone playing with their food instead of eating it? Were people urging their tablemates to sample what was on each other's plates? Did anyone's eyes light up with surprise when they first put a bite in their mouths? More often, these were better indicators of how good the food was than asking people how they liked their meals.

As he stood back and scanned the room, Lorenzo spotted Jenny talking animatedly to two women at one of the tables by the windows. She seemed to have gotten over her incident earlier in the evening, as he knew she would. She was smart and driven, two qualities that would make her an excellent physician. The women she waited on were obviously people she knew. One was petite with dark, curly hair and a wide smile. She laughed at something Jenny said, and her eyes danced with amusement. He could only see the other woman from the back, but something about her height and the blonde ponytail bobbing behind her head felt familiar to him. He went to a nearby table and began chatting with the customers—two middle-aged couples away for the weekend—about their stay on the island, what they had done that day, and then finally, how their meal was. Pleased with their praise, he moved on to another table.

As he neared the table occupied by the brunette and the somewhat familiar blonde, he heard one of them say, "I wonder if there will be any outdoor challenges. You know, like using a charcoal grill or something like that."

He turned toward them and saw the dark-haired woman make a face and shake her head. "No, I doubt it. They tend to stay inside where the studio setup is unless they're team cooking for a special occasion, a wedding or banquet of some kind."

"They do that?" the blonde asked, her voice full of wonder, or perhaps fear. "They cook for someone's wedding or special occasion?"

"Sometimes. Depends upon the show and where they film. Anyway, what made you wonder about cooking outdoors?"

The blonde responded, "My dad and I used to barbecue on charcoal all the time. I think I could handle that challenge well."

Lorenzo stopped in his tracks. The blonde. She was the one from the meeting, the one who was almost hit by the car. No wonder she seemed familiar to him. He started to turn away when he heard Jenny call, "Lorenzo, are you on your evening rounds?"

He was forced to turn back and smile. "I am, Jenny. How are things going out here?"

"Much better than the last time you saw me." She gave him a cheerful smile. "Come over here, I want you to meet someone."

Lorenzo put on a wide grin as he followed her to the table. Café girl—an unimaginative name that suddenly popped into his head—turned around and looked up at him, her startling blue eyes wide with surprise. He suddenly realized he was seeing those eyes in his dreams. It unnerved him.

"Lorenzo, this is Tori Baker, a local EMT, and Holly Peterson, who owns Sand and Sugar Café. Both are good friends with my sister."

Lorenzo bowed slightly. "It's nice to meet you, Tori. And it's nice to see you again and formally meet you, Holly."

Her perfect mouth formed a small 'O', which she hurriedly turned into a smile before reaching out her hand.

"It's nice to officially meet you, Lorenzo, was it?"

He couldn't tell if she was trying to be snide, but her smile seemed genuine. He took her hand like he had on the day they met, but this time, he noticed that it was small and soft, and he wondered how she kept it like that working in a kitchen all day. He found himself relaxing as he looked into those eyes.

"Yes, Lorenzo. My parents are Paul and Maria. Their parents were immigrants and wanted their children to have American names, but my parents wanted us to have authentic Italian names. Go figure."

He wanted to kick himself. Maybe he was too relaxed. What a stupid thing to say. What was wrong with him? Even Jenny was giving him a peculiar look, her brow raised and head tilted to the side.

Holly, however, laughed and said, "Parents and their choice of names. Can you guess which day of the year I was born on?"

"It's a nice name, Holly," he said, feeling like he was in a dream now with those jay-blue eyes dancing before him.

A silence fell over the table, and Lorenzo realized he was still holding her hand. Like before, he gently, and reluctantly, let go and reached for her friend's hand.

"It's nice to meet you, too, ah—"

"Tori. It's nice to meet you, Lorenzo," she said with a smile and a sideways glance toward Holly as she shook his hand and released it. "Are you, um, one of the chefs competing in the show, or are you sending someone else? I think that's what Holly said, that you had a choice between going yourself or sending someone in your place."

Lorenzo stood to his full height. "I'll be the chef representing Speziato. And what about you?" He turned to Holly. "Will you be doing the show yourself?"

She looked him square-on and straightened in her chair, doing her best to exude confidence though he detected some reticence. "I will. I have a few employees, but none who have any training, so they'll be staying at the café with the former owner, Diane. She's going to step in for me while we're taping the show."

Lorenzo nodded. "And your training? Where did you go to school?"

Holly's confident gaze faltered. "I, um, I taught myself to cook. And Diane. She taught me to make donuts. My mom taught me a lot, but mostly, I taught myself. I don't have a culinary degree. I have a degree in hospitality and management."

She bit her lips tightly together as though expecting an admonishment, but something about her honesty, and perhaps the vulnerability she tried to hide, touched him. "Then you probably have an advantage over many of us. You've never had anyone telling you what you're doing wrong."

He meant it as a compliment, but she visibly bristled at his words.

"Yes, well, I'm sure Gideon will have no problem telling me everything I do wrong." She stood and tossed her napkin onto her chair. "Now, if you'll please excuse me." She turned abruptly and walked toward the restrooms.

Lorenzo opened his mouth. "I didn't mean—"

"It's fine," Tori said. "Showtime jitters. She'll be okay." Tori gave him a forced smile.

"Well, I'll let you get back to your food. It was nice meeting you both."

Lorenzo hurried back to the safety of his kitchen. Strike two, and he didn't even know he'd stepped up to the bat.

***

Holly took several breaths and looked in the mirror, reminding herself of everything Tori had said. She was typically calm under pressure. She could handle stressful situations and troublesome people. She did not get easily rattled. So why did this guy, *Lorenzo*, get under her skin the way he did? Why did she let him bother her?

The door opened, and Jenny walked in looking concerned. "You okay?"

"Fine," Holly said with a huff. "Your boss is a jerk."

Jenny's head snapped back, and her eyes widened. "Lorenzo? A jerk? I mean, he's tough to work for, but in a good way. He strives for perfection and expects the same of his employees, but honestly, he comes about it in the kindest way. He's demanding and doesn't cut anyone a lot of slack, but he can be gentle and even humble which really says something considering he's probably the best cook I've ever known, and he definitely knows it." Jenny gulped a large breath of air and put up her hands. "I didn't mean that in the way it sounds. I mean, I know you're a good cook, too. I mean, I'm sure you'll more than hold your own against him. I mean," she shook her head. "I'm not helping, am I?"

Holly laughed and placed her hand on Jenny's shoulder. "It's okay. I know what you mean. It's just that I've met him twice now. Okay, just once officially, but both times he said something so condescending that I wanted to hit him. Is he really that big an egomaniac?"

"Isn't everyone in his profession? Well, present company excluded." She smiled. "But seriously, I don't think he is. He knows he's good, but he really wants to help others around him succeed as well. I mean it, Holly. He's a good guy. You'll see."

Holly had her doubts, but she knew Jenny was a good judge of character.

"I'll take your word for it. And I guess I'll find out for myself soon enough."

Holly thanked Jenny and returned to her seat. Her cacio e pepe had gone cold, but Tori had managed to finish every bite of her risotto di seppie. Holly was only on her third mouthful by the time Jenny was back at their table.

"For you," she said to Tori. She held out one hand in which she had a small dish with a rich-looking, perfectly molded chocolate circle of creamy delight with a sprinkling of nuts. "Chocolate panna cotta topped with toasted bits of almonds."

She then presented her other hand to Holly. In it, she held a wide-rimmed bowl containing sliced cherries swimming in a dark red, gooey sauce, topped with a dollop of cream and a drizzle of honey. "And for you, cherries poached in red wine with mascarpone cream." She placed the decadent dessert on the table. "On the house."

"No, Jenny, you didn't have to do that. Will this come out of your tips?" Holly hated that Jenny felt compelled to treat them.

"No, no, it wasn't me," Jenny said. "It truly is on the house."

"But, who…?"

Jenny gave Holly a beguiling smile. "Take a guess." And with that, she strolled away, leaving Holly more perplexed than ever about the incomprehensible Lorenzo.

***

"Who are you again?" Holly asked the young man who showed up late the following night, after she had closed the café and gone home. She'd met with the show's psychologist that day, which made her even more nervous about the show.

"I'm with *Neighbor vs. Neighbor*. I have a packet for you about the show. You are…" He looked down at the label on the package. "Ms. Holly Peterson, right?"

"Yes. Does this mean I'm in?"

The young man raised an eyebrow and frowned "In?"

"I passed the mental health exam?"

"Oh, that. Yeah. Everyone passed."

"Oh." That surprised her though she didn't know why. She knew everyone except Lorenzo, and even he, jerk that he was, seemed normal. But what was normal?

"Okay, so what's this?" She reached for the packet.

"It's a basic outline of each day on the show, when you'll be picked up each morning, what to wear, what to expect, what you'll be doing each day, that kind of stuff."

"Stuff besides cooking?" Holly opened the book and started flipping pages.

"A lot more than cooking." The twenty-something turned to go but called back, "See you on set."

Holly closed the door and started reading. "I start every day with hair and makeup before doing interviews? What kind of interviews?" She sat down in a nearby chair and began reading.

"Listen to this," she said to Tang, who had wedged himself into a small space beside her on the chair. "Apparently we get short cooking lessons each day to help us learn to be better chefs in high-stress situations. And on Sunday, we have the option of taking the day off or attending a cooking class with Gideon and the judges."

She looked down at the cat, who looked about as interested as a cat ever looks when his owner is talking.

"That's pretty cool, don't you think? I mean, you always have something new to learn, right? I've read online that this is the way Gideon operates. He comes across all critical on his shows, but he's really all about creating the best chefs. I always wondered how true that is."

"Listen to this," Holly read from the book. "He says, 'If you want to become a great chef, you must work with great chefs. That's exactly what I did and what I want for you.' He goes on to say, 'I cook, I create, and I'm incredibly excited by what I do, but even I've still got a lot to learn.' Wow. This surprises me. I thought he was much more arrogant than that."

Tang looked up at her with one eye open.

"What? You didn't think that, too? I do follow him on Insta, and he seems to be a cool husband and father who laughs a lot and really loves life. But I'm not stupid. I know that almost everything on there is staged. He probably has a publicity person post everything that makes him look good. Right?"

Tang stretched, pushing his paws against her leg as if to say, *enough talking. I'm trying to sleep.*

"Fine. I'll give him the benefit of the doubt."

She continued to look through the book. "This is some great stuff," she said to herself.

"I knew this would be demanding but I had no idea it would also be so educational. Never in my wildest dreams did I think I'd be taking cooking lessons from the great Gideon Randall. And so much time goes into those little video clips. I always wondered when they did those. They definitely can't pull people aside and just start interviewing them in the middle of a crazy busy cooking challenge."

She looked down at the sleeping cat and yawned. She had a lot to learn before the show started, but for now, she still had a restaurant to run and needed to get to bed. She wondered if she was the only one who was completely clueless about this whole cooking show thing.

***

The restaurant was dark. All the customers had gone back to their homes or their hotel rooms.

The chef sat at a table and looked up from the ledger, letting his gaze wander out to the dock where a single boat gently rocked back and forth. The past few years had not been kind, and the family was counting on this summer, this restaurant, to lead them away from financial disaster. The world was weighing on the chef's shoulders. It was a heavy load to bear.

This competition could really change things. It could mean the key to the future or the demise of a dream. So much was riding on the skills everyone thought had been handed down from generation to generation, but what if they were all wrong? What if those skills, that intuition, that ability to thrill and tantalize taste buds had skipped a generation? What if all of this had been an act since day one?

And therein lay the problem.

It all *had* been an act since day one. Everyone else in the family had just the right genes. They could all cook with one hand tied behind their backs, identify by smell alone every spice in the cabinet, and tell the difference between a flank steak and a ribeye with blinders on. Only one person lacked all that talent. Only one family member had always cheated, always found ways to reproduce the family recipes without any real skill or know-how, always been able to hire the right people to keep those secrets from everyone else, and even convince the family that the skills and intuition had been passed down successfully to the next generation. Now, the whole world would know. Because the chef had to compete. It couldn't be the hired help who showed up to the set on day one ready to flay the competition (no pun intended, though Chef Bobby Flay was an idol to be admired). The only way to keep the family from knowing this dirty little secret was for the chef to compete in person.

He looked back down at the book in his hands. How was he going to pull this off? Could he really convince Gideon Randall and everyone else on the island and in the world that he knew what he was doing?

This would either be the greatest accomplishment in the history of gastronomic greatness, or it would be the biggest crash in the whole chronology of the culinary arts. The imposter would be exposed or be extolled. Only time, and a building full of chefs, would tell.

Hey there, everyone. It's Jake, your favorite grill master here. I've been grilling practically since I could walk. There's not a meat I can't barbecue, smoke, or skewer. And veggies? Give me any veggie, and I can make it better cooking it outdoors. [Jake flashes a killer smile at the camera as he tosses a piece of chicken in the air over a grill.] I'm doing this for my old man, who taught me everything I know. I'll be home before you finish your treatments, Dad. [The man wipes a tear.] I love you.

Chapter Four

Holly woke up in a state of complete dread. No, that wasn't quite right. Holly hadn't woken up because she'd barely slept in the first place. How was she going to make it through the first day of the competition without any sleep?

She threw off the covers and made her way to the shower. As she lathered and shampooed, she gave herself an internal pep talk. She could do this. At least, she could get through one day. Maybe if she made it through the first day without being a complete disaster, she could make it through the next. Her eyes sprang open as water ran down the back of her head and spilled over her shoulders.

Why hadn't she looked at it like that before?

Her mother always told her, take each day in life one day at a time, or each challenge, one challenge at a time. Don't try to tackle every day or every worry all at once.

She blinked and looked through the mottled glass of the shower door to her blurry image in the mirror. She had become a pretty good cook, maybe not a professionally trained chef, but a good cook with fancy ideas and the ingenuity to make them work. Isn't that all she needed to do to get through this?

Holly reached for the towel hanging over the top of the shower as she turned off the water. She felt more confident, more able, and more composed. She'd spent the past month binge-watching every one of Gideon's shows and had gained a new appreciation for him and his expertise. She'd also gained a lot of knowledge, and some of it harkened back to what Molly had said the night she told her girlfriends about the show. Cooking and baking were science. But Holly had learned that they were much more than that. They were experimentation. They were taking something familiar and building upon it to create something better. Holly didn't know about science, but she knew all about taking something familiar and making it better. She'd been doing that her entire life.

As she dressed and ran a wide-toothed comb through her fine hair, she thought about all the advice that Molly and Diane had given her in the past weeks. She'd had lessons in coming up with new recipes, mingling spices to achieve just the right flavor, tweaking things that would normally take a long time to cook or bake to cut the time, and learning what flavors work together. There were times that Holly was having so much fun, she forgot this was all to prep her for the big competition. Even Freddy got into it and started showing up for work when he was off so that he wouldn't miss one of Molly and Diane's lessons in the art and science of cooking and baking.

By the time she reached the kitchen, Holly wasn't sure she could eat. She didn't know how much food they would eat on set, and despite her breakthrough in the shower, she was still nervous and had no idea what to expect. She was looking forward to having day one out of the way so that she didn't have to face quite as much of the unknown.

Opting for a butter and jam-topped, homemade English muffin—which was so much easier to make and tastier to eat than she imagined—Holly filled a travel mug with a strong cup of coffee and, suitcase in hand, went out to wait for the bus that would pick her up. Ready or not, she was outside, thirty minutes early. Gideon made it clear that he would wait for no one.

***

"Ouch!" Lorenzo jerked back quickly then leaned closer to the mirror. A bright red spot of blood bubbled up on his chin. He put down the razor and reached for a styptic pencil. He had never been good at shaving, especially when he was nervous. Almost every first date and school dance from the tenth grade through college, began with him nicking himself with his razor. The blood clotting pencil had quickly become his best friend as an adolescent.

"How's it going in there?" Antonia called. "Do I need to call someone to do stitches?"

"Very funny," he answered behind the closed door.

"I know you, big brother. How many cuts so far?"

"Just one," he said picking the razor back up. "But if you insist on pestering me, I might not survive getting ready." He heard Antonia laughing as she moved down the hall.

He finished shaving without another incident and began getting dressed. Had he already put on his deodorant? He wasn't sure. A quick sniff of his underarm gave him the answer, and he reached for his lucky shirt. It was the one he was wearing when he got his first kiss, the one he had on the day his father taught him how to filet a sea bass—which he had done expertly the very first time—and the one he was wearing when the bank accepted his application for a loan to purchase the restaurant. When his fingers touched the first button, he stopped. Should he be wearing this on day one of taping, or should he save it for a later day when the competition was fierce? Maybe he should wear it both days. Nobody ever noticed what guys wore, right?

By the time he walked into the kitchen, Antonia and Marissa were setting out homemade crisp bread with butter and jam, cereal, and cappuccino. Both women stopped what they were doing and stared at their brother.

"I can't believe you're both up already. It's not even dawn."

"Oh, no, Lorenzo. Not that shirt," Marissa said, ignoring his words and shaking her head.

"What's wrong with it?" He looked down at the shirt and back at his big sister.

Antonia answered, "It looks like you've had it since you were fifteen. Oh, wait, you have had it since you were fifteen."

"But it's my—"

"Nope. Don't say it," Marissa said. "You know how much Mamma hates it when you say that. Superstitions are sacrilegious."

"And since when did you become Mamma?" he asked as he picked up his cappuccino.

"Since I had kids of my own. Besides that, it looks awful. It's faded and wrinkled, it's worn so thin, I can see your dark chest hairs through it."

"That's not true," he said, looking down at his shirt and realizing it might be true.

"It is true. You can't go on national television looking like that." Antonia took the coffee from his hand and put it back on the table before leading him down the hall by his arm. "Come on, we'll find you something to wear that makes you look like a twenty-eight-year-old professional chef and not a high school freshman. And then I'm inspecting your suitcase to see what other awful things you packed."

Lorenzo sighed and resigned himself to the fact that his sister was probably right. Too bad he wouldn't have her with him all week to decide how he should be dressing.

Twenty minutes later, a newly dressed—and suitcase repacked—Lorenzo found himself being pushed out the door after a series of well wishes, hugs, and unnecessary tears. An onlooker would have thought he was going off to war.

I suppose I am in a way. I just hope I'm not the first casualty of the battle.

He stood by the curb in front of the house he was renting to buy. He glanced at his watch and realized he was early, but he supposed that was a good thing. One thing Gideon had stressed was that nobody was to be late, or they would be out before they began.

***

"Very good," Gideon told the group of twelve chefs who had gathered outside the locked community center. "You all passed the first test. I expect you to be ready for the bus on time if not early every morning. Be ready to work hard, to think on your feet, and to bring your best game to the competition. Now, who's ready to see the studio?"

Holly inhaled deeply and let out her breath. Her heart was beating wildly, and she felt a bit lightheaded. None of the contestants had much to say on the short ride. She wondered if they all felt the same way she did. Scanning their faces, she tried to gauge their feelings. Dawn and Jane, longtime friends, exchanged looks and brief smiles as they headed toward the door. Jerry— Holly's former boss—and Bob greeted each other with a handshake, both wishing the other good luck. Jerry had given Holly a hug and told her good luck as well. Robby, head chef at JR's, held the door open for Kayla and asked how her father was doing. Jane followed Kayla, saying good morning to Robby and asking how his new granddaughter was doing. Walt was having one last smoke before entering the kitchen, a habit Holly couldn't stand, especially from someone who cooked her food, though she knew many cooks and kitchen staff smoked. She took one last breath of fresh air, thankful Walt was several feet away, then reached for the door.

"Allow me," Lorenzo said as he pulled open the door and held it for her.

Surprised, Holly blinked before saying, "Thank you."

"You're welcome." He followed her inside and then said, "Good luck today."

She turned back toward him, wondering if he was being sarcastic or even demeaning, but the look in his eyes was genuine.

"Thanks. You, too."

Lorenzo smiled. "Look, I know we got off on the wrong foot, but I really do wish you well. My sister is a big fan of your pastries, and I want you to know that I think you're going to be a real contender in there."

She almost didn't know what to say.

"Dinner the other night was wonderful. You're going to give all of us a run for our money." She smiled as best she could, given the level of her anxiety now.

"Thank you. I owe it all to my parents."

Hmm, that was a bit of humility she didn't see coming.

"Well, I guess I'll see you in there." She gave a little wave and walked toward the closed door that separated the lobby from the large room where the taping would happen. Everyone stood and waited for Gideon, who had disappeared, to open the doors. Three crew members, all wearing headsets, rushed toward them and handed out white aprons that displayed their names and *Neighbor vs. Neighbor* in bold red lettering. As Holly tied hers around her waist, a crew member held a hand signaling them to be quiet.

The crew member said loudly, "Doors open in three, two…"

Then the doors opened, and the contestants entered the arena, unsure if they would be preparing lamb or were being led to the slaughter themselves.

***

The lights were blinding. Lorenzo resisted the urge to put his hand over his eyes. He'd been told ahead of time that he was at station six, but he followed the instructions they'd been given to stand in the back of the room until their name was called.

One by one, Gideon introduced each of them to the camera—which was even more nerve-wracking than Lorenzo expected—and showed them to their stations which were paired in six groups of two. Dawn was introduced as the owner of the Seaside Grill and led to the first cooking area. Next to her was Bob of Prime Rib and Rockfish. Several feet away from their area were stations three and four, occupied by Jerry of Ropewalk and Anna of Uno Taco Dos Tequilas.

Lorenzo looked at the remaining seven chefs standing with him and wondered who would be called to station five. He hoped for Kayla, as the local caterer was a known entity and kind person, but he had to refrain from gasping when the owner and head chef from Sand and Sugar Café was sent to station five. Lorenzo was caught so off guard, he missed his own named being called and only responded when one of the others nudged him to go forward. He was suddenly so nervous, he wasn't sure he'd remember the difference between a spatula and spoon rest.

He smiled and gave a wave to the future viewers as he made his way to his station. Holly offered a crooked smile, and he couldn't help but wonder if she felt as nervous as he did. He did his best to return his attention to Gideon and realized he'd missed the next pair of stations entirely.

Kayla was at station seven to their left along with Dockside's Family Style Restaurant owner, Walt, at station eight. Lorenzo watched as station nine's Jake, a blonde-haired, blue-eyed model type in casual designer clothes, was introduced as a YouTube barbecue influencer. He was joined by Jane of Captain Morgan's Seafood at the pair of stations behind Lorenzo and Holly. Finally, stations eleven and twelve were occupied by Robby, the chef at JR's, and Cynthia, a Tik Tok home chef who couldn't have been older than Antonia.

Gideon pointed to the back of the room, and Lorenzo turned around to see the doors opening again, through which two more famous chefs entered to join Gideon. Lorenzo recognized both from the hours of streaming cooking shows Antonia had insisted he watch. Christina Carlson was a petite blonde with sparkling green eyes, a wildlife biologist turned baker. She was the owner of a renowned bakery, Cupcake Castle, and a former judge on one of Gideon's most famous shows. José Gaitán, a chef, cookbook author, and humble philanthropist, was also familiar to Lorenzo. Though Latino instead of Italian, both men shared a long line of chefs in the family and were passionate about bringing their heritage of ethnic foods to the masses.

Crew members encouraged the chefs to applaud before someone—the director, Lorenzo presumed— yelled, "Cut."

Gideon turned away from the cameras and looked at each chef.

"Great job, everyone. Okay, leave on your aprons, go grab some coffee and get something to eat. There's plenty of food set up in the lounge. You'll be called one at a time to do your bio clip. After the bios, we've got some publicity shots to do before your cooking lesson. We'll go over what you're making and offer advice, then we'll shoot the competition after lunch. Be prepared to be cooking all afternoon. It's going to be a long day."

***

"Here we go, everyone," Gideon said once they were all gathered on set that afternoon. "Remember, you're all here because you're good at what you do. You own or work at businesses that people support and want to succeed. Yes, this is a competition, but you are neighbors and colleagues, probably friends. It's a small island, and no matter what happens here this week, that fact will remain. You may be competing against each other, but don't let that ruin the quality of life you have here. Just continue to support each other like always, do your best, give it your all, and have fun."

Holly was a bundle of nerves, and it wasn't just because she was going to be on national television. She hadn't given any thought to being in a work area this close to another chef, and she certainly hadn't expected to be sharing her space with Lorenzo. It took everything in her to focus on Gideon's pep talk. She tried a deep-breathing technique that Tori taught her. When the red light on the camera was illuminated, she pasted on a smile and listened carefully to their host.

"Your first task will be simple and no-nonsense. You'll be cooking a regular breakfast, but not something I can get at McDonald's." The contestants laughed as expected. "I want a carb, I want breakfast meat, I want eggs, but don't give me boring buttermilk pancakes or scrambled eggs. I want it to be special, with personality and flair. You have a whole pantry full of flours and spices and a refrigerator bursting with flavor. I expect your dishes to reflect that. Everything will remain available to you throughout the competition, but there are limited quantities of some items, so you need to know your ingredients from the start. You have one hour to get this right. And the clock starts now!"

Holly couldn't believe it when their task had been revealed that morning after their first cooking lesson. She'd spent hours upon hours learning to bake lofty soufflés, grill perfectly temped steak, and sauté vegetables she had never heard of. She was not expecting to begin the competition with the meal she did best.

She didn't waste a minute running to the refrigerator and grabbing milk, eggs, Italian breakfast sausage, and parmesan and ricotta cheese. She almost knelt and thanked Heaven then and there when she spied the ricotta and grabbed it before anyone else. She hurried over to her station and dropped them onto the stone surface before rushing to the pantry and picking out flour, sugar, several different spices, and breadcrumbs. Every station was already equipped with salt and pepper, oil, and fresh maple syrup. If she remembered her recipes, she had everything she needed.

She put a generous amount of oil in a frying pan, then filled a saucepan with cold water and put both on the stove. Meanwhile, she mixed the sausage with some dry mustard, nutmeg, and cayenne pepper. She glanced at the water before forming the sausage mixture into balls. As she worked, she resisted the urge to look around, but she couldn't help hearing the whir of blenders and clashing of pots and pans mingled with people talking to themselves and an occasional word that she was certain would be bleeped out of the final cut.

Once the water was boiling, she added four eggs. She only needed three, but she was a lifelong Girl Scout and knew to always be prepared. She set a timer for six minutes and went back to the sausage. She made four flat oval patties with the sausage balls and left them until the eggs were ready. She moved on to her specialty, something she made regularly at the restaurant to the delight of her customers. She cracked open two eggs and separated them from the yolk, then combined the yolks with the milk and cheeses, whisking them together gently but not over-beating them. The timer went off, and she lifted the saucepan from the stove and set it in the sink letting cold water run over the soft-boiled eggs.

"Fifteen minutes down," Gideon yelled, and she heard groans from one of the other stations. Suddenly, their host was standing between her and Lorenzo, who she was surprised to realize was still there, cooking beside her, as much in his own world as she had been in hers. She noticed Christina and José talking to some of the other chefs.

"And what are you working on, Lorenzo?"

"I'm making a family favorite. Pea, prosciutto, and pecorino frittata."

"Homemade frittatas in an hour?"

"Yes, Chef."

"Gutsy move. I hope it's completely cooked when it hits that tasting table."

"Yes, Chef."

Holly listened with interest while not taking her eyes or her mind off the egg whites she was whipping into soft peaks. She wondered if Lorenzo would pull it off. After tasting some of his food, she felt certain that he could, but the pressure was definitely on.

"Holly, I imagine you're used to cooking breakfast foods under pressure."

"Yes, Chef. Every day."

"Those peaks look nice. Tell me, what will they be used in?"

"Chef, I'm making ricotta hotcakes with Scotch eggs." She stopped whipping and turned off the water, reaching in to feel the temperature of the eggs.

"You're making Scotch eggs for a Scottish chef? Bold move. If they don't taste like my mother's eggs, you may be the first one sent home."

"Yes, Chef. I understand."

Gideon moved on and Holly carefully peeled the eggs. She placed the eggs onto the sausage ovals, molding the sausage around the eggs. She put some flour in a bowl, beat the eggs into another, and poured breadcrumbs into a third bowl, creating an assembly line. She gently dipped the egg and sausage creations in each of the bowls—flour, beaten eggs, then breadcrumbs— and rested them on a plate.

"Thirty minutes to go!"

She needed five to six minutes to cook the eggs and about four minutes to cook the hotcakes, which had to be piping hot when presented. However, she still needed to garnish the plates before they could be served. She needed to use these next thirty minutes very carefully, or her food would be cold and unappetizing.

Holly looked over at Lorenzo's station. Judging by the aroma of onions, garlic, and other mouth-watering scents, she guessed that his main course was in the oven. She watched him cut artisan bread into smaller squares and place it in the oven, then whip together some berries, sugar, and cinnamon. She wondered what he was making, but she needed to think about her own dish.

Holly went to the display of herbs and chose several nice pieces of rocket, one of her favorite herbs. She washed and broke it into three-inch pieces. She got out three plates and placed them on the counter beside the rocket then glanced at the clock.

"Fifteen minutes, everyone! Start thinking about plating and getting those garnishes ready."

Holly breathed a sigh of relief. She was doing great on time. She carefully laid each Scotch egg in the hot, sizzling oil, noting the time. She then prepared another pan, lathering it generously with butter. She watched the clock carefully, adding her hotcakes to the buttered pan at the right time and keeping an eye on the eggs.

When the countdown began to the end of the first competition, Holly was carefully plating her breakfast, garnishing it with the rocket. As she set her plate on the counter to be judged, she breathed a sigh of relief. The angels must have been watching over her, giving her the confidence that she needed to get this thing started. Unfortunately, she knew it would all be uphill from here.

***

Lorenzo wiped the sweat from his brow with the end of his apron after setting his plate on the counter. He was nervous that his frittata would be runny, and he wasn't sure how these highly esteemed chefs would feel about his twice cooked toast with butter and quick-set jam.

Despite reading the book and seeing the outline of each day, Lorenzo experienced one surprise after another. After their food was cooked and plated, the judges sampled everything right there at each person's station. They didn't say anything and didn't reveal their thoughts. The chefs ate while the food was hot, taking their time to try each dish, making notes on everything but not saying a word. It had been two hours since they disappeared behind the curtain, and Lorenzo's nerves were shot.

Now, the competing chefs all stood in a huddle as they watched the judges pretend to taste their food for the first time. Lorenzo scanned the other plates, already knowing what they all contained. The contestants had plenty of time to talk about their creations, what went well, and what went terribly wrong.

Now, laid out on the counter before the judges were pancakes layered with thick cheeses or heavy creams and fresh fruits, crepes filled with sweet and savory ingredients, French toast that looked light and heavenly, and bowls of baked goodness that he could smell from across the room. They all looked amazing despite being ice cold.

Lorenzo swallowed hard as Gideon introduced the first dish.

***

"Here, we have traditional French toast served alongside eggs baked with spinach, mushrooms, goat's cheese, and ground sausage." The camera zoomed in on the plate.

Christina took a bite of the baked eggs. "Mmm, so good," she said with a mouthful of food. "And hot!" She fanned her mouth and the contestants laughed. "What a taste. The spinach and mushroom blend so nicely with the goat's cheese and sausage. Wonderful flavor. Unfortunately, the egg is a bit undercooked."

"I agree," said José, shaking his head. "It's a shame. This would've been a nice dish, but you need to get that egg just right for it to work." He took a bite of the French toast. "Good flavor. I can taste the cinnamon and butter with hints of vanilla. Nothing is too overpowering. It's just a little boring."

"I have to agree," Christina said. "I would like to have had a fun variation on the French toast."

Gideon tsked. "We wanted a traditional breakfast with personality and flair, and we got undercooked eggs and bland French toast."

They moved on as the camera caught the contestants nervously shifting while they stood and watched.

"This is an interesting take on some old favorites," Gideon said while the camera panned the plate. "We have corn fritters with avocado salsa, accompanied by baked potatoes and chorizo."

"Wow," José said as he chewed. "This I did not expect. Taste that jalapeño. Just perfect. What a great twist on morning hash browns."

"And these corn fritters," Christina said, wiping a spot of salsa from her chin. "José, this will take you back to your mother's breakfast table."

"Mmm, no." He looked at the camera. "Sorry, Mama, but this is better. Again, wow."

The camera focused on Anna, who was beaming with pride.

They went down the line sampling crispy pancakes with hot chocolate sauce, a croque madame breakfast sandwich, gluten free coconut pancakes with fresh palm sugar syrup, and a potato rosti with salmon, egg, and hollandaise. Some were uncontested hits, others failed either on the imprecise preparation or paltry presentation.

Gideon pointed to Holly's dish, and a camera and microphone caught her quick intake of breath. "This chef made ricotta hotcakes and Scotch eggs."

"Brave move," Christina praised. "Have you tasted them?"

"Not yet." Gideon chuckled. "And I doubt I'll be insulting my mother on national television." He jabbed José with his elbow.

"You first," he said to Christina.

She dug in and took a bite. The camera zoomed in on her face, reflecting delight as she chewed. "Mmm. Mmm, oh my gosh. This makes me wish I was Scottish. Oh, my goodness. Did your mother make this when you were a kid?"

Gideon nodded. "All the time." He picked up a fork and scooped a bite into his mouth. His eyes widened as he looked at José. "Oh, wow. I might have to take back what I said. Sorry, Mum," Gideon said into the camera. "This is delicious."

José cut into the pancake and chewed, then cut off another bite. "Perfection. It's not easy getting that cheese and milk ratio right. Too much, and the pancakes are thin and runny. Too little, and they're thick and gummy. These are just right."

"And the perfect accompaniment to the eggs, don't you think, Gideon?" Christina asked.

He nodded and continued to chew, moving them on to the next dish. He swallowed and wiped his mouth with a napkin. Though Lorenzo attempted to look discretely at Holly, the camera picked up on his movement and zoomed from one to the other. Holly quickly wiped her eyes and sniffled a few times, and Lorenzo smiled.

Interesting, thought the cameraman.

Then the camera focused on Lorenzo as Gideon said, "Next is a pea, prosciutto, and pecorino frittata with double toasted bread topped with butter and a fruit spread."

"A frittata made from scratch and cooked in under an hour?" José asked, his forehead wrinkled in either disbelief or concern.

Gideon shrugged. "We'll see. Cooking at a higher temperature can yield a burnt or too hard bottom with overcooked cheese, but undercooking will result in an absolute mess. Who's going to be brave enough to give it a try first?"

Christina looked dubious, her mouth askew and one eyebrow raised, but she cut into the frittata. "I like that it's served right in the mini cast-iron pan with garnish and all. It's just how I would want it to come out of the kitchen."

"That really seals in the heat and lets it keep cooking just a bit longer," Gideon said. "Which might be just what this chef was hoping for." He, too, cut into the cheese-topped dish that resembled a personal pan pizza as the camera followed his fork to his mouth.

"Mmm, nice," Gideon said. "This chef has cooked this before. Just the right blend of seasonings. Taste that paprika and those chives. Delightful."

"What about the eggs?" Christina asked. "Too soft, too hard, or just right?"

José chimed in. "Just right. Amazing."

"It is. It's a really nice dish." The camera followed as Christina picked up a piece of toast and bit into it. "Nice Italian touch to go with the ethnic double toasted bread, and the fruit spread is perfect, but I'm not sure this is what we were looking for as far as the bread item."

"He spent all his time on the frittata," Gideon said.

"But what was he doing while it was cooking?" She shook her head. "Pity. I really liked this one."

The camera showed Lorenzo's head drop to his chest. He closed his eyes and let out a breath. Not escaping the notice of the camera or microphone, Holly shifted toward Lorenzo.

She whispered, "Don't worry. It was still one of the best dishes so far, and it's only the first battle."

Without lifting his head, he turned toward her and smiled. The camera captured that, too.

"Thanks," he mouthed to her.

The chefs were finishing the final dish, and in a flash, they disappeared behind a curtain.

The chefs congratulated each other and smiled, some trying not to let their feelings show. The camera, however, caught everything.

***

"There you are." Anna said when she found Holly by the pool. "Day one is over. What do you think?" She sat down in a vacant lounge.

Holly collapsed deeper into the lounge and breathed loudly, even though she was still basking in the glow of the day. She was convinced that the first day would be her last day, and to think that she was awarded top chef in round one. She could hardly believe it.

"Exhausted is an understatement. Everything hurts, both physically and mentally. I'm not even sure I can remember everything that happened today. It's such a blur."

"I agree." Anna reached over and grabbed Holly's hand. "And you came out on top. Congratulations! Can you believe it?"

"No, I really can't." Holly shook her head.

"I feel bad for Jane, but someone had to lose. I'm just happy it wasn't me."

"We're safe to do it all over again tomorrow," Holly said.

"I can't wait!" Anna said enthusiastically. "We've got this, girl. I have confidence in us."

Holly smiled, but she didn't agree. She'd won the first battle, but the war was just beginning.

***

"Viewers may know that Chincoteague Island is a barrier island in the Mid-Atlantic," Gideon says, standing on a sand dune with the water to his back. "Behind me is Assateague Channel, and the land over there is Assateague Island, which lies partly in Virginia and partly in Maryland."

Gideon turns and points to the landscape and across the channel to the land beyond.

"This is the land of the famous Assateague Ponies and the Chincoteague Pony Swim," Gideon continues. "These horses are believed to have come to the islands after a Spanish shipwreck hundreds of years ago. The famous pony auction has been taking place since at least

1835 and was the inspiration for the book and movie, *Misty of Chincoteague*. My daughter read that book when she was little." He smiles at the memory.

"Chincoteague is a small island with a big history, and we plan on showcasing the island's uniqueness throughout the season."

Hi, I'm Bob, and I'm the head chef at Prime Rib and Rockfish, a seafood restaurant on a floating dock on Chincoteague Island. I grew up rock fishing with my dad and my older brother, Mick. The thing I hated most about fishing was the cleaning of the fish, so Mick always volunteered. [Photographs of Bob and Mick fishing flash onto the screen.] When I was sixteen, Mick was killed in a car accident, and my life spiraled. I got into drugs, I drank, I almost got kicked out of school more than once. Then one day, my parents told me I had to move out or clean up. They insisted I get a job. I saw an ad saying the restaurant was hiring someone to clean fish. Imagine that. I saw it as a sign from Mick that if I took the job, he'd be right there with me cleaning every fish. [Bob wipes tears from his eyes.] I went from cleaning fish to learning to cook fish, and that sparked my interest in all kinds of cooking. Now, I'm going on thirty years as a chef, and I've loved every minute of it, especially ordering someone else to clean the fish. [Bob flashes a killer smile with a mouth of perfect, pearly whites.]

Chapter Five

"One day down, eleven to go," Gideon said when they all arrived the next day. "I know it's hard to say goodbye to someone after just one day. It's an emotional way to start out, but that's how it goes. And don't feel too badly for Jane. She'll be hanging out at the Harbor spa all day getting a massage and having her nails done."

Everyone laughed.

"Congratulations again to Holly who was the top chef in yesterday's competition. Congratulations to Jerry who won the elimination challenge. Don't let yourself get that fricking close to losing again. Yesterday was an easy day. We should have had the hardest time ever choosing winners, but that didn't happen. I can't imagine what some of you were thinking in there. Come on! You need to be better than that. Make sure your food is cooked all the way through, your sides are worthy of your meal, and you're representing the best your restaurant has to offer. We want to bring people to your town, not scare them away. Now, chefs, let's get to work on round two!"

Everyone cheered, and Gideon went inside. Holly blew out her breath and said a silent prayer that today would go as well as yesterday. She felt eyes on her and looked up to see Lorenzo staring at her. He quickly looked away, and she felt the warm glow of a blush coming on.

Kayla bumped Holly with her elbow. "I bet you're feeling pretty good after yesterday, aren't you? Congratulations."

Holly's cheeks grew even warmer as she turned toward Taylor's family friend.

"I was so surprised. I really thought I'd be out on day one."

"What?" Kayla said, drawing back with wide eyes. "You're kidding, right? Your food is amazing."

"My breakfast foods and sandwiches are okay, but I don't know how I'm going to keep up in the rest of the rounds."

Kayla shook her head and started to say something but was interrupted by the crew member they now knew as Rachel.

"Time to get started, everyone. Lots on the agenda for today."

Holly didn't have much time to enjoy Kayla's praise. She needed to concentrate on day two, and only God— and Gideon—knew what would be thrown at her this afternoon.

***

"Did you know it would be like this?" Holly asked.

Lorenzo took a long drink of water and looked around. All the contestants had just come from hair and makeup and were waiting in line for more interviews which would be used for the show's promotions and for the clips shown throughout the competition.

"Nope," he said honestly. "I just thought we'd be cooking. That whole book listing everything expected of us each day really threw me for a loop."

"Same. I had no idea that these shows worked this way."

"Congratulations, by the way. Your breakfast really impressed Chef Randall."

She squinted at him and pursed her lips, giving him the impression that she was scrutinizing his words for some kind of insult. He resisted flinching and wondered how he managed to get them off on such bad footing. Finally, she spoke.

"Thank you. Breakfast is my specialty. I'm not confident that I'll do as well with the other dishes."

Lorenzo shook his head. "That's not what I've been told. My sister says your sandwiches are amazing."

"Your sister?"

"Antonia. She's my manager. One of the things she likes to do is eat often at the other eateries on the island to get a feel for what they're cooking and what the customers like. She's young, but she's smart with a good head for the restaurant business." He leaned closer and said conspiratorially, "But don't ever tell her I said that."

Watching Holly laugh, Lorenzo had a sudden realization. He liked her laugh and wanted to hear more of it.

"Lorenzo, your turn," Rachel called and motioned him to the room where the interviews were taped.

"See you in the kitchen," he said to Holly with a smile. She almost smiled back, and he could tell that she was still judging him, trying to decide if he was trustworthy or at least someone worth talking to. The fact that she spoke first that morning was a good sign. Lorenzo didn't like thinking that she disliked him. Not her in particular, but anyone. He'd struggled with self-esteem issues as a youngster. Being the middle kid in a family of do-gooders, great chefs, and naturally talented people made one question their own abilities. Those feelings didn't go away easily.

No matter how successful his restaurant might become, Lorenzo knew that he would always be a fraud. He just didn't have the talent that the rest of the family had. It was only a matter of time before everyone knew it.

***

Diane surveyed the damage. All the food was lost, everything in the walk-in and the freezer.

"How could this happen?" asked Christy.

"The electric company says that Holly called late last night and told them there was a problem, that the electricity needed to be cut off for the next week."

"Why would she do that?" Christy asked.

"She didn't," Molly said irritably. "She doesn't have a phone, remember?"

"None of that matters now," Diane said. "I've gotten it straight with the electric company. What matters is that we've got no food. Everything in the walk-in and freezer was way over temperature, and there's no way to know for how long."

"Okay," Christy said. "So, we need to order new food. Do we have an inventory of what was lost?"

"Freddy and I have been working on it," Diane said. "But without food, we can't open, and if we don't open, we don't make money to buy food."

"There isn't anything we can serve?" Christy asked.

Diane shook her head. "Not much. There was so much that Holly prepared before she left. She baked and froze desserts, made hollandaise sauce with her own secret ingredient, spent hours kneading and baking the baguettes and croissants she uses for sandwiches. She even froze soups she prepared all month long. She put hours into making sure we would be covered."

"We've got to make this work." Christy said. "Holly can't know what happened, she can't lose the café. She's got so much talent, and she put her entire inheritance into this place."

"Well, we need to figure out how to keep things going here. What if we did a fundraiser?" Molly asked.

"You know, like one of those GoFundMe things. We tell people what happened and stir up some sympathy for her. It might even bring in more customers."

Diane liked the way they were thinking, but there was one problem. "Well, we need food in order to have customers."

"I think we can handle that," Christy said. "Just give me an hour, and I'll take care of everything."

"You're going to replace everything Holly prepped over the course of an entire month in one afternoon?" Diane knew that was a stretch, to say the least.

"Not quite, but I can come close. Freddy helped her do a lot of the prep, and Molly can find the files in her computer with her secret sauces."

"You can?" Diane asked.

"Well, I've never done it, if that's what you're asking. But can I? Of course. It's not rocket science. And even if it were—"

"She can do it," Christy said. "Now, we just need to get permission to use some temporary kitchen space and find more cooks. And I've got that covered."

"You do?" Diane asked.

"I sure do. Come on, Diane, what have you told me over and over again since the day Molly and I came to this island?"

"We're all family here, and we look out for one another."

"All for one, and one for all," Christy said. "And I know just where to start."

***

"So, are you ready for day two?" Lorenzo heard Anna ask when she and Holly emerged from the women's restroom.

"As ready as I can be," she answered.

"Lorenzo."

He turned at the sound of his name and smiled at the chef walking up to him.

"Walt," the man said, reaching out his hand. "I just wanted to tell you how much I enjoy your cooking."

"Thanks, Walt. I appreciate that."

"You're welcome. Well, let the best chef win."

Lorenzo stood still and watched Walt walk away. He was an odd man, angry one minute and friendly the next. Lorenzo almost laughed at the thought. He supposed most people would describe him the same way if they saw him in the kitchen. He guessed he and Walt had that in common.

Rachel appeared at the door and called everyone to their stations. Once they were all in place, Gideon recapped the day before and once again congratulated Holly on her top dish, and Jerry for saving himself from elimination.

"Okay, today we're really pushing you all to a much higher level. I hope everyone knows how to open a bottle of wine."

The contestants laughed as expected.

"You know I do," said Cynthia the Tik Tok chef. "Since I turned twenty-one in May, and I've been keeping the island liquor store and bars in business."

"The real question is," Gideon continued. "Can you cook with wine?"

A curtain opened to their left, and a wall of wines were displayed, some on shelves and some in wine fridges. There were dozens of bottles. Lorenzo could see small labels on the shelves denoting where each wine was produced.

"As you can see, you have lots to choose from," Gideon said. "But you must choose wisely. Not all wine is good for cooking, and not all dishes are enhanced by adding wine. And there's only one of each bottle, so if you need a particular wine for your recipe, you better find it fast. Start the timer…now!"

The director yelled, "Cut." Everyone exhaled, knowing another long day was underway.

A couple hours later, they all knew what they were cooking and were back at their stations.

Lorenzo hurried to the walk-in and grabbed chicken thighs but came up short on fresh anchovies. Luckily, he found a can and decided that would have to do. He looked long and hard but was able to come up with only a jar of capers and a bottle of olive oil before he dashed to the wine wall and perused the Italian wine selections. He chose a nice bottle of pinot grigio but took a quick peak at the Italian reds. How could he get Gideon to partner with his Aunt Marta's family vineyard in Valpolicella? That was something he'd have to find out.

He grabbed a package of angel hair pasta and a pound of butter. He dropped those at his station and went in search of fresh rosemary, garlic, and an onion. He rarely used onions in his own kitchen. Good Italian food didn't need them, but he wasn't sure what the American judges would say if he left it out. By the time he reached his station, he had decided against using it. Why ruin his grandmother's recipe? He set it aside and began prepping his pan.

"What are you making?" Holly asked as she seasoned the chicken breasts she'd chosen.

"Rosemary chicken with tomato sauce. It's my grandmother's recipe."

Holly smiled. "Mine, too. Chicken and red wine casserole with herb-flavored dumplings. It's a far cry from what I'm used to making, but this was one of my favorite recipes as a kid, so my grandmother taught me to make it. I never thought I'd be making it for something like this."

"Onion!" Anna yelled. "I didn't grab an onion, and there aren't any left!"

"I've got you," Lorenzo called as he loaded a pan with olive oil and reached for the onion he'd abandoned. He tossed it through the air to Annam who caught it. A few whistles sounded, and someone yelled, "Get that guy a jersey."

"Gracias," Anna called, and they all bent their heads back toward their work.

"That was nice," Holly remarked.

Lorenzo held out his hands. "You heard what Gideon said. It's okay to be nice and share."

"They sure don't show that on TV." Holly checked the temperature of her pan and began adding chicken. She glanced at the pan Lorenzo had simmering. "I love the smell of rosemary. I'd like to try that sometime."

"I'll make it for you sometime," he said automatically. He found that he liked the idea.

***

"Scotch eggs yesterday and Venison stew today?" Gideon asked. "What's going on here? Did you all call my mum in Scotland and ask her for a list of my favorite meals?"

The camera caught Holly and Dawn looking at each other, smiling.

"The flavor's wonderful. Not gamey. That's a danger with venison," Christina said. "And the soda bread is spot on." She looked at Gideon and said in a British accent, "Hear that? Spot on."

Gideon rolled his eyes. "Everybody's sucking up today. José, what do you think?"

"I like it a lot. It's hard to win with something like venison because perfect seasoning is difficult to achieve, but this one is, what did you say, Christina, 'spot on'?" The judges laughed. "I think this is going to give the rest of the dishes some very tough competition."

"I agree. Here's something else you don't eat every day." Gideon pointed to the next plate, and the camera zoomed in on the dish. "Herb and lamb cobbler."

"A bit like shepherd's pie, right?" José asked. "Not something I've ever tried, I don't think."

"This will be interesting," Gideon said. "It usually takes twice as long to cook, so let's hope the flavors mingled the way they should."

The camera zoomed in on Bob as he drew in his breath and held it.

José took the first bite and made a face. "I'm not a fan of raw carrots, especially in a casserole. These didn't cook at all."

"Way too much onion," Christina said with a sour look on her face. "Onions should enhance a meal, not overpower it. Too many chefs make that mistake. Maybe if it had cooked longer and the flavors had time to cultivate, it would be better, but I'm not a fan."

The camera moved. The skirt steak with shallot pan sauce was a hit, and the judges praised the perfectly cooked steak. Jake's grilled spareribs with a pinot noir barbecue sauce was declared a "real treat." Anna's sautéed chorizo accompanied by colorful paella rice and slices of "well-cooked and delicious" red, yellow, and green peppers, was a frontrunner.

The camera caught Holly smiling at Anna, and Anna did a little happy dance.

"Here we have chicken and red wine casserole with herb-flavored dumplings." Gideon frowned. "Another casserole. Can't you all come up with anything better? Casseroles aren't exactly fine dining foods."

"Don't knock it 'til you try it," Christina said. "My mother's casseroles could stand up to any gourmet meal."

"Well, let's see about this one," Gideon countered.

"Perfectly cooked chicken," Christina said after taking a bite.

"I love the herb dumplings," José chimed in. "You can really taste the thyme and parsley without them over-powering the buttery goodness of the dumpling. Gideon?"

"Not bad for a casserole."

The camera zoomed to Holly smiling.

"Rosemary chicken with tomato sauce." Gideon pointed to the next dish. "A family recipe, I'm told. Let's see if it's a family that knows anything about cooking."

The camera moved closer as the chefs each took a bite.

"Oh, wow," said José. "The chicken just melts in your mouth. And taste that rosemary. Delicious."

"I'm not the biggest fan of anchovies, but they really make this dish," Christina said as she took another bite. "And the capers add just the right amount of saltiness."

"And this person used no onion," Gideon remarked. "Yet the flavor is powerful. Perfectly seasoned. Nice job."

Christina took a bite of the next dish and began coughing. The camera followed her hand as she reached for a glass of water. A close-up showed José's face turning red as he chewed. Another camera spied Walt flinching, then moved on from him to the dish in question.

"What the—" Gideon's expletives ended in a choking fit. "What happened to this braised beef?" He downed a glass of water, spilling some of it down the front of his shirt in his haste to drown the food.

"I like it," José said despite the red face. He, too, reached for a water.

"You like it? I could hardly swallow it." Gideon wiped his chin and looked down at the dish. "There's heat, and then there's a deadly inferno. Christina?"

She put up her hand and took another long drink of water. "I like spicy foods, but this is over the top. And the braised beef should be the star of the show."

"Why the cranberry gravy?" José asked. "That's my question. The fruit and the spice just don't go together. I like the heat, but that cranberry must go."

"The vegetables are overcooked," Christina said. "Overall, this whole dish is a big disappointment."

"Here, we may have something special." Gideon said. "Jerry, I understand that you used my personal recipe for coq au vin, correct?"

Jerry answered, "I did, chef. We make it in the restaurant, and it's very popular. Of course, I've tweaked it a bit to make it my own."

"You tweaked my recipe?" Gideon asked, eyebrows raised. The camera went back and forth between the two men.

"I did, Chef. You once said that every great chef finds his or her way to make their mark on a recipe."

"Well, I guess the proof is in the pudding, or the coq au vin," Gideon said, prompting everyone to laugh.

"The chicken is a little dry," Christina said. "But it has a lot of flavor."

"The flavor is definitely different. What kind of wine did you use?" Gideon asked.

"I appreciate you including local wines in the selection. I chose a blackberry wine made at a local Eastern Shore winery. I like that it has the basic essence of the traditional burgundy, but it gives the dish a local flair."

"Nice touch. Tell me, how well does the dish sell in your restaurant?" Gideon asked.

Jerry smiled. "One of the most popular dishes on the menu."

"Can't beat that," Gideon said. He clapped his hands together. "Well, that's the last one. Shall we go chat?" Gideon asked, and the cameras followed them from the room.

After the judges returned from their huddle behind the curtain, they declared Dawn the top chef of the day, saying her venison stew was far and away the best they'd ever tasted. Gideon then announced the contestants for the elimination round. Bob and Walt took their place on the elimination platform and waited to hear what they would be cooking.

***

"I'm standing at the top of the Assateague Lighthouse," Gideon says into the camera. "As you can see, we have a spectacular view of both Assateague and Chincoteague Islands. Vast marshlands cover large areas of the islands, but there are also hiking trails, bike paths, and, of course, beautiful ocean beaches."

The camera pans the panoramic view, zooming in on the white foam waves caressing the sand, fenced in by tall marsh grasses.

"The original lighthouse was constructed in 1833 and stands 142 feet high. The lights, once candlelit and now electric, are still in use today as navigational aids and can be seen over nineteen miles out to sea. And the best part about this magnificent view is that it's free! It's just one of the many delights our crew has discovered during our filming here."

***

Lorenzo left his cottage and walked across the yard. He stepped onto the boardwalk that ran along the waterfront behind the main building. It was the perfect evening—warm but not too humid with a gentle breeze stirring the water. It was quiet along the narrows, and it reminded Lorenzo why he and his father chose this out-of-the-way resort town for his restaurant over the busy city of Baltimore.

He gazed over the water and watched a white heron slowly step out of the marsh which lined the channel that separated Chincoteague and Assateague Islands. Some of his fellow chefs were taking out the paddle boards and kayaks offered to them by the Harbor. He smiled, knowing they probably had little to no time to do this during an ordinary summer. He spied Holly, her blonde hair in its typical ponytail, sitting on the dock, and he went to sit next to her.

"Nice night," he said as he slid off his flip flops and dangled his feet next to hers. "Phew. That's cold."

"It's still early in the summer. In August, the water heats up. Some."

"Ah, yes, the chilly Atlantic."

Holly laughed, and he was reminded what a nice laugh she had.

"Too bad about Bob. I like the guy," Lorenzo said.

"Me too, but I guess someone has to lose."

"Yeah. How are you feeling after day two?"

"Nervous for the rest of the week. I pray I can keep getting dishes I know how to make, but my repertoire is limited."

"Do you? Pray, I mean?"

He knew it was an odd, out-of-the-blue question, so he wasn't surprised by the look she gave him. He wasn't even sure himself why he asked it.

"I do. Why?" she asked warily as though he was a door-to-door evangelist.

"I don't know. I just wondered."

"Do you?" she asked, her eyes filled with curiosity now that he'd broached the subject.

"Not as much as Mamma would like."

Holly laughed. "Ain't that the truth."

"Seriously, though. I just realized recently that I haven't been to church since I came here. To the island, I mean, not here as in the Harbor. It used to be a natural part of the week that I never thought to question. We didn't open the restaurant on Sundays until eleven, and the doors stayed locked until after the 7:30AM Mass. My parents were pretty strict about it."

"Not mine," Holly said. "We sometimes went on Christmas or Easter, but that was it. Christmas, mostly, I guess. And I think that was only because we would spend the holiday with my grandparents, and they never missed Sunday Mass. My grandfather went every day."

"My nonna, too. She said she couldn't start her day without spending time with the Lord."

"What made you bring this up? There must be a reason."

Lorenzo stared at his feet as they swayed back and forth under the water.

"I think it was making Nonna's dish today. I wondered if she was looking down on me, cheering me on. Then I thought, is she disappointed that I haven't made any effort at all to spend time with the Lord in months? I don't know. Maybe it's just too much down time in the evenings. It's throwing me off balance."

Holly was quiet as she watched Dawn and Jane steer a tandem kayak close to the shore.

"We should do that," she said.

"Do what?" Lorenzo asked, following her gaze, assuming she wasn't talking about Mass. "Oh, no. I don't think so."

"Why not?" She looked at him and cocked her head to the side.

"I've never…I mean, it probably takes a lot of energy, and we need that for the show."

Holly drew back and assessed him. "You've never kayaked before?"

"Well, I grew up in the city. There wasn't time for vacations. We went to Italy once when I was younger, but I don't remember much about it. Someone had died, I think. Nonna's mother? Or was it Nonno's?"

He looked up at the sky as though whomever it was might somehow supply the answer.

"So, you've never kayaked." Holly's question turned into a statement.

"I've never kayaked," he admitted.

"Okay, tomorrow evening, we kayak."

"What about the show? The days are exhausting, we should conserve our energy."

Holly shook her head. "Tomorrow evening. I mean it. If you're going to live on an island, you have to live like you're on an island."

Lorenzo looked back at Dawn and Jane who seemed to be lazily hanging out in the boat, their paddles draped across their laps.

"I guess I could give it a try."

"Good. It's a date."

He looked at Holly and saw her face redden. She gave her head a little shake. "I mean—"

Lorenzo smiled. "I know what you mean. It's a not-date-date."

Holly smiled back. "Exactly." She let out a puff of air. "Now, I'm going to head inside and take a long bath and enjoy a cup of chamomile tea before heading to bed." She stood and stretched, and Lorenzo watched her with a new kind of awe he couldn't quite explain.

They bid goodnight, but he sat a little longer thinking about their conversation. Holly was more interesting than he first thought. And someplace deep inside, he wondered what she looked like with her hair down, splayed across a pillow.

***

It was well past midnight, and Seaside Grill had been closed for a few hours. A flashlight shone the way from the pried-open back door into the wine closet.

Known across the island for its wine selection, the restaurant boasted an amazing array of wines from all over the world. No wonder she was so good at cooking with wine. She had an arsenal at her fingertips.

Fairly certain there wasn't any way someone could hear anything, he pulled one bottle from the wall and smashed it on the floor. He waited a few minutes, breath held, and listened for voices or movement. Assured that he was still alone and undetected, he smashed another, then another. He kept going, his heart beating faster with each new bottle he slung to the ground. He felt exhilarated, more alive than he'd ever felt before. Forget making phony calls to disrupt a business. This was much more satisfying.

Once all the bottles, save one, were on the floor, and he was standing in a sea of wine, he took several deep breaths, letting his heart slow down. Wine ran into every corner of the room, seeping across the threshold and soaking into the empty cardboard boxes in a corner. He pulled the last bottle from the shelf and walked away from the mess, his head starting to feel woozy from the heavy scents of the mingling wines.

He stopped just beyond the spilled wine and removed his shoes, careful to make sure the spreading liquid covered his footprints. Then he walked in his socks to the back door and slipped out as quietly as he had entered.

"My name is Dawn McNally, and I'm the owner and head chef at Seaside Grill. I started cooking as a little girl in my grandmother's kitchen. [Photos of Dawn and her grandmother dissolve in and out of the frame.] I always wanted to be an attorney, so I studied hard and made it to law school, but something was missing in my life. I sat in class and was totally bored. By the time I graduated, I hated everything about the law except when it came to the food industry. I made that my specialty, and I spent a few years helping new start-ups get licensed, understand the codes, and protect themselves from litigation over stupid things like hot coffee and fish bones in their filet. After five years, I turned in my briefcase and picked up a spatula. I've been cooking ever since. My husband, Ted, and I bought this place about ten years ago, and we don't want to ever do anything else."

Chapter Six

Just before taping on day three, Holly and Kayla found Anna in tears.

"Oh, honey, what's wrong?" Kayla asked, dropping to the floor beside Anna's chair and taking her hand. Holly pulled over another chair and sat beside Anna.

"I didn't know this would be so hard." Anna's tears began to pour faster. "I miss my kids. I miss my baby. He's so little, and I've never left him before."

Holly and Kayla exchanged sympathetic looks.

Kayla patted Anna's hand. "Sweetie, your baby is fine. Marcos is a wonderful husband. I'm sure he has everything under control."

Anna shook her head vehemently. "He's never had all three kids at once. What was I thinking? I should have sent someone else in my place."

"Who?" Holly asked. "Who else on your staff is as creative and talented as you? They all follow your lead."

"But my babies. They need me." Anna sniffled and took a breath.

"Of course, they do," Holly said. "But you're not going to be gone forever. Everyone is going to be just fine for a couple weeks."

"And Anna, you're doing so well," Kayla said.

"She's right, Anna," Holly encouraged her. "You almost won yesterday! You're destined to be top chef soon. You can't quit."

"You really think so?"

"Absolutely. Just wait and see." Holly squeezed Anna's hand. "Just think of how proud of you your family will be when everyone who watched the show starts flooding to your restaurant."

"Holly's right, Anna. You can't quit now. Besides, with Jane and Bob gone, we gals are still tied with the men. We need to stick together and start showing them who the real pros are."

Anna looked from one to the other and offered a feeble smile. "I am doing okay, aren't I?"

"You're doing more than okay," Kayla said. "I think you're my top competition, and I say that with both reverence and love."

"Come on, Anna. We're about to head in. You've got this." Holly stood and reached out her hand. Anna took Holly's hand and stood.

"Um, guys, how about a hand for me?"

They looked down at Kayla crouched on the floor and began to laugh. Both women reached for Kayla and pulled her up.

"I'm not as young as you two are."

"To be honest," Holly said. "I was thinking of leaving you down there. Your skirt steak was one the best meals of the day, according to the judges."

"Look who's talking, miss perfect herb dumplings," Kayla said with a smile.

"You know what?" Anna said. "When this is all over, we should all take turns making some of our best dishes for each other. We don't get to do things together very often, and we should change that."

"I love that idea," Kayla said. "We could take turns going to each other's restaurants, and on my turn, we could use my backyard. It would be fun."

"I'd want to really get to know each other and be friends. And I want to support each other's businesses more and leave the competing for the camera," Holly told them.

"Me too," Anna agreed. "Let's do this."

They all high-fived each other before heading over to the others. As they walked, Lorenzo sidled up next to Holly.

"What was that all about?"

"Anna missed her kids. She has a baby at home, not yet one, and she's feeling guilty about leaving him. She was on the verge of quitting. Kayla and I talked her into staying."

"Hmm," Lorenzo said.

"What?" She looked at him, trying to figure out what he was thinking.

"She's impressive," Lorenzo said. "Kids, marriage, and a fabulous restaurant. I don't think men give women like her," he turned to look at Holly, "like you, enough credit."

Holly smiled. "Thanks, but I'm not able to fill Anna's shoes or Kayla's. Maybe someday, but for now, I'm just watching and learning."

"I'm not a woman, and I feel like I'm learning from them, too, from everyone. Day two, and I'm already seeing what others do, how they do it, and how I can improve." His honesty surprised Holly.

Just then, Rachel appeared at the door and told everyone to get ready. Holly was seeing Lorenzo in a whole new light, but she would have to put those thoughts aside until after today's competition.

***

"Go, Holly, go!" Anna, Kayla, Dawn, and Cynthia cheered Holly on, giving her instructions and calling out the time left on the clock.

Lorenzo wanted to join them, but all the other guys were cheering for Jake.

When did it become a battle of the sexes?

Gideon talked up the round as Holly and Jake fought to stay in the competition.

"Today was all about seafood, and you guys live on an island! Everyone should have sailed through this task like Kayla, but you two are trying to save yourselves because your dishes were lacking in almost every area. Holly, you needed to elevate your game. You can't keep relying on your knowledge of breakfast and comfort foods. Jake, barbecued cobia fish takes finesse and can't come out like rubber. Now's your chance to show us what you've really got."

"Yes, Chef!" they both yelled without looking up from their work.

Gideon went to Holly's station and observed her for a few moments before commenting.

"Okay, Holly. For this round, you must elevate pasta by turning it into an amazing seafood dish. What do you have in the works for us?"

"Chef, I'm making a crab carbonara with lemons and capers."

Holly tossed the cooked pasta with olive oil and turned to check on the sizzling oil and garlic. Lorenzo could smell the garlic and hoped she knew it was ready. He found himself breathing a sigh of relief when she began adding the capers.

"I take it this isn't a dish you serve at the café."

Holly chuckled, but Lorenzo knew it wasn't her normal laugh, the laugh that did something to him deep inside that he wasn't ready to explore.

"No, Chef."

He watched her stir the capers and freshly ground pepper into the oil and garlic.

"Where did you learn to cook this?" Gideon asked.

"This is my first time, chef," she said. "But I'm good at trying new dishes. My parents weren't big cooks, so I ended up making a lot of our meals. I never thought I'd own a restaurant or café though. Manage one, yes, but never own one and do the cooking. But I like the challenge."

"Good. You're going to need that attitude in this round. The challenge is on."

Holly wiped her forehead and added the reserved pasta water to the pan, turning the heat up to medium, and Lorenzo nodded to himself. So far, she was doing everything right. She might not have cooked this before, but it was one of the most popular dishes his parents served back in Little Italy. It wasn't difficult to make, but it tasted decadent to the palate. That's why he had whispered the suggestion to Kayla and urged her to convince Holly to make it. When they were making their dishes earlier, she'd told him about some of the seafood dishes she'd made growing up, and he mentioned this dish as one that wouldn't be too far outside her comfort zone. He'd given her a few pointers that now seemed to be serendipitous strokes of luck.

He turned his attention to the conversation between Gideon and Jake. The smell of bacon filled the air as Jake's pan popped and sizzled.

"Clams and bacon are a great combination," Gideon was remarking about Jake's linguine with clams, bacon, and tomato.

"Yes, Chef. And bacon makes everything even better."

"Spoken like a true man," Gideon said with a laugh. "You're not using canned clams, I see. That's standard in a dish like this."

"Elevating Chef, elevating. Going above and beyond the standard. The clams are steaming now."

"Don't over-steam them, Jake. That will bring that elevation crashing like a lead balloon."

"Yes, Chef."

"Ten minutes left," Kayla shouted. "Come on, Holly!"

Lorenzo shifted his attention back to her. She was pouring the egg yolks into the pasta mixture while stirring vigorously. This was a crucial step. If her rhythm was off even just a bit, the mixture could be too thick or too runny. When she seemed satisfied, she began gently adding the crab and lemon.

He looked at the clock. She had plenty of time to finish seasoning, plate the dish, and add her garnishes.

"You've got this," Anna called.

Without meaning to, Lorenzo found himself cheering her on as well. "Come on, Holly. It looks great. Don't forget the sea salt."

"Hey," Jerry said, elbowing Lorenzo in the ribs. "What gives? Whose side are you on?"

"I didn't know it mattered." Jerry laughed, and Lorenzo focused on Holly. "Plate and garnish, Holly. Time's almost up."

Holly and Jake were both concentrating on garnishing their dishes. Just as Holly added a couple lemon wedges and a slice of garlic bread, time ran out.

"Time!" Gideon yelled. "Hands up!"

They both stepped back from their stations, hands in the air, and double high-fived each other. It was the moment of truth.

It seemed like hours before the decision was made, but not that much time had passed.

"Both dishes were very good," Gideon said. Christina and José nodded in agreement. "But we all three agree that only one truly rose above the typical pasta dish. Jake, you went from rubbery and tasteless fish to perfectly steamed clams. Holly, your uninspiring crab melts paved the way for a beautiful blend of crab, lemons, and capers. But only one of you can stay to compete another day." He looked back and forth as tensions rose in the room.

"I'm sorry to say that the chef going home today is…Jake."

Lorenzo held back the urge to shout in relief, but the women all whooped and hollered.

"Jake, you brought your A-game, but unfortunately, it wasn't enough. Best of luck to you."

Jake hugged Holly and then the others. He shook hands with a couple of the men and did a manly hug with the others, their bodies leaning into each other for that awkward one-handed pat around the back. Lorenzo shot his hand out and told Jake, "Good job. I'm looking forward to subscribing to your show."

"The Island BBQ King!" Jake yelled to them as he headed out the door.

Gideon turned back to Holly. "Good job today. You're a better chef than you give yourself credit for.

Don't be afraid to step out of your comfort zone. You can create more than sandwiches. From here on out, everything gets elevated. Got it?"

"Yes, Chef," she said, looking ready to drop from exhaustion.

"Okay," Gideon said, clapping his hands after the camera stopped rolling. "Wrap-up interviews, then you're done for the day. Get a good night's sleep. Tomorrow's going to be the hardest day yet."

*****

"Operation Save the Sand and Sugar is on," Molly announced as she plopped herself down at the counter.

"You hung all the signs?" Diane asked.

"Yep, and I had Jared take some to the flight center, too. Everyone there loves the café."

Just then, the café phone began ringing. Diane answered and smiled.

"Hello, Ronnie. Yes, you heard right. The Sand and Sugar is in trouble, and we don't want Holly walking away from her big chance to draw a crowd to the place."

"We all want to help, the whole family. We'll all donate some money, but I have a load of crab meat saved up in the freezer that Trevor and the boys caught. Can we donate that?"

Diane wanted to cry. "Oh, Ronnie, you're the best. I know Holly and Kayla are competing right now, but this is exactly what I always tell these girls about our little island. We're all family."

"Of course, we are. Kayla may be my daughter, but I know Christy, Holly, and their friends have become daughters to you. Whatever you and Holly need, we'll try to help you get it."

When they finished their call, Diane laid the phone back on the cradle, but she hadn't taken her hand away when it began ringing again. She answered, giving a thumb's up to Molly.

"Hi Kate. I just hung up with your mother-in-law."

"Good. I figured she'd want to help. I do, too. I know I can't talk to Holly this week, but can you find some good pictures of Holly, both in and out of the café?"

"I think so, why?"

"I'd like to run a story on her in the Chincoteague Herald about how she's making a new start with one of the oldest and most beloved businesses on the island. In addition, I'm going to run ads for free all week, urging people to stop by for donuts and sandwiches."

"Oh, Kate, you're wonderful. Thank you."

"You're quite welcome. When I was in trouble and didn't know where to go, this island opened its arms to me and pulled me in for a hug and then gave me a home. I'm all about giving back."

"That's what we do," Diane said through tears.

"It is. That's why I'm doing the same for Dawn."

"What? Dawn? What happened to her?"

Diane listened as Kate reported the news, that some kids had broken into the restaurant and destroyed her wine collection.

"Oh my. Do they know which kids did this?"

"They don't, and Dawn doesn't have cameras or a security system. Whoever thought we'd need those around here?"

"I hear you," Diane said, looking around the café. "I guess we've seen enough evidence over the past several years, though, that shows the world and its problems have found our little haven."

"You're right about that. Send me those pictures when you get a chance, and I'll send Lylah over to ask you some questions."

"Will do." Diane said goodbye and hung up.

"What's wrong?" Molly asked.

"I guess our little island is starting to have big world problems."

***

"Welcome to the Pony Express Nature Cruise," says Gideon, his blonde hair waving madly in the wind. "We're on a U.S Coast Guard certified tour boat that's giving us a tour of the island from the water. We're going to get a close-up of the wild ponies, look for some very special migratory birds, and we may even see a dolphin or two."

Gideon lifts a pair of binoculars strapped around his neck and points to the sky. "I'm told that a ruddy turnstone has been seen this morning, a remarkable species to add to my life list. I'm hoping to also see a bald eagle while we're out today."

He lets the binoculars rest against his chest and looks back at the camera. "After our cruise, we may take in some kayaking as part of our tour, but for now, we're going to enjoy the wind and the waves and see what other wildlife we can spot."

He returns to watching the sky as the view widens to encompass the island and sea landscape.

****

"Are you sure you aren't too tired?" Lorenzo asked as he eyed the boat warily.

Holly laughed. "Don't even try to get out of this. You'll see how relaxing it can be. Just do what I tell you to."

She coaxed him into the front of the kayak and handed him a paddle. He seemed more nervous than she expected. She knew he was a city boy, but really, it was just a kayak. She wasn't taking him aboard the Titanic.

"I'm going to sit in the back and steer. You just paddle how I tell you. When we get out a little, we'll sit back and relax."

She climbed into the kayak and told him to follow her lead.

"How can I do that? I can't see you."

"We'll start with one paddle on the right—that's starboard—and then lift it out of the water and take it the left—that's port. Then back again. Back and forth in nice, easy moves. Got it?"

"Why can't they just say right and left?" He asked.

"Because a boat's direction always changes, but no matter where you are on the boat, which direction it's heading, or which direction you're facing, everyone is clear on which side we're referring to. Starboard is always this side of the boat." She tapped the right side with her paddle. "And port is always this side." She raised the paddle and tapped on the left. "Even if you were facing me, this would be starboard." She paddled on the right. "And this would be port." She shifted the paddle and paddled on the other side.

"What about the front and back? They have names, too, right?"

"Yep. The bow and the stern." She paused and made a face. "But I don't know if we use those for small crafts like kayaks and canoes. I'll have to look that up when we get home."

"So, where is home to you?" he asked.

"Here, of course," she answered but then understood what he meant. "I guess you mean, where was home?"

"Well, yeah. Where did you grow up?"

"Here and there." She made a few strokes before letting the paddle rest in her lap. "Let's stop here and float a bit. Sometimes you can see the ponies from here. They like the marsh."

"Military?" Lorenzo asked, and Holly was momentarily confused.

"Oh, yeah. Dad was in the Coast Guard."

"Ah, so that's where you learned about boats."

"Boats and other things. Like, how to make new friends every three years or so, how not to get attached to people or places or even things, how to never try out for school plays or sports teams because you never knew when Dad was going to come in and announce that you were moving again." She sighed. "Sorry. It wasn't a bad life. It just wasn't a stable life. We never knew where we were going to end up or for how long. But it was better than being in the Army or Navy because we always knew we would be on some US coast and not whisked away to a foreign land, though I wouldn't have minded seeing the world."

"You must've liked living on the coast. You ended up here."

"Yeah, that's the ironic thing. I'm not a beach person. Can't stand sand. I mean, I really can't stand it."

"Yet you moved to an island."

Chuckling, she said, "I moved to an island because I went to college at Saint Louis University. It has the third best hospitality school in the nation, met my mother's criteria as a Catholic school, and offered me a nice scholarship. What it didn't have was water. I had no idea how much I loved the water until I didn't have it. I also didn't realize how much I hate living in urban areas."

"Baltimore has water but it's about as urban as you can get."

"And it has cruise ships, which is what led me to Baltimore for a time."

"You lived in Baltimore?" He quickly turned, trying to look at her, and the kayak wobbled.

"Whoa, Lorenzo. Let's not end up in the water."

She waited until the boat stopped rocking.

"I was based in Baltimore, but I lived on a cruise ship."

"I can't say I've ever known anyone who lived on a cruise ship before."

"It's why I went into hospitality. I loved being on ships, but I had no desire to go into the Navy or the Coast Guard. I'd had enough of that life. I thought a cruise ship was the perfect alternative."

"And was it?"

Holly was quiet as she watched the marsh for a moment, wondering if any ponies were nearby.

"It was horrible, to be honest. We worked long hours, had no days off for months at a time, had to deal with the most obnoxious passengers, and had no privacy." She shook her head. "Like a lot of military kids, I didn't have any brothers or sisters. Dad was gone a lot, and Mom had a hard enough time with one kid. She didn't want more. Going from an only child with my own room and a big house to hang out in, living on a cruise ship felt stifling. And then there was the partying. After hours was awful for anyone who wasn't into the party scene."

"Which you weren't, I take it."

"Not for me. I just never got into all that. I was happy to sit and read or go for a dip in the pool. But I missed doing this, just being out on the water in my own boat on my own time."

"Did you travel anywhere fun?"

"Only to the Caribbean. A lot. And if I had a few hours off, I often kayaked or snorkeled, but only if I had a friend on board who would go with me. Nobody has any idea just how many young women disappear from cruise ships and tropical islands every year."

"How long did you do that?"

"Two years, then I just wanted the island with the ship. I was familiar with Chincoteague, being so close to Baltimore, and I'd come here as a kid when my dad was stationed at Portsmouth, Virginia. I remembered liking it here."

"Where are your parents now?"

"Monterey. They wanted Dad's last port to be in sunny California, and I suspect they'll stay out west. They like the lifestyle. I'm more of a small town, quiet life kind of gal."

The sun was touching the tops of the trees, and Holly knew it was time to head back in.

"Ready to go? It'll be dark soon, and morning comes early."

"You know, you might have twisted my arm to get me out here, but I could sit here all night," Lorenzo said in a low, far-away voice.

Holly thought about the man sitting in front of her, of his life with brothers and sisters, his home that never changed, and the friends who were probably the same ones he'd had all his life.

She felt like she, too, could stay here all night, with him. The feeling that came over her at the thought was the nicest one she'd felt in a very long time. But then, reality hit her. They were living in a strange fantasy world not unlike the life she lived on the cruise ship. Nonstop days dealing with one crisis after another and nights that went by too quickly even if the view was incredible. And when this was over? They'd return to their normal existence in professions that didn't often cater to the best family lives. Then again, his family seemed to have it together.

"Holly," she heard him whisper, breaking the spell of twilight. "Look. Over there." He pointed, and she turned her gaze toward the marsh.

"Phantom," she breathed.

"You recognize him? How?"

"Taylor is kind of obsessed with him. He's sired many of the ponies on the island. He keeps to himself most of the time, so that's why she named him Phantom. He's like a ghost who stays in the shadows until he shows up out of the blue."

They sat and watched him for a few minutes, but the night sky was beginning to darken.

"We'd better go," Holly said. She lifted her paddle and started to steer them back toward the Harbor.

"Holly," Lorenzo said, his voice low. "Thank you. For getting me out here and telling me about yourself. I needed that."

"You're welcome, Lorenzo. I needed it, too. It's been a long time since…" She let the words trail off.

"Since?"

"Never mind. This was really nice. But if you want to get back before it's completely dark, you'd better pick up that paddle and get to work."

She hadn't said, *Since I didn't feel any pressure to have feelings for a guy or act a certain way*, but she'd thought it.

***

The instincts of a former sniper never fade. There wasn't a noise in the night, or even a shift in the air, that Zach didn't hear or detect.

He looked at his phone. 1 a.m. Was EJ home? His curfew was midnight, and he didn't typically push his limits even though he was getting ready to head to college in the fall. Maybe he lost all track of time and was just getting home.

Zach tossed off the covers and stealthily walked down the hall, another trait that was still ingrained in him like the desert sand. He tapped lightly on EJ's door, but there was no answer. He gently turned the knob and peeked into the room, where he heard EJ's light snore before he made out the shape on the bed. Zach started to pull the door closed and then recalled the scene in *Ferris Bueller* where the not-so-sick kid faked his sleeping body. Zach moved across the room like a panther and gazed at his stepson's forehead just above the bedsheet.

After quietly closing the door, he walked to the next room which Todd, the younger of the two, inhabited. Like his mother, Kayla, Todd still had the occasional nightmare, a remnant of the harrowing night he'd been kidnapped and left for dead on the beach. Luckily for them all, Nick, Zach's best friend and the newest police recruit, had found him. Still, Kayla had a hard time pushing away the dreams. Like mother, like son.

Though almost ten, Todd was nestled with his favorite teddy bear. He looked much younger than he was, but that had been true even before his teacher had lured him and two other boys from their homes. Zach resisted the urge to scoop up the little boy and hold him, but Todd was sleeping soundly, no signs of any bad dreams tonight.

Perplexed, Zach went to the stairs and listened. His body stiffened at the unmistakable sound of the kitchen door being closed. Though the sound was low, and care obviously had been taken to not make any noise, Zach's ears were better trained than most and picked up on the faint click even from the top of the stairs.

Relying on his honed instincts, he slowly made his way down, one step at a time. If someone was still in the house, Zach was going to get the jump on him. His bare foot touched the hardwood floor as he eased himself down onto the first level.

He didn't have a weapon, but weapons were sometimes overrated for a man of his training. Though he spent his days looking through the scope of a rifle, he was just as good with his bare hands.

Zach peered around the corner, but the kitchen was empty. Moreover, he didn't feel anyone watching him or sense another being in the room. The hairs on his neck were still in place, and his heart was beating at a normal pace. He let the rest of his body relax and stepped into the kitchen.

Everything appeared normal, but Zach knew that it wasn't. Something was off. He looked around and wished he could place what it was. If Kayla had been there, she would have known in a second. He wished he could FaceTime her, take her on a tour of her own kitchen, but he didn't have that luxury while she was competing.

Careful not to touch anything—after all, he was certain someone had been in the house—he examined every surface. Nothing looked disturbed. Then, Zach noticed the door to the storage room was slightly ajar. That wasn't right. The boys knew they weren't allowed in there, and Zach didn't even allow himself to enter the sacred space unless he and Kayla were cooking. Even as the one doing the cooking this week, it felt strange to him to enter the room without Kayla there.

It was built to be a dining room, but Kayla had long ago turned it into a home office for herself and a homework center for the boys. Over the winter, Zach had knocked out the back wall and expanded the room so that it now housed a dedicated office space for Kayla and a large storage area for her lesser used appliances and the many pantry staples their business needed.

As soon as Zach opened the door, he knew something was wrong. Even with the lights off, he could sense it, hear it.

He flipped the switch and jumped back with a jolt. The room was literally crawling with ants. In the short amount of time between Zach's waking and his entering the kitchen, the ants had managed to take over the entire room. If he hadn't detected someone in the house, the ants would have found their way into every bag and box in the room by morning.

Zach looked at the floor and saw several ant colony terrariums, the kind kids used to buy at hobby shops when Zach was a little boy, that promised hours of enjoyment watching the insects hard at work in their glass home.

Something larger caught Zach's eye, and he quickly went to a corner on the far side of the room. An empty box lay on the floor and scurrying away were several large, ugly roaches. He closed his eyes and let out a long breath. Kayla was going to be devastated. Not only were they going to have to pay to get someone here to professionally exterminate, but they were going to have to inform the health department and line up a series of pre and post-treatment inspections. Worse, all the food in the room was going to have to be thrown away and replaced.

That wasn't even the worst of it.

This had been done on purpose. Someone had targeted Kayla, and Zach had no idea why. Kayla didn't have an enemy in the world. And none of Zach's enemies would have any reason to retaliate like this if they could even find him.

He picked up the phone and texted Nick. He wanted to keep this as quiet as possible, to protect Kayla's business, but he was going to report it to the police.

He spent the rest of the night clearing the bugs from the room, throwing away food, and trying to figure out how to break the news to Kayla when she returned home.

You know, I thought it was going to be me in the elimination round today. [Jerry chuckles nervously.] When I stepped in to take care of Ropewalk for my mom after she got sick, I thought it would be temporary. I had no idea I'd end up enjoying being in the kitchen. Mom was the chef in the family. [The camera cuts to a photo of Jerry and his late mother before going back to him.] I try to do my best, but my head chef is really the star of the kitchen. I should've sent him instead! But so far, I'm holding my own. [He laughs and shakes his head.] Kind of.

Chapter Seven

"Today, we're changing things up a bit. So far, we've cooked breakfast using standard ingredients. We've cooked with wine and with seafood. Today," Gideon paused for dramatic effect while the cameras panned the room.

Lorenzo wanted to roll his eyes. If only the home viewers knew how all this was really done. They weren't even going to be cooking for hours. And they would get a lesson on whatever dishes they would be making. Not enough to make them experts, but enough to let them know what basic ingredients should be used or what sides go best with the main protein. They could make their own choices and change things up during the competition, but the lessons were meant to make them better chefs.

"We're cooking international cuisine but with a twist."

They all looked at one another. Holly raised an eyebrow, Lorenzo shrugged. Every day had a twist. What would make this one different?

"You're going to blindly choose the country that your recipe comes from."

Lorenzo saw Anna's jaw drop and had to clench his teeth to keep his own jaw from doing the same. He'd been cooking Italian his entire life. What if he got something he'd never even eaten, like Pad Thai or something he'd never heard of from Namibia or Zimbabwe?

"When I say go, you'll grab an envelope from the table in front of me and get to work making something from whatever country is named in the envelope." There were no envelopes on the table, but Lorenzo knew that clip would be added in later. "Now, get ready, get set, go!"

Nobody moved, and the director called, "Cut!"

"Great job," Gideon said. "Let's get my chefs out here!" he yelled to the set managers.

Two hours later, their heads were full of recipe ideas, spice combinations, and cooking techniques from around the globe. They were ready to choose their envelopes and then begin meal planning.

When the cameras rolled and they were given the cue, the nine remaining contestants sprinted toward the table with the envelopes. Lorenzo said a quick prayer as he reached for one and hurried to his station before pulling it open.

He frowned as he looked at the name of the country: Singapore.

Well, that wasn't great, but it could be worse. He surmised that Asian cuisine wasn't all that different from Italian. They both used rice and pasta along with chicken and beef. It was the spices that would be tricky, but he could handle this.

"What did you get, Holly?" Gideon asked.

"Israel, Chef."

"Ever been there?"

"No, Chef."

"You've got your job cut out for you."

"Yes, Chef." Holly frowned. Lorenzo offered an encouraging smile, but she had looked down and was staring at the paper in front of her.

"Dawn, your country?"

"Poland, Chef."

"Ever been?"

Dawn laughed. "No, but my maiden name is Wolski!"

"You'll have to live up to the family name," he told her.

"Yes, Chef."

"Jerry?"

"Thailand, Chef."

"Are you familiar with Thai food?"

"No, Chef, but I guess I'm about to figure it out."

"Good attitude. Anna?"

"Germany, Chef."

"Ever cooked German food?"

"Yes, some. I can work with this."

"I like the confidence. Lorenzo?"

Lorenzo's head shot up. "Singapore, Chef."

"Any experience with Singapore cuisine?"

"No, Chef, but I know it uses a lot of rice and noodles, and I can work with those."

"Again, nice confidence. Keep that up. Walt?"

"Ireland, Chef."

"Nice. Do you serve Irish pub food in your restaurant?"

"No, Chef, but we serve a killer chicken pot pie. I think I can manage an Irish pub version."

"Sounds good. Kayla?"

"Brazil, Chef."

There was a confident smile on her face as she looked toward Holly who was smiling and nodding at her friend. Lorenzo wondered what that was about.

"Any experience with Brazilian food?"

"Yes, chef. My husband and sister-in-law lived all over the world, and we cook a lot of international recipes for our customers."

"Including Brazilian?"

"Yes, Chef."

"Good for you. How about you, Robby?"

"Ghana, Chef."

"Ever cooked a recipe from Ghana?"

"No, Chef, but I know they use a lot of chicken and peanuts."

"That's a start. Last but not least, Cynthia?"

"France, Chef."

"Have you been to France or cooked French food?"

"I spent a semester there in college, and I've cooked some French food on my channel."

"Great. We've got quite the range of experience. It should be an interesting show."

"Cut!" the director called again, and Gideon's chefs raced in to advise the contestants. Once they had their recipes, the show would resume.

***

Great. Just what I need, a recipe I have no idea how to cook.

He looked around as everyone else began planning their dishes, and he felt anger rise from deep within.

Anybody else in my family would laugh at this. They'd whip out some old family recipe that could be tweaked and manipulated to create the perfect dish for whatever country they'd chosen. But not me. He felt the tension in his jaw and glanced at Kayla. *And of course, she's an expert at cooking Brazilian food.*

He turned his gaze to look at Holly, then Dawn. Neither one seemed stressed except for the usual pre-show jitters of coming up with a recipe. He shook his head in disgust.

Why hasn't anyone contacted the show about what's been going on in their restaurants? Why aren't they stressed or packing their bags? How are their businesses surviving without them?

He sighed audibly and quickly glanced around to make sure nobody heard him.

I have to win this. Somehow, I have to get that top prize. My reputation, my family's reputation, and my restaurant depend on it.

He wondered who he'd have to target next and how he would do it. He was running out of ideas, and this competition was far from over. He needed people on the outside to start contacting the show to tell them these chefs were needed back home. Weren't they all supposed to be crucial to their businesses? Why were they still here? How could he get rid of the top chefs?

***

Holly rolled the dough and quickly glanced at the oil heating in the pan. Her chicken was marinating for the little time she had to infuse it with spices and moisture.

"You good?" Lorenzo asked.

Holly nodded and smiled at him. "Thank you for giving me the idea to make the pita without yeast. I didn't know that was possible."

"Mamma makes the best pita. Her cousins on the Zollo side of the family export olive oil that's better than you could ever imagine. I used to make a whole meal of just fresh pita dipped in olive oil."

"Does she always make it without yeast?"

"Yep. She says, why waste time waiting for the dough to rise when you can make it just as good without the wait?"

Holly laughed. "My kind of woman."

"You must make a lot of things with yeast."

"I do, but I don't mind too much. I often make the dough for my rolls and croissants in the afternoon and bake them in the morning. The shop always smells like bread at one stage of preparation or the other."

She finished cutting out the pita and dropped the first round into the pan.

"Start your hummus prep. You want it to be chilled," Lorenzo advised.

Holly didn't know why he was helping her so much, but she was grateful. She'd learned that, unlike the way it looked on TV, most of the contestants actually helped each other out with advice or through sharing ingredients. She imagined that would change as they got into the final rounds, but she hoped not. She always wondered how the contestants on those shows got so close after spending a couple hours a day trying to get each other eliminated, but now she understood.

The competition itself was such a small part of the day. They spent a lot of time learning to improve their skills and as much time sitting around waiting to finish interviews. There was quite a bit of getting to know each other, or in most of their cases here on the island, getting to know each other better. And then there was the evening time when they were the only ones at the Harbor. Even the crew stayed somewhere else other than those tasked to make sure no rules were broken. There was a lot more downtime than Holly imagined. Sometimes it felt like she was on a strange, at times very intense, mini vacation.

"How's the chicken and rice coming?" she asked Lorenzo.

"Not bad," he answered as he coated the cooked chicken with oil. She looked past the meat and read the label on the bottle—sesame oil.

How does he know these things?

"I just hope I can keep all this moisture in the chicken. Poultry is my least favorite thing to cook. I can't stand a dry meat; it's so easy for poultry to come out dry even for the best chefs."

"I know what you mean, but you look like you know what you're doing." She held the chickpea can over the sink with her hand carefully pressing down on the opened lid.

"Wait, stop. Don't pour out that aquafaba. Use that instead of water. The hummus will taste better."

She stared down at the can of chickpeas. "Really? I thought you were always supposed to drain beans."

"No, often you want that liquid to enhance the flavor. Just check to see how salty it is, and adjust your salt as needed."

"Lorenzo, how's your dish coming?"

"Great, Chef. I've got the chicken resting, and I'm getting ready to take the rice from the stove."

"Are your sauces done?"

"Yes, Chef. All done."

"Good. Don't forget the bok choy. You'll want that green on the plate."

"On it, Chef."

Holly pressed the button on the food processor while Gideon looked over what she had made so far.

"You made pita from scratch?"

"Yes, Chef."

"No yeast?"

"No yeast, Chef."

"I hope it's fluffy. You're almost out of time. Get that chicken cooking. If it's raw, that's strike two against you."

"Yes, Chef," she said as her stomach knotted.

"You'll be fine," Lorenzo assured her. "Get some hummus into the fridge quickly, then put your chicken on the stove. You've got this."

He made her feel like she did have this, and she marveled at how he was able to effortlessly cook his own dish while still paying attention to hers. She supposed this was what good chefs did. He maintained a quality kitchen that ran smoothly and sent out the best food under his watchful eye and expertise. She was more than impressed and not at all jealous. Their kitchens were very different, after all.

"Fifteen minutes, everyone! Get that food cooked!" Gideon yelled. "I don't want to see anything raw come out of this kitchen. Understood?"

A chorus of "Yes, Chef" filled the room along with a wave of panic.

***

"The article is killer," Molly said as she slammed the newspaper on the table. "Kate highlighted everything Holly does for the community as well as what happened with the electric company."

"That's great," Diane said. "I hope some of those people she's volunteered with at the soup kitchen will make a donation."

The bell over the door jingled, and Molly and Diane turned to greet the first customer of the day.

"Hello, Nick," Diane said. "Pony pork doughnut and a Coke coming up." She started for the display. "Any clues about Diane's place?"

"Ongoing investigation," he said. "But no, nothing yet. Taylor told me about the trouble you had, and I guess you've heard about Kayla's house. Is the electric company making things right here?"

"Well," Diane frowned as she bagged his donut. "They turned the power back on, but insurance is going to need to come through with a check for damages, and the inspector couldn't get here until later today. That's why we're asking for donations. What happened at Kayla's?"

It was Nick's turn to frown. "Uh, you'll have to ask Zach about that." He held out his hand to Molly with his payment when she handed him his soda, but Diane shook her head. Molly pulled back her hand.

"Nick, after all the years you've been coming in here, you know our policy for first responders and military."

"Not this week," he said. "We'll all be in for all our meals, and we'll all be paying. No arguments from anyone here, you got it?"

Diane beamed. "Thank you, Nick. We really appreciate it."

"I know. We all owe you and Holly for more than just donuts and drinks. You take care of us."

"Looking back at the events around this island the past few years, I'd say it's the other way around, but the truth is, we all do our part to take care of each other."

"You got that right," Nick said. "See you ladies at lunch time."

After he left, Molly turned to Diane.

"Do you think it's strange? That something happened to both Holly's and Dawn's restaurants while they're in seclusion taping the show? And now it sounds like something has happened at Kayla's, too."

Diane mulled it over for a moment. "Hmm… Hopefully it's just a coincidence. One had nothing to do with another. Our problem was a mix-up on the part of the electric company, so that doesn't count."

Molly didn't say anything. Diane might believe that, but Molly's keen intellect wasn't sure. She was still learning from Jared about his beliefs in God's providence, but religion aside, she did not believe in coincidences. She was going to do a little investigating of her own. After all, the department had a busy month ahead of them.

***

"It's the battle of the J chefs," Gideon said as they watched Jerry and JR's Robby in the elimination round. "Two days in a row, Jerry. Let's see if you can overcome elimination twice."

"What do you think?" Holly leaned over and asked Lorenzo.

He thought for a moment before answering. "Could go either way. They're both good. I've eaten at both their places, and I like them and their food."

"You must have a lot of time off. You seem to have eaten almost everywhere."

He looked at her out of the corner of his eye, then turned his gaze back to the two men vying to stay alive. Did she resent that Antonia had been to her shop but he hadn't? Her voice hadn't sounded annoyed, but he wasn't sure.

"I made a point of eating at all the restaurants while my place was being built. I never made it to yours. You were still renovating at the time." He glanced over to see if that satisfied her, but her expression was neutral.

"Jerry, move your towel!" Walt yelled a split second too late. The towel erupted into flames, and someone shouted, "Fire!"

Jerry picked up the towel with the tongs he had in his hand and began turning this way and that.

"The sink, Jerry, the sink!" Gideon yelled and let loose several choice words.

Lorenzo saw a light go off in Jerry's brain as he jumped to the sink and dropped the towel in while turning on the faucet.

"Check your duck, Jerry!" Gideon yelled again.

Smoke was coming from the oven. When Jerry yanked open the door, a black cloud billowed out, causing him to cough. He waved his hands in front of him to dissipate the smoke.

"Looks like your duck is cooked," Walt said with a laugh. His tone was good-natured, and everyone chuckled, but the reality of Jerry's situation was lost on none of them.

Another good chef was going home.

***

Kayla popped open the expensive bottle of champagne and started pouring some into everyone's glasses. They were all gathered in the communal room after Kayla's second top chef status had been awarded.

"This is really nice of Gideon," Holly said as she watched Kayla pour the golden liquid into her glass.

"Well, two wins in a row is a big deal," Anna said, holding out her own glass.

"Anyone hearing news on the home front?" Walt asked.

Anna shook her head. "No, how would we?" She frowned. "We don't have phones."

"I try to listen out when the staff is talking," Robby admitted. "But I never really hear anything interesting."

"I do the same," Jane said. "I'm here all day, and I've gotten to know the housekeepers and other staff pretty well, but they don't disclose anything that's going on outside of this place."

"It's hard," Walt said, "not knowing what's going on in the real world. I've hardly spent a day away from the kitchen in the past twenty-five years."

"Well, regardless of whatever is happening out there," Cynthia remarked. "I think we women are doing a great job here."

"You are," Lorenzo agreed. His was the last glass to be filled, and he held it up. "To the women chefs of Chincoteague. You all blew us guys out of the water today."

Holly blushed, knowing that it was Lorenzo's tips and advice that pushed her ahead of him that afternoon.

"I think we all did well today." She gestured toward Robby with her glass. "Well done, Robby. Your apple-stuffed duck was amazing."

"Thanks, Holly. I feel bad for Jerry, though."

Jerry laughed. "Why? I was supposed to be serving smoked duck, not smoking duck!"

They all laughed. Holly loved that they could hang out and laugh together at the end of the day. Even when the competition got fierce, they were all friends when it came down to it.

"Anybody up for a walk on the beach?" Bob asked. Jane jumped up quickly.

"I'll go," she said, and the two left together.

"What's up with that?" Robby asked.

"It makes me happy," Anna said.

"What does?" Cynthia asked.

Anna replied with a knowing grin. "Bob's wife was Jane's best friend. She passed away last year. Cancer. Bob was devastated, but Jane helped him keep his place afloat while he grieved. She went back and forth between the deli and his rib place, making sure everything was running smoothly, but in the end, she closed the deli and went to work at Captain Morgan's Seafood. Her husband ran off years ago with his assistant, and Jane's whole life became the deli. Suddenly, she had someone and something else that needed her as much as her work did, maybe more, and that was a good thing for her, especially after the deli closed. And she's good for Bob."

Though Jane and Bob had been gone for several minutes, everyone looked toward the door through which they had left.

"Oh, that's so romantic." Cynthia cooed. "I feel like we're in an episode of *Passion Island* instead of a cooking show."

"Do you actually watch that trash?" Jake asked, grabbing a beer from the fridge.

"Of course, I do," Cynthia said. "My whole group from college is obsessed with it. It's the main topic of conversation in our chat group."

"You twenty-somethings don't know what good TV is," Walt said. "You all have a good night. I think I'll head to my room. This old man is beat."

"Old man?" Kayla said with a laugh. "You didn't that far ahead of me."

Walt winked at her and nodded. "Good night, all."

Dawn claimed exhaustion as well and headed to her room. Jerry invited Lorenzo to join him, Jake, and Robby in a low-stakes poker game, but Lorenzo declined, claiming he wasn't good at poker. Holly wondered about that. She bet he had a great poker face.

"I'll join you," Kayla said. "But beware, Zach taught me all the tricks he knows."

"If Kayla's in, I'm in," Anna said. "You did mean to include the women, right Jerry?"

Jerry's face reddened as he nodded. "Oh yeah, of course. All are welcome."

"I want to watch this," Cynthia said, and Holly wondered if it was the game she was interested in or Jake, who she was following closely behind.

"Alone again," Lorenzo said, and Holly felt her pulse quicken. As she looked into his dark brown eyes, she couldn't help thinking that Cynthia might be right. There was definitely something in the air tonight.

***

"We've got a real treat in store for you tonight," Gideon says. In the background, a tall rocket reaches toward the sky. "We're at the Wallops Island Flight Facility, just off Chincoteague, where we're waiting for the countdown to begin." He turns and gestures toward the rocket.

"It's the annual Student Launch, and we're looking at a Terrier-Improved Orion rocket that is scheduled to launch in five minutes." Gideon turns toward a young man with an enthusiastic smile. "What can you tell us about the rocket, Jared?"

Jared pushes his glasses up on his nose and answers. "My students have been working on this one for a while. The rocket has a bi-phase propellant system with a thrust of approximately 19,000 pounds when it launches, dropping to 3,000 pounds in around 25 seconds. Its payload weighs around 500 pounds and should reach an altitude of about a hundred kilometers."

Gideon looks overwhelmed. "Yeah, okay, can you explain that in chef's terms?"

Jared laughs. "It's like using a pressure cooker, Chef Randall. Steam is trapped inside the cooker, and when the temperature goes above the boiling point of 212 degrees, the pressure builds, equaling about thirty pounds per square inch. The more pressure, the heavier the load, and the more steam it will propel when opened."

Gideon chuckles as the countdown can be heard behind them. "That works, Jared, thanks. I guarantee the chefs here on Chincoteague understand what it means to be under pressure. Well, guys, I think we're about to take off. Don't miss your chance to visit Wallops and see a rocket launch. I'm going to watch this baby go up, and then I'll see you all back in the kitchen."

***

They returned to the dock, dangling their legs in the water. Holly wore shorts and a tank top. Lorenzo noticed her skin was so pale, it was almost translucent in the twilight. Her blonde hair glowed, and he felt a strange sensation, like he was sitting next to an angel like the one in the painting that hung on his wall when he was little.

"Did you have an angel painting hanging in your room when you were a kid?" He surprised himself by asking.

Holly squinted as she looked at him sideways. "An angel painting?"

"Hmm, guess not," he said.

"No, really. An angel? What kind of angel?"

He picked at a loose splinter on the dock. "All us kids had a painting of an angel in our rooms when we were growing up. Antony and I had one of St. Michael the Archangel hovering over a little boy. Antonia and Marissa's was an angel guiding a little girl and little boy over a bridge. Adrian—he was the only one who got his own room until he moved out and Marissa took it—he had an angel holding a baby in her arms."

"Wow. That's a lot of angels."

Lorenzo looked up to see her smile and wondered if her red lips tasted as sweet as the Amarena cherries his mother coveted. He pushed the thought away as he remembered Cynthia's comment about their private resort setting. That's all they were, these feelings he had. It was the setting, the remoteness of their situation, and their equal pairing of males and females. His brain was playing tricks on him.

He ignored whatever it was his heart was doing.

"Everyone I knew had one. I thought every kid in the world grew up with an angel watching over him until I visited a friend from school who wasn't Catholic. I noticed that none of the bedrooms in his house had an angel or a crucifix. I didn't mention it, of course, but I thought it was strange—not that we had them, but that they didn't."

"I like the idea of guardian angels," Holly said. "Everyone needs someone to watch over them at some point in their lives."

"You know, I like it, too. I think that's why I noticed it at that kid's house. I almost felt sad for him, that he didn't have an angel watching over him sleeping at night or the Lord watching from the cross."

"What was it like having brothers and sisters?"

Lorenzo shrugged. "Noisy, messy, annoying. But at the same time, comforting. I never had a moment's peace, but I was never lonely. I hated sharing a room, but when it was my turn to get the single room, after Marissa went to college, I had a hard time sleeping without talking to Antony before closing my eyes. I ended up talking to God a lot."

He looked down, slightly embarrassed for admitting that, but Holly seemed to understand.

"Sometimes, God was the only person I had to talk to as well. My parents socialized a lot, and I had a hard time making close friends because we moved so much. I didn't have a real best friend until I moved here and met Taylor."

"Tell me about her," he said.

"Taylor? Why?"

"Why not? What makes her your best friend?"

Holly cocked her head to the side and looked up at the moon slowly rising in the sky. "She's nothing like me. She's loud and quick-witted. She owns an award-winning landscaping company she built with her dad. He died from a heart attack a couple years ago, and instead of breaking her, it made her stronger. That's when she went after his place with the Saltwater Cowboys."

"Ah, so she's the one," he said, nodding. "I've heard that caused quite the stir."

"It did, and I was so proud of her for fighting for it. She's strong and smart and has guts. I guess I gravitated toward her because she was everything I wanted to be."

Lorenzo watched the shadow cross her face.

"Holly," he said quietly. "You're all those things."

She gave him a weak smile and shook her head. "I'm none of those things. Okay, I guess I'm kind of smart, but the rest? Nope. Just a wannabe."

"Didn't you buy a restaurant with no experience in owning a business or any culinary experience?"

"Yeah, but—"

"Pretty gutsy."

"I don't know about that."

"And you didn't crack when you went into elimination. You could've flaked out. Gideon put a lot of pressure on you, but you excelled. Sounds like a strong person to me." She didn't say anything. He continued, "And you're fighting every day for your place at the top."

"I'm not so sure…" She looked away.

Lorenzo couldn't stop himself from reaching up and lightly touching her chin, gently turning her face back to his.

"I am," he said quietly, his fingers lightly caressing her soft skin. His eyes held hers for several moments before they dropped to her lips. When he looked back up, there was something in her eyes, something unsure, and not entirely about herself. He had crossed the line.

Lorenzo took his hand from her chin and forced himself to look away. He cleared his throat.

"It's getting late." He looked at her and smiled. "Another long day in store for us tomorrow."

Holly nodded. "Yeah, we'd better turn in."

He stood and started to offer her a hand, but she pushed herself up and wiped the sand from her shorts.

A noise made them turn, and they watched silently as Bob and Jane made their way, hand-in-hand, toward the little cottages. They parted ways when they entered the lit area between the buildings and looked to be saying goodnight before they each headed to their respective cottages.

"Good for her," Holly said quietly.

"Lucky man," Lorenzo said, wondering if there was a lucky man waiting for Holly somewhere on the island.

"Thanks for keeping me company," Holly said before she began moving from the dock.

"Any time," Lorenzo said, and he meant it. For the first time since he heard the news about the competition, he wasn't looking forward to it ending.

***

He paced his room and wondered what to do next. Why had there been no word about the house? No news about the bugs or the ruined food? And still nothing about the café or the busted wine. This was not good. He thought somebody would've contacted Randall by now to say the business owners were needed at work. Why hadn't any of the competitors left the competition to save their businesses?

He knew Kayla's husband was a consultant for the local PD. Why hadn't he contacted Randall?

He knew everyone thought the café's loss of electricity was merely a mix-up, and the police were certain that kids had broken into Dawn's place. There wasn't any reason for the former Ranger, or whatever his division was, to think they were connected. But it made him nervous, nonetheless, especially since Kayla had won again. He couldn't strike twice, not without knowing what was going on with that husband of hers.

He'd just have to go in tomorrow and continue being his charming self, giving tips and offering advice, making his family recipes and showing his skills. So far, nobody had figured out that he was a phony. He just had to make it through another eight days of competitions. Would he be able to keep up his façade for that long?

Unfortunately, he had no choice. He was in this to win, and he had to do that at all costs no matter who got in his way.

Maybe he was going about this all wrong. He was only targeting the top chefs, but maybe he needed to make sure one of the underdogs was hit. And he knew exactly which restaurant to hit next.

Hola, everyone! I'm Anna, and my husband, Marcos, and I own Uno Taco Dos Tequilas. Yes, I love Shakira! [Anna does a little belly dance for the camera.] We grew up cooking Latino food, and what I especially love to cook is seafood. We spent a few years in Miami running a Latino restaurant, but we didn't like the heat. We like mild winters and short summers, and that's what brought us to Chincoteague. A friend told us about a restaurant being up for sale, so we sold our business and home in Florida and brought our children to the Mid-Atlantic. We cook seafood and local favorites with a Latin twist. You've never eaten anything like our signature recipes, and I know my cooking is going to win over the judges.

Chapter Eight

Holly awoke feeling unrested and jittery, and it had nothing to do with the show. She went through her morning routine, hoping to ease herself into a feeling of comfort, if not confidence, but she felt off. She couldn't stop thinking about the night before.

She was pretty sure Lorenzo had wanted to kiss her, and it terrified her. They were station mates (as she referred to them in her thoughts). They also seemed to be friends, but they barely knew each other. Besides all that, he was smart, good-looking, good-natured, well-liked, and fun to be around—everything Chad was.

They looked nothing alike and had starkly different backgrounds, but they had many of the same personality traits. Yet there was still something mysterious about Lorenzo. He talked about his childhood, his siblings, his parents, and his grandmother who was a big influence on them all. But he didn't have much to say about himself, not really, and there seemed to be a part of himself that he was holding back, though she honestly didn't know what it was or why she felt that way.

She couldn't help but compare that to Chad.

"Meow," came a hungry cry from Tang as he entered the little bedroom. He'd made himself right at home in the little Harbor cottage, and she was grateful for that. She worried whenever he had to adjust to someplace new, especially now that he was so old. Holly picked him up and sat him on the neatly made bed—a habit she couldn't abandon even at the resort.

"Good morning, baby. I'm having issues today."

Tang let her cuddle with him, though he wasn't typically the warm and fuzzy type, especially before he'd been fed.

"You know, Chad had all the right traits, as far as I could tell. He had a thriving marine business and came from a good family, but all that time, he was holding back something important." Holly sighed.

"Meow," Tang answered, a little angrily this time, and Holly knew he was more interested in breakfast than in hearing her lament about Chad. She put the cat down and followed him to the tiny kitchen.

Chad had been holding back the most important thing she could imagine. He had no intention of getting married. Ever. He didn't want kids and didn't want to be tied down. Oh, he let her go on and on about their future and the number of babies they would have and how they could manage two businesses between them. All the time, he knew it was never going to happen.

What kind of guy does that?

What kind of guy looked at a girl the way he looked at her, made her think she was the center of his universe, and set her heart racing with the slightest touch, but didn't open up to her or tell her the truth about himself?

The bigger problem was that Holly was no longer certain if she was asking the question about Chad or about Lorenzo.

She placed the food bowl on the floor then returned to the bedroom. She looked at herself one last time in the mirror, pulled her ponytail tighter at the base, and took a deep breath. Looking more confident than she felt, she left to join the others on the bus to the community center. She had no idea what this day was going to hold and didn't know if she was ready to handle it, cooking or otherwise.

***

"Dad? Are you here?" With an unsettled feeling, Angela Stevenson walked through Dockside Family Style Restaurant and called for her father, though she knew he should be at the taping.

"Danny?" She called for her brother, but there was no answer.

A chill ran down her spine, and she instinctively began rubbing her bare arms. In all the years their family had owned the restaurant, she'd never arrived in the morning and found the back door unlocked. For ten years, she'd gone by as soon as she got the kids to school and picked up the books and checks from the safe and taken them home to do the accounting. She'd never had this feeling like she wasn't alone.

Angela reached into her pocket and pulled out her phone. She activated the screen that held the instant button for 911 and took a few steps toward her father's office behind the kitchen. Everything seemed to be in place, and his door was locked. When she opened it with her key, nothing looked askew. The safe was locked, and upon opening it, she found the money and the books from the night before.

On her way back through the kitchen, Angela stopped to look around. She stiffened when she saw a mound of spilled salt, or maybe sugar, on the floor outside the pantry. She knew the place was swept and mopped every night just before the staff headed out and locked the doors. Odd that this was missed. She opened the pantry and gasped.

The shelf that held all the seasonings and spices was empty.

"What on earth…?"

She went inside the room and swept her gaze across every shelf. She wasn't crazy. There wasn't a single spice, dried herb, or sack of flour or sugar anywhere to be seen. She was flabbergasted. Who in the world would throw out all the seasonings and baking ingredients without replacing them?

Perhaps there'd been a problem of some sort. Bugs? Moisture? Maybe someone had done a date check, but how could the whole lot be bad? She'd have to ask Danny about it.

At that moment, Angela's phone rang. She recognized the number of the school.

"Hello? Yes. Oh my gosh, is she hurt? I'll be right there."

Angela didn't think about the missing items again until a couple hours later when she received a panicked call from her brother.

***

"Hey, Chad. How's it going?" Zach laid a few items on the counter and smiled at the young man who used to date Holly.

"Great, Mr. Middleton. Find everything you were looking for?"

"I did, thanks." He watched Chad add everything to the computer. "You heard from Holly since the show started?"

Chad frowned, the smile gone in an instant, replaced by a scowl he didn't try to hide. "Why would I hear from her? She's not allowed to call. Besides, I wouldn't be someone she'd call even if she had an emergency. We broke up, you know."

"Oh, I'm sorry to hear that." He feigned surprise and kept his eyes on Chad.

"Yeah, whatever. I tried to go by there the day everyone found out about the show to wish her luck, but she blew me off. I guess she's already moved on."

Zach knew that wasn't true. His sister, Kate, knew everything about everyone on the island, and Holly's best friend was Nick's wife. No, he was positive Holly was not seeing anyone.

"Too bad. I like Holly. She's a nice girl."

"Yeah, well, nice girls want marriage and kids and all that forever stuff. I'm not into that."

And he wasn't. He was a cocky kid who dated Taylor once upon a time, and Nick didn't care for him at all. Zach could see why.

What do women see in men like that?

"Well, I hope everything's going well for her with the show. She's done a great job with the café," Zach said, pushing for any info the kid might give him.

Chad's expression turned to one of pity. "Yeah, shame about the thing with her food storage, I mean the electricity getting turned off."

"I heard it was some kind of error with the electric company. That's a big error. Cost Holly a pretty penny."

Chad's eyes filled with remorse, but Zach didn't see any guilt, and he was good at reading people. He'd had a lot of practice reading body language.

"I bet. That really is too bad. We didn't work out, but you're right. Holly's a nice girl. She didn't deserve to have that happen to her."

Zach sized him up one more time before deciding it was a dead end. He took his purchases and waved.

"Well, thanks Chad. Have a great day."

Chad waved goodbye but didn't say anything. Zach had the feeling that breaking up with Holly was weighing on him more than he wanted to let on.

***

"How did I feel? Well, I felt bad, of course," Lorenzo said. "Jerry's a nice guy. But someone has to lose, a lot of someones. There can only be one winner at the end of the competition."

"Do you think it will be you?" Toby, the interviewer asked.

Lorenzo shrugged. "I'd like to think so. Going in, I was certain I had an advantage, growing up in a restaurant, but now that we're this far in, I'm not so sure. I've got to hand it to them, the others are quite the competition, and most of them grew up in restaurants, too."

"Who do you think is the one to beat?"

Lorenzo frowned. What was this guy looking for? Thinking back to some of the shows he and Antonia had binged, Lorenzo smiled.

He puffed his chest and mustered all the bravado of his older brother, Adrian. "I think it's obvious that I'm the one to beat. I'm one of only four who haven't gone to elimination yet, and I don't plan to get there. I'm taking this one all the way to the end."

"Great. Perfect. Thanks. Can you send in the next person?"

Lorenzo smiled as he left the room. That was kind of fun. He missed yelling at people and telling them what they were doing wrong in the kitchen, but that's mostly acting, kind of like these interviews. Oh, he lost his temper plenty, and he hated for anything to go wrong in the kitchen, but he was a softie on the inside, and they all knew it.

"What are you smiling about?" Cynthia asked as she passed him in the doorway.

"Just looking forward to a good day," he said. He was starting to get into the groove of this whole thing, and he was actually excited about cooking today. He hadn't looked forward to cooking in a long time.

***

"The time starts now!" Gideon threw his arm, the clock started. Holly finally felt like her head was in the game. She had a hard time with the interview that morning, and she felt guilty for avoiding Lorenzo. Instead, she spent the time between filming with Cynthia, Anna, and Kayla and forced herself not to glance in Lorenzo's direction. With the announcement that today's segment was going to be a sandwich challenge, Holly was ready to display her skills.

She'd barely needed any coaching from the pros, and the biggest question she had was which of her popular, self-styled sandwiches should she make?

"What have we got today?" Gideon asked, starting with her station first this time.

"Well, if I had more time, I'd bake my signature croissants which I use in my French Heaven sandwich—butter and brie cheese melted over sliced mushrooms and topped with a raspberry glaze."

"Now, you're just teasing us. That sounds amazing. Since you don't have time for dough to rise for croissants, what will you do instead?"

"Well, Chef, I opted for my Greek Isle Sandwich instead. It's one of the most popular things on our menu, and I think the judges will love it."

"Tell us about it. I can see you're slicing figs." He gestured toward the fruit she was handling.

"Yeah, they give the sandwich just the right sweetness and provide a great texture that makes a spread unnecessary. I love that because a spread can ruin a sandwich, making it soggy. I hate a sandwich that just falls apart when you're trying to eat it."

"It's a bold move. Most people don't think of figs as a sandwich ingredient except as a jam, and not using a spread can make a sandwich dry, turning the bread to paste in the mouth."

"Agreed, Chef, but the addition of feta cheese helps with that. Arugula adds a peppery flavor, and prosciutto provides a protein and the saltiness a good sandwich needs."

"So, no addition of any spices? Not even salt and pepper?" His brow went up as he looked at her ingredients.

Holly shook her head. "None needed. Trust me." She smiled confidently, knowing that Insley, the camerawoman, as soaking up their exchange and her confidence.

"Let's hope you're right." Gideon turned to Lorenzo, and Holly listened to their banter while she prepared the feta.

"Lorenzo, I'm sure you have a take on some kind of Italian sandwich. Am I right?"

"Yes, Chef. I'm making an Italian-style grilled cheese."

"And how are you elevating a grilled cheese for our judges?"

"First, I'm using mozzarella instead of American. For several obvious reasons."

"Sure, but that's just the beginning, I hope."

"Of course, Chef. I'll be grilling it with slices of tomato and spinach leaves."

"Replacing the butter with olive oil?"

"Yes and using sun-dried tomato pesto as the spread along with a balsamic reduction."

Gideon pointed to Holly. "You heard what your opponent just said about soggy bread ruining the sandwich, right?"

"Yes, Chef. It will be balanced just right."

"You better be right about that." Gideon moved on to interviewing Kayla. Holly heard her say she was elevating the tuna sandwich to a spicy panini.

"Another meal right up your alley," Lorenzo said. Holly turned to see him looking at her with a normal, friendly smile. They were back to being friends and station mates. She almost breathed a long sigh of relief.

"It is, but I'm sure tomorrow, I'll be a nervous wreck again. What about you? I've never seen your lunch menu. Do you serve sandwiches?"

"We do, but not this one." He frowned. "Gideon's right. It's hard to get the right balance and keep the bread from falling apart. My mamma is the expert at making these. Her customers love it, as do all us kids, so I thought I'd give it a try."

"It's kind of too bad Jake's gone. I'd love to try one of his pulled pork sandwiches."

"I always heard Jane's deli sandwiches were the best," Lorenzo said. "She'll be disappointed she didn't make it this far."

"Let's just hope we both make it to tomorrow."

She arranged the figs on the bread while Lorenzo carefully placed his sandwich onto the ribbed cast-iron skillet, pressing down on it to get the perfect lines on the sandwich.

"We'll make it to tomorrow," he said without looking up. "It's making it to the next day that worries me."

"Why? We don't have any idea what that day will bring."

"Exactly," he said, and she felt a jolt in her gut.

He was right. If this was today's challenge, an easy one that everyone seemed confident about, then what would the next challenge bring?

***

"I love the tanginess of the lemon and dill." The camera zoomed in on Christina as she licked her lips after tasting Cynthia's chickpea salad sandwich.

"The mashed chickpeas give it a great texture, especially combined with the avocado slices," Gideon remarked.

"I could do without the sprouts," José said, pulling a long bean sprout from his mouth and holding it out to the camera. "Something more substantial and spicier like jalapeños would have added to it."

"I disagree," Christina said. "I love the flavor as it is."

"Let's move on." Gideon pointed to the next plate that the camera focused on. "Here we have a tuna salad panini with lemon juice and chopped celery and pickles."

"Interesting choice," Christina said. "I never think of a tuna fish sandwich as something that can be elevated." She took a bite and nodded, puckering her lips in a good way. "But I like it. The Tobasco sauce combined with the lemon and dill flavors really do bring this to a whole new level."

The camera zoomed out to encompass the two judges.

"Pour on the heat," José agreed. "This ain't your mama's tuna fish sandwich!"

"I agree. The spice is just right. How about a Greek sandwich next?" Gideon said, moving to the next plate. "This one combines sliced figs, pressed feta, prosciutto, and arugula on ciabatta bread."

"What a nice combination," Christina said, as the camera followed her lifting a piece of the sandwich to her mouth. "No spread?"

"None." Gideon said.

She took a bite and slowly chewed the sandwich. The camera focused on her face, and the background faded. She shook her head.

"It doesn't need it. The figs and feta harmonize in a moist and creamy blend that sends my mouth soaring. And the saltiness of the prosciutto and the peppery arugula provide the perfect amount of spice. Wow. Holly, you know how to make a great sandwich."

Another camera caught Kayla elbowing Holly who beamed with pride.

"I like it," José agreed, as the first camera moved over to him. "And I'm not a big fan of figs or feta, so if I like it, it has to be good."

"One of the best sandwiches I've ever tasted," Gideon said.

In the other lens, the contestants all turned toward Holly, whose face was reddening at the praise.

The camera zoomed out to show Gideon and the judges eyeing the next selection.

"Here we have a spicy mayo and veggie sandwich."

"Look how they cut off the crust," José pointed out. "Sometimes, a sandwich just needs that, to be crustless."

"Like Mum used to do," Gideon said.

"Aw, your mummy cut the crust off your sandwiches, Gideon? How sweet," Christina teased.

The camera caught them all laughing before Christina bit into her slice of the sandwich. She made a face and put her hand to her mouth, forcing herself to chew and swallow.

"Um, not for me." She put the sandwich down and reached for her glass of water. "It's more like a pasta salad without the pasta, and the plain white bread does nothing for it."

"Yeah, I agree." José nodded. "If I had taken this in my lunchbox, I would have been teased throughout lunch."

A camera zoomed in on Robby. His eyes were wide with shock, and his jaw dropped. Dawn patted him on the back.

"It definitely needs a protein to break up the mayo." Gideon said. "It just feels like a mayo sandwich that someone added veggies to without thinking through what would make it taste good." The camera panned to the sandwich and then moved to the next selection.

Gideon announced, "Here's an interesting take on your classic club sandwich. Instead of plain mayo, it has a homemade dressing of mayo, sour cream, lemon juice, and lots of spices. To further elevate it, the chef used toasted sourdough bread."

"I love this," Christina said with a mouthful of food. The camera zoomed in closer to her face as she wiped a bit of mayo off her chin. "I love the dressing. And avocado? Who adds that to a club sandwich? Mmm."

"I couldn't agree more," José said as the camera moved to him chewing. "Dawn, the only thing that would make this better is a different lettuce. Bibb lettuce, or better yet, butter leaf. Now, that's worth having leftover turkey."

Dawn nodded but beamed with pride, and the camera caught the other women giving her their thumbs up. She received a wink and a "good job" from Walt.

"Here's something completely different," Gideon said as the camera zeroed in on a tortilla. "It's called a summertime quesadilla, which the chef says was created by a friend. It has mushrooms, spinach, basil, and mozzarella cheese, grilled until everything blends, and the tortilla is slightly crunchy. Then it's topped with a balsamic glaze."

"I love a good balsamic glaze," Christina said as the camera followed her picking up a slice and taking a bite. "Mmm, this does not disappoint. Wow. I could eat this every day."

They continued to praise the Mexican-style sandwich as the other camera caught Anna accepting a high five from Holly.

"Two more to go," Gideon said. "Here, we have an Italian twist on a grilled cheese sandwich. And another play on balsamic glaze."

Gideon explained Lorenzo's sandwich as the camera zoomed in on the plate. As soon as José picked up his slice, part of the bread fell away.

A camera zoomed in on Lorenzo's shocked face. He looked down and shook his head as the others turned toward him with pity.

"Well, this isn't good," José said.

"Not enough reduction of the balsamic vinegar," Christina said as she tried to take a bite of the rather messy sandwich. "The flavors are all there, but the execution is a failure." She looked at the contestants. "Here are a couple tricks to try when using balsamic reduction on a sandwich. First, you could toast the bread before making the sandwich. Even if you're going to grill it, the toastiness on the inside of the sandwich will stop the bread from soaking up the liquid, and it won't affect the grilling. In fact, the extra crunch adds great texture. Another trick is to use olive oil both inside and outside the bread. While the outside oil, used instead of butter, will help get that beautiful coloring and flavor as it grills, oil on the inside will provide a barrier between the bread and the liquid. Of course, if the reduction is thick enough, those tricks will just be added precautions and shouldn't be necessary."

The judges finished by discussing Walt's sandwich, keeping the camera crew busy and the contestants holding their breath. The elimination round would soon follow.

***

The cranked-up air conditioner on the bus back to the resort gave Lorenzo chills as it blew over his sweat-soaked clothes. He ran his hand through his hair and tried not to think about the day. He had humiliated himself, and the whole world would witness it when the show aired.

Nobody said anything to him, and he guessed they knew he didn't want to be bothered. He stared out the window as he silently beat himself up inside. His warm breath steamed the cold window, and he resisted drawing a frowning face like a sullen child.

As he stepped off the bus, Robby held out a hand. "Better luck tomorrow, Lorenzo. You were a formidable opponent."

It was then that Lorenzo really felt bad. He'd been sulking like a petulant child when he had no need to do so. He had indeed humiliated himself, but not on the show. It was his display of self-pity and bruised pride that did the honors, not his digression into the elimination round.

"Thanks, Robby. It was a pleasure and an honor to face you."

Was acting as though he'd just taken part in a duel his mind's way of making him look and feel better? He turned and found himself looking into Holly's eyes. In those pools of blue, he saw disappointment. She had believed him to be a better man. Her lowered opinion of him cut him to the core. He almost winced but didn't look away.

"I was a jerk today. I'm sorry."

Holly's eyes softened. "No, it's okay. I've been there, remember? You'll bounce back tomorrow."

"Maybe on the show, but what about as a person in their eyes?" He gestured to the rest of the group who had exited the bus and were heading toward their cottages. "Or in yours?" He again met her gaze.

"My eyes have seen a lot, including men brought down by their own pride. It's not the pride that leads to the fall. It's what one does next that determines what kind of person he is and what others think of him. Remember, God may have been willing to forgive and forget the eating of the fruit, but the denial of wrongdoing and not owning up to their responsibility led to Adam and Eve's expulsion from the garden."

Lorenzo found himself smiling. "I thought you said you weren't much of a churchgoer."

"That doesn't mean I don't listen when I'm there. Chin up. Things will get better if you admit that you messed up and move on."

Lorenzo watched her walk away and tried to ignore his growing feelings. He was already participating in one reality show. He would not get sucked into another.

***

Holly avoided going out to the dock. Instead, she changed into her swimsuit and headed to the pool. Anna and Cynthia were already bobbing up and down in the saltwater. After laying her towel and book on a lounge, she descended the steps into the warm water.

"I love this pool," she said. "Why aren't all pools filled with saltwater instead of chlorine?"

"Good question," Anna said. "I'm trying to soak for a little bit every evening. It's doing wonders for my skin."

"Your skin is already perfect," Cynthia said. "I wish mine was that golden color all year long."

Anna laughed. "Try being this color all year long and see where it gets you. My mama and papa have to work longer and harder than others just to prove they're good enough to be here."

Cynthia looked down. "I'm sorry. That was insensitive of me."

"No hay problema," Anna said with a smile. "All is forgiven. And thank you for the compliment."

"What was with Lorenzo today?" Cynthia asked Holly as they settled along the wall of the pool, their legs outstretched and moving as though they all were synchronized swimmers. "I mean, he's not the first to face elimination, and he didn't even lose."

Holly shrugged. "Bruised pride, I guess. I said something to him after we got back, and I think it snapped him out of it."

"I hear he's a bear to work for." Kayla said. "I'm told he's a Grizzley most of the time, yelling at his employees and barking orders, but a teddy bear when someone needs consolation or a pep talk. Jenny says he turns on and off like a switch."

"Yeah, that's what she told Taylor. She seems to really like him though. She enjoys working at the restaurant." Holly thought of all the help and advice he'd given her over the past few days. "I think I've seen the teddy bear side a few times this week. I guess the Grizzley was bound to show up at some point."

"You know, it's not a bad combination. Zach's the same way."

Holly knew Kayla wouldn't elaborate. Zach's past as a ruthless sniper was well-known on the island as was his fierce loyalty, abounding compassion, and steadfast love for his family and friends. She looked up to Zach and hoped to find someone as kind and loving as him, someone not like Chad. Which led her back to her own dilemma.

"Do you think he's hiding something?" she asked.

"Who? Zach?" Kayla asked.

"No, Lorenzo. Do you think he's hiding something about himself that he doesn't want us to see?"

The others were pensive for a moment.

"Well, he's very quiet," offered Anna. "But that doesn't mean he's hiding anything. I think he's shy."

"I'm not sure about shy," Kayla said. "And I'm not sure about hiding something. I know a little about that." She laughed. "A lot, actually. Eddie and Zach hid plenty from me, but both were trying to protect me."

"Did you know," Holly asked, "that they were hiding something?"

"Well, with Eddie, I thought it was an affair, so yeah, I totally knew. We'd been married for almost ten years, so I knew he wasn't being honest. When he was killed, and the truth came out that he was working with the FBI to gather evidence on his boss, it all made sense."

"And Zach?" Anna asked.

Kayla smiled. "With Zach, it was different. I didn't really know him at all. I wanted to, but he was elusive, getting close then pulling away. He didn't know how to reconcile his past with my past, knowing that Eddie had been shot. It was a long time before he admitted that he was afraid. Sometimes, I think that's what men hide the most—the fact that they're afraid."

"Of what?" Holly asked.

Kayla shrugged. "Could be anything. Afraid of something in his past, afraid of the future, afraid of being found out that he is or isn't what people think. There are dozens of things, at least, that people, especially men, don't want to admit they're afraid of."

Holly thought of Chad and how he was afraid of commitment. She'd never fall for that again. But what was it that Lorenzo was afraid of? What was it he didn't want her to know?

***

Lorenzo could see the three women in the pool and the men and other ladies going in and out of their meeting room and walking toward the docks. Everyone seemed to be doing their own thing tonight, unlike the gathering the night before. He was at loose ends, unsure whether to eat crow and join the group—acting like the elimination round and his childlike behavior afterward were nothing—or stay away and lament his own shortcomings.

He was less concerned about his performance in the kitchen and more with his childish petulance on the way back. His siblings always told him that his moodiness was his biggest stumbling block and that he needed to be a kinder and gentler person all the time and not just when someone was hurting. They always said that a person's pain was often invisible, that the way you reacted toward and around them could make all the difference in the world. It was advice he too often ignored.

Suddenly, all the stress and emotion of the day got the better of him, and he felt bone-weary tired. Though he longed for a dive into the pool and a walk on the beach—preferably with Holly—he took a long, hot shower and got ready for bed. He knew he would be fast asleep the second his head hit the pillow.

He just had one thing to do before he went to sleep. He needed an assurance that a day like today would not happen again, and he knew how to make that happen. He needed to talk to the one person who could help him.

***

"It's a perfect day on the beach." Gideon, clothed only in a modest bathing suit, stands in the surf, surrounded by sand and water. "One of the best things to do while on Chincoteague Island is visit the beach on Assateague. The National Seashore is thirty-seven miles long and the perfect place to spend a hot, lazy day."

Gideon walks up the beach to a blanket laid out on the sand. "While here, you can try your hand at sand fishing, walk the beach combing for seashells, or just soak up the sun. By the way, you can take up to a gallon of seashells home with you."

He gets down on the blanket and stretches out. "Now, this is the life. You can go fishing or shell collecting, but I'm going to lie right here and relax. And then I'll see you back in the kitchen."

***

He disconnected the call from the Harbor and smiled. He looked at the time and knew he had a while before it would be dark and even longer before the place was quiet. He had time to do some research, which was good, because they were both out of ideas, but he thought he had the beginning of one forming in his brain.

A couple hours went by before he had a plan.

Their first ruse might've worked if Holly didn't have Diane working in the café while she was gone. Diane knew just what to do to keep the restaurant in business despite losing all their food. And between the two women, they had too many connections on the island. That pitiful newspaper article on Holly stirred up enough sympathy that everyone on the island was pitching in to keep her place going until she could build her inventory back up.

Then there was Dawn's restaurant. That was the biggest hit, but it alerted the cops. Thankfully, the island had had trouble with teenage boys blowing off steam in the past, and everyone assumed that had happened again.

It was Kayla's business that worried him, or really, her business partner. Her husband was a scary dude with a reputation that preceded him. He'd almost been caught when Zach had awoken. Or maybe he never actually slept. Maybe it was ingrained in him to always keep one eye open, alert to any and all threats. He didn't want to be caught in Zach's crosshairs, not figuratively, and certainly not literally.

The worst part was none of it had worked. None of them had quit the show like he thought they would. They were all threats and needed to be taken out, but how? Their partners, friends, and families were too powerful and too good at running things to worry them or let them leave the competition. Did any of them even know what had happened to each of their places? Would everyone on the island want to protect and help a guy like they have for the women? So far, it didn't seem that way.

He thought people would be just as outraged when Dockside was hit but nobody seemed to care. Maybe stealing all the spices wasn't enough. The police were stumped when the restaurant's staff tried to convince them that the pantry had been cleaned out of all the key staples. They just shook their heads like it had been some kind of joke. They'd told the staff to call the owner if they wanted, but it was doubtful that Chef Randall would even pass along the message. And that was just fine. If all it did was confuse the police, then all was good. After all, everyone knew Walt was no threat. He was just one of the underdogs.

Later that night, when all the businesses on the island were closed, and the residents and tourists alike were lulled to sleep by the salt air and gentle tide, he headed to Anna's Uno Taco Dos Tequilas. She was a major threat, but he knew exactly what to do to get her to ditch the competition and head home. He was beginning to like this game.

I'm Walt, and my family runs the Dockside Family Style Restaurant. My parents opened this place in 1975 and ran it until Mom got sick, and Dad got tired. [Old family photos at the restaurant faded in and out of the screen.] It was their American Dream for themselves and us kids. My last wife thought I loved the restaurant more than her and made me choose. Well, because of that restaurant, I'm on TV, so I think I made the right choice. Watch out, you chef wannabes. I'm going to take this thing all the way.

Chapter Nine

"What is up with you guys?" Gideon said, shaking his head. He had divided the contestants and was yelling at the only two men standing to his left—Lorenzo and Walt. The expletives he'd already spewed at them seemed to be spent. "You're not holding your own. Every one of your lot has faced elimination, none of you has made anything I'd serve in one of my restaurants. You want to draw people to your businesses? You've got to step up your game. You're the last two. The women are killing you. Are you ready to show me what you've got?"

He finished the sentence by labeling them both something even Lorenzo would never say in his kitchen. When Gideon had exhausted his tirade, he turned toward the remaining five to his right.

"Keep it up, ladies. I know where I'll be taking my wife to dine the next time we're on the island."

Gideon's right-hand, Rachel, stepped into the room and cautiously approached.

"Um, Chef Randall, sir." She cleared her throat. "There's something I need to talk to you about."

Gideon looked at her with fire in his eyes, but his respect for her had been apparent since day one. He took a deep breath before he spoke calmly and politely.

"Now, Rachel? Is it important?"

They all knew it must be, or she wouldn't be interrupting. Lorenzo saw her eyes dart across to where the women stood then flicker back to her boss.

"Yes, Chef. Very."

Gideon cursed again, but not at Rachel specifically. "Hold those thoughts." He turned and followed her from the room.

"What's that about?" Lorenzo heard Anna ask.

They were all perplexed. Nobody else spoke for several minutes as they awaited his return.

"Anna," he called and motioned from across the room. "We need to talk to you."

Anna looked at the others before hurrying away. Lorenzo had a very bad feeling about this.

It was a good fifteen minutes before they returned. Most of the group had taken seats in the chairs set aside for the crew, but Cynthia had dropped to the floor, and Lorenzo stood propped against the closet station. The first thing he noticed when they entered was that Anna's eyes were puffy, and her face was red. Lorenzo had two sisters, and he recognized the symptoms of crying immediately.

Without saying a word to anyone, Anna walked out of the room letting the door close behind her. Nobody else moved. Lorenzo could hear birds chirping outside and the air conditioner kick on, but the silence in the room felt like a wet blanket had been thrown upon them all. After several seconds, Gideon emerged looking upset, a mix of anger and disappointment.

"Anna is leaving us," he said as he shook his head. "She did nothing wrong. She's not being sent home. She's had an emergency that she must deal with."

"Can you tell us what happened?" Walt asked. "We've all known each other and our families for a long time. Anna didn't grow up around here, but she's one of us."

Gideon sighed. "Anna asked that I only tell you that she's sorry she can't continue and that you all are not to worry about her. She wants the competition to go forward and wishes everyone good luck."

He paused for a moment and looked around the room. Lorenzo was certain Gideon felt the same thing he did—confusion, sympathy, a desire to know what happened coupled with anxiety and guilt about continuing. Everyone loved Anna. She was like a daughter to the older women and a sister to the rest, and her presence would be missed.

"Okay, we've got a lot to do today." Gideon calmly said once the news had sunk in. "Hair and makeup, cooking lessons, filming of the food challenge announcements, recipe prep, filming of the episode, then wrap-up interviews. We're on day six, everyone, so let's keep our heads in the game."

There was no shouting. No profanities were thrown around. Gideon was kind and gentle, coaxing them like five-year-olds on the first day of kindergarten. Like good little boys and girls, they all nodded and replied, "Yes, Chef."

***

The competition was difficult, not from a cooking standpoint, but from a mental one. Holly felt the shift as soon as Gideon told them that Anna was leaving. A heaviness fell over the room, and nobody wanted to move, as though anchored in their places, a gravitational pull so strong only Molly or Jared would be able to understand it. At that moment, Holly felt an overwhelming loneliness. She missed her café. She missed Diane and Molly and Taylor. She missed her weekly girls' night and their summer get-togethers with their families or significant others. For a split second, she envied Anna, but then she remembered the state in which she'd left, or at least what they knew about her leaving. Something so big and awful had happened, Anna felt she couldn't stay.

The day did not go well for anyone. Cynthia cut her hand badly with a knife, and the medic had to administer stitches. That set them back quite a bit as they had to wait for Cynthia to be ready, then they had to start the filming and their meals over from scratch. Lorenzo burned his dish, and Walt dropped an entire baking sheet as he attempted to remove it from the oven. Holly's dish wasn't coming together at all, and she was on the verge of tears. Finally, Gideon stepped in.

"Enough, guys. This isn't working today. Let's get rid of the cameras and just have a talk for a minute." He called for someone to bring chairs, and he motioned for everyone, judges included, to join him in an open corner of the room. As the crew set up the chairs, Gideon rubbed his hands together and seemed to be gathering his thoughts.

"Okay. The afternoon has been a total loss, but that's okay. I think we need to talk this out and then call it a day."

Holly settled back in the chair and heaved a long sigh. She was worn out, physically, mentally, and emotionally. Looking around at the weary faces, she was certain everyone else felt the same.

"I'm sorry about Anna. I really am. She's a great chef, and I know you all thought highly of her. This is not what she would want. She cheered on every one of you and wanted the best for everyone. She's doing what she needs to do, and you all need to do what you came here for. If anyone thinks they can't handle this anymore, I need to know now."

Holly looked around. Kayla stared off into space. Lorenzo was studying his hands. Cynthia cradled her injured hand. Holly wondered if the cut was throbbing. Her own head throbbed, so she empathized. Walt had his elbows on his knees and hung his head low, and Dawn anxiously fingered the pendant she wore around her neck.

"Okay, then. We're all in?" Gideon asked, as though he was one of the ones wearing an apron. One by one, they all nodded, and Gideon stood. "I'm calling the bus. Go back to the Harbor. Get a massage, soak in the pool, or take a walk on the beach. Find a way to decompress, and we'll start from the top tomorrow. We'll just do the challenge, elimination, and wrap-ups, so the bus won't bring you here until ten. You can sleep in." He started to turn away but then shifted back to look at them. "Oh, and Kayla and Anna requested a Catholic Mass at the Harbor on Sunday before the group cooking lesson. Obviously, Anna won't be there, and initially, I said no, but maybe I was wrong. It's a day off for those who want it, but if people want a service of some kind, I'll try to make it happen. Does anyone else want to attend Mass or request another service?"

Holly thought about it for just a moment before slowly raising her hand.

"I think I could use that."

Lorenzo's hand gradually went up as well. "Me, too."

Kayla suggested, "Bob and Jane might want you to ask about the Methodist Church. I believe they both attend there."

"Jerry's Baptist," Dawn said. "You'll need to ask him. I don't know about Robby or Jake."

"Anyone else?" Gideon asked.

Cynthia shook her head, and Walt continued staring at the floor between his legs as though he was so lost in thought he couldn't hear anything being said.

"Is this normal?" Holly asked. "I mean, we aren't supposed to have any contact with the outside world, right?"

Gideon shook his head. "No, it's not normal, and I've never done it before. Like I said, I told them no at first, but nothing about this entire week has seemed normal." He let out an angry breath, and Holly and Kayla exchanged looks. What did he mean by that?

"I don't like the idea of breaching our bubble, but if doing this makes everyone feel better and gets you back on track, I'll do it."

"Thank you," said Kayla. "I knew when I asked that the answer would be no. I appreciate you changing your mind."

"Well, they must agree to the terms. Rachel will check with them and see what we can work out." He clapped his hands together once. "Get your things together. The bus will be here shortly. Take care of yourselves, and Cynthia, don't forget your next dose of ibuprofen."

They watched him leave, then they quietly headed toward the front of the building, walking like zombies in need of a feeding.

***

"It was must have been bad," Lorenzo told Jerry and Bob over another round of beer. Jake had gone for a run along the beach, and Walt was so upset about whatever forced Anna to leave, he had excused himself and gone to his room.

"And nobody knows what happened?" Bob asked.

Lorenzo shook his head. "Nope. It was clearly something big though. Anna was having a ball and was one of the top chefs. I think she was really getting into the whole thing and letting her creative cooking juices flow."

"I suppose we'll find out when this thing is over. And I'm ready for that." Jerry took a long pull from his bottle. "I miss my wife and kids. I miss the everyday rhythm of the restaurant. I'm bored to death already, and it hasn't been a whole day for me. How can you stand it?" he asked Bob.

Bob shrugged as a shade of red crept up his face. "I've found ways to keep busy."

"You old dog, you." Jerry said, patting Bob on the back. "I'm glad, real glad. You two deserve something good to come out of this."

"Oh, I don't know if it will last. It's a funny thing, being trapped here all day without any pressing needs or the stresses of everyday life. It's like living in a dream world that will burst as soon as we open our eyes to reality."

"It doesn't have to be that way," Jerry told him. "You could make a go of it. I hope you'll give it a try. Jane looks awfully happy these days. Happier than I've seen her in a long time."

Bob grinned. "She does, doesn't she?"

"What about you?" Jerry turned to Lorenzo. "You're spending a lot of your free time with Holly."

Lorenzo nearly spit out the mouthful of beer and had to swallow carefully so it didn't backtrack to his nose. He shook his head as he coughed.

"No, we're just friends. Nothing more."

"Are you sure about that?" Bob asked. "That's what I thought about Jane and me."

"I'm sure," Lorenzo assured them. "I've been down that road before, and it's not worth it. I came down here to get away from all that and concentrate on building a business."

"Funny," Bob said. "How things like *all that* sneak up on you when you least expect it."

"You know," Jerry told him. "I never thought I'd settle down and *all that*, but here I am with a wife, three kids, a house with a mortgage, and a restaurant on the water. It's a pretty good life, if you ask me, and I can't wait to get back to it."

"Well, I'm glad it worked out for you, Jerry. And Bob, I'm sure it will work out for you, too. As for me, I don't need those entanglements in my life. Speziato is enough for me. I'm married to the restaurant, the staff are my kids, and that's a good enough life."

"Good enough isn't what we're made for, my friend," Bob said. "Believe me, I was content with good enough after I lost Sue, but now I'm thinking I want more than that. I want to relive what made us great, and I think I have a chance to do that. Take it from someone who had it all at one time and watched sickness and death take it away. If you want a chance at happiness, go for it. Don't settle for good enough."

Lorenzo stood and guzzled the rest of his beer. "Thanks for the advice, Bob. I'll keep it in mind." Though, as he said the words, he knew the truth. No matter how attracted he was to Holly, it wasn't worth it. Bob might be willing to take a chance at another heartache, but Lorenzo was not.

***

"You don't think this is more than a coincidence?" Zach asked Nick over lunch at the café. They met regularly at the café after their favorite lunch place, the deli, closed.

"I don't know, man. Holly's was an error of some kind, a misunderstanding. It could've been a group of kids at Dawn's just like Paul said. Your place, well, I don't know what the heck happened there. I mean, that was definitely a targeted attack. Walt's was odd, but his son swears someone broke in and stole all his stuff, and Anna's, well, that was scary. Still…"

"Nick, so far, five out of the twelve people on the show have had something happen to their restaurant or business. That's not just a coincidence. It's a pattern."

"Paul doesn't want us jumping to any conclusions. We have no evidence that suggests that the incidents are related. Other than being on the show and owning food businesses, none of the people have anything in common that would make them targets. They're all chefs, sure. They have that in common, but nothing that ties together what happened. He still thinks it may be kids taking advantage of the owners being away."

"Except that's the commonality. All the places that have been hit are owned by the chefs, not some other entity they work for. It seems to me that someone is sending a message."

"And what's the message?" Nick asked.

"I don't know," Zach admitted. "To quit? To stop the show?"

"You mean, someone on the island might not want the show to take place? Why? It benefits everyone."

"Again, I don't know." Zach shrugged. "Just do me a favor. Talk to Paul about putting surveillance on the other restaurants. See if anyone is lurking about or trying to cause trouble. I don't think we've seen the last of this."

"Will do, but we're all hoping these were unrelated incidents that will come to an end."

"It's wishful thinking, Nick. I'm sure of that."

Nick stood and handed cash to Zach. "It's my turn to pay, but I've got to go. Paul's questioning Anna at one, so if you want me to look closer at all this, I'd better see if I can sit in."

"Thanks, Nick. I appreciate it."

Zach sat back and thought about what had happened the night before. Though Uno Taco Dos Tequilas was locked up tight when Marcos and the kids went to bed, Marcos had been awakened during the night by the carbon monoxide detector going off. At that point, the smell of gas was already overwhelming. He got the kids out from their above-the-restaurant home and checked the kitchen to find one burner had been turned just enough to release the gas. Thank Heaven they had a detector and that it worked. If he hadn't heard the alarm, if he hadn't gotten his family out in time, if the door at the top of the stairs hadn't been closed while they slept, or countless other scenarios had or hadn't taken place, they would not be alive today. The thought made Zach sick.

What if, instead of bugs, someone had turned on the gas in Kayla's kitchen? They could've been in and out undetected, before Zach heard a thing, and the carbon monoxide could've spread throughout the house. He winced. Their boys were asleep at the top of the steps with no door to stop the gas from rising. How long would it have taken for them to…

He couldn't complete the thought. In his mind, he saw Marcos and his kids standing outside the restaurant, one of them not even walking yet. How did the perp get in? And why? And why leave the gas on in a place where people lived right upstairs? Did he know they were there? He did if he was local. The good news was, Marcos and Anna's family made it out safely. Zach didn't want to think about what might've happened to himself and Kayla's boys.

***

Molly washed the table with care, a lot more care and attention than usual. She leaned a little closer to the next table, trying not to be obvious. Her senses were on high alert, and that brilliant mind of hers was absorbing everything that was being said. When Nick left, she moved on to another table before being summoned by a customer on the other side of the café.

All afternoon, she devised a plan, never breathing a word to anyone about what she was going to do. All she had to do was convince Jared to drive her off-island to pick up some supplies. Luckily for her, he rarely questioned her scientific pursuits.

***

"This was the best idea you've ever had," Holly said to Dawn as the masseuse pressed down on her shoulder blades, kneading her sore trapezius and deltoid muscles.

"Oh, you're not kidding," Dawn moaned from the table to the right of Holly.

From her left side, came another moan. Kayla murmured, "I think I've died and gone to Heaven."

"I can't believe Cynthia passed this up to go kayaking," Dawn said between satisfied sighs.

"I can," Kayla breathed. "Have you seen Jake without a shirt?"

"Kayla!" Holly blinked at Kayla's admission.

"What? It's true. His build is almost as nice as Zach's."

"TMI," Dawn said before admitting, "Though, to be honest, I've envied you more than once."

Kayla laughed. "Don't be too envious. He snores."

Holly smiled. "Do you miss it? The snoring? I've heard that when loved ones are apart, the snoring is something they miss, like it's a loss of some kind of comforting feeling."

Kayla snorted. "No way. I love my husband, but I don't love that. I haven't slept this well in five years."

Holly wondered if Kayla's first husband snored and if she missed it after he died, but she wasn't going to ask. Instead, she began to wonder if Lorenzo snored but hastily pushed the thought aside. She needed something else to focus on.

"What do you think happened to Anna?" she asked.

The room grew silent except for the soft music flowing from the overhead speaker.

Dawn said, "It must've been bad. Really bad."

Holly knew Dawn was thinking about her own family and business.

"Do you think she's okay?" Holly asked.

"I don't know. Without knowing what happened, there's no way to tell."

"Anna was already struggling," Kayla said. "She felt guilty about leaving her baby and missed her family, but I think she had made up her mind to stay. Something awful must've taken place."

Holly spoke up, her voice tinged with worry. "What do you think it was, Kayla?"

"I don't know. I hope it has nothing to do with her doing the show or leaving the kids with Marcos. It must be something big though. There's no way Zach would let me know if something was wrong at home, especially if he thought he could handle it or if it would upset me. How many others in our group have someone at home who would be able to do everything on their own without letting us in on what was happening?"

Kayla was right. Diane would never call to tell her anything that wasn't an absolute emergency. Would Antonia contact Lorenzo? Holly didn't think so. They had a whole family who would rush in to help without him needing to know. Jerry and Dawn had spouses who worked alongside them. Walt had kids who worked for him. She didn't know about Jake, Cynthia, or Robby. Bob's daughter was his right-hand person, and Jane had a fiercely loyal staff who would not call unless someone literally died. Holly shuddered at the thought. She didn't want to think about this anymore.

"You know what? I think we're going down a rabbit hole here. Anna's husband or one of the kids could've gotten sick, or there could've been a death in the family. I mean, I'm not wishing that on her, but we don't even know what happened. It makes no sense to get worked up about it."

"You're right," Dawn said. "We're here to relax, not to undo everything these wonderful ladies are working so hard on."

Holly decided Dawn was right. She tried her best to let the masseuse release the tension she was feeling.

She'd never had a real massage before, and there was no reason to ruin it. She breathed deeply, doing her best to let thoughts about the outside world be released through the laying on of the masseuse's hands.

***

"I'm standing outside the Herbert H. Bateman Educational and Administrative Center at the Chincoteague National Wildlife Refuge." Gideon gestures to the building behind him. "This is where we'll begin our visit to the refuge. Come on, follow me." He opens the door and walks inside, followed by the camera.

Gideon speaks quietly as he walks around the center. "Inside, we find all kinds of displays that tell us about the wildlife in the area. Displays show what flora and fauna are present during the different seasons, and videos tell the history of the area. There's so much to read and watch, you'll want to give yourselves lots of time here. If you still have a question, you can ask the volunteers and park rangers. I learned that the island is actually growing and not shrinking like other islands."

Gideon exits the building, and the scene changes to a wooded trail. "You can walk, run, bike, and even drive through the refuge. You'll meander through woodlands, marshes, and beaches and will see birds, ponies, and other animals."

Gideon's wife, Tara, walks up to him from the trail. "Time to go," she says with a smile.

"We're off on a hike," Gideon says. "I'll see you back in the kitchen."

***

After dinner, the first all week that was served at a reasonable time, Lorenzo walked down to the dock. He'd become accustomed to finding Holly there, so he wasn't surprised to see her sitting with her legs dangling in the water.

"Mind if I join you?"

"Go ahead," she said, looking up with a smile. "It's a beautiful night if you don't mind the humidity."

"I guess I don't mind it then." He sat down, slipped off his flip flops, and plunged his feet into the water. "The water's still cold."

"Yeah, but it's getting warmer. Kind of." She grinned, and his heart picked up its beat a little.

"What do you think is going on with Anna?"

Holly heaved a long, heavy sigh. "I don't know, and to be honest, I can't keep thinking about it. We're only halfway through this thing, and if I'm going to stay in, I need to stop thinking about what's going on out there, on the rest of the island, and concentrate on what's going on within our bubble. Does that sound mean?"

Lorenzo shook his head. "No. I get it. Worrying about what might be happening, especially since it probably has nothing to do with us, can throw all of us off our game."

"Exactly. I've made a personal decision not to think about anything else except the competition."

He wondered if that extended to whatever he was feeling about her, about them.

"Okay, let's forget about our restaurants and everyone else's for a while. Tell me more about yourself."

Holly laughed. "I think I told you everything interesting."

"I doubt that."

She turned her head and peered at him with narrowed eyes. "How about we talk about you instead? Tell me about you."

He shrugged. "There's not much to tell. I have four siblings. My parents own a restaurant. My grandparents—"

"About you." She cut him off. "Tell me about you. What do you like to do outside of the restaurant? Any girlfriends, kids, pets back in Baltimore who you left behind?"

"You think I left kids behind? You have that low an opinion of me?"

"No, no, I just mean, tell me something about Lorenzo the person, not about Lorenzo the chef."

He thought it over for several seconds. How much should he tell her? How much did she really want to know? He decided honesty was the best policy, especially since he had the same questions about her.

"I'm twenty-eight, went to twelve years of Catholic school where I dated half the girls in my class." He looked at her. "It was a small class."

"How small? I had over four hundred in mine."

Lorenzo laughed. "I can't even imagine. I had sixty."

"So, you dated thirty girls?"

"Well, I'd say only a few count. I had my first crush on a girl when I was six."

"You started young."

"Her name was Sister Mary Ellen. She had the deepest green eyes, a gentle voice, and welcoming smile. And I thought her chalkboard handwriting was the neatest I'd ever seen."

"You had a lot of handwriting analysis experience at six?"

"I had a romantic heart at six."

Holly reached down and scooped up a handful of water from the channel, drizzling it on her bare legs as she spoke, her eyes on the water droplets falling from her palm.

"And now? Are you still a romantic at heart?"

"Not so much," he admitted. "I found out love isn't all it's cracked up to be."

Holly let the last droplet fall before turning to face him. "Same."

"Okay, now that we got that out of the way, what else do you want to know?"

Holly didn't answer. She just looked out over the channel for what seemed like an eternity before she turned back to Lorenzo.

"Who was it?"

He blinked and tried to figure out what she was asking. When he did no more than stare, she drew in a breath and asked, "Who broke your heart? Besides Sister Mary Ellen, already married to God and undoubtedly much too old for you anyway." She smiled a gentle, nudging smile, and he found himself talking before he gave himself time to think about it.

"Her name was Grace. She was beautiful, smart, an accomplished musician." He pictured her. She was tall with the longest fingers he'd ever seen. When she slid her bow across her violin, it was hard to tell where the bow ended, and her fingers began. He cracked the knuckles on his own fingers absent-mindedly as he pictured her, sitting tall and proud, eyes closed, long dark hair cascading down her back, swaying to the rhythm of the piece she played. "We met right after she moved to Baltimore to play with the symphony. She rented a house in the neighborhood, my Aunt Marta's house, and the sound of her playing filled the air every morning, a private concerto just for us, her most adoring fans."

"And you adored her most of all," Holly said quietly.

"I was smitten from the first time I heard her play. I'd open my bedroom window as I was getting ready for work and hum along to her playing. One night, she came into the restaurant to grab a late dinner, but we were closing. When I realized who she was, I stayed late and made her dinner. When she found out what I'd done, she invited me to join her."

"That does sound romantic," Holly said, returning to playing with the water. Lorenzo wondered if it was a nervous response. Was his story bothering her? If so, he wanted to know why.

"What happened?" Her question broke into his thoughts.

"She started coming in regularly. I learned her schedule and started making special dishes for her on the nights I knew she would come in late, and we would eat together by candlelight in the closed restaurant. Sometimes, we played music and danced." He smiled at the memory.

"I meant," she hesitated. "What happened to her? How did she break your heart?" She was looking at him now, her top teeth tugging at her lip, and despite having Grace on his mind, it was Holly's lips he wanted to taste.

"She got an offer to play for the Orchestra of the Vienna State Opera." He shrugged, knowing that pretty much summed it all up, but apparently, it did not.

"Okay. And?"

"They take only the very best, and the very best of the very best are then eligible to audition for the Vienna Philharmonic, the most prestigious orchestra in the world. She had to be with the Opera for at least three years before she could even try out. And if she was accepted? There would be no other place for her to go."

"And you didn't want to go with her?"

He opened his mouth to speak, but the words didn't come. Instead, he let out a long breath and shook his head.

"I would have followed her to the ends of the earth."

"She didn't want you to go." It was not a question, and he could see that she understood what had happened.

"I wanted to marry her, but it wasn't the life she wanted. She had big dreams, and they didn't include pregnancy, raising kids, or having to go home every night to a husband who couldn't share her with her music."

"I imagine that would have been difficult. For both of you."

"And we both knew it. My parents never really approved. They knew it wouldn't end well, but I was too stubborn and too much in love to listen."

"I understand," she said with a sigh.

"You do?"

"For me, it wasn't anything as romantic. He dated my best friend for a bit when they were in high school. Before I moved here," she qualified. "He wasn't anyone or anything, not like an accomplished violinist, but I thought what we had was special."

"And he didn't?"

Holly shook her head. "He didn't. He loved me, I believe that, in his own way. But he doesn't have any desire to be married or have kids. It's not that being married would prevent him from running off to Vienna. He's just not interested. Taylor tried to warn me, but…" She held out her hands and shrugged.

"His loss is another man's gain," Lorenzo said, putting his arm around her and pulling her close. "But I do suggest you not fall in love with a musician."

Holly laughed and laid her head on Lorenzo's shoulder. "Noted. And I advise you to stay away from marina-owning, baseball cap-wearing pretty boys."

"I can assure you, that won't be a problem."

He felt her take a deep breath and let it out, and he pulled her in a little tighter. They watched the night fall until the sky was bejeweled by stars, then Lorenzo reluctantly let her go and bid goodnight. They didn't touch again as they walked toward their cottages, but somehow he could still feel her head on his shoulder and her body encircled by his arm. From somewhere deep inside, he heard a symphony playing. The thought made him smile.

Hey there, everyone! I'm Cynthia, and I'm the island's only TikTok chef! [Footage from TikTok overlays Cynthia's voice.] I make everything from healthy cuisine to heavenly, filled-with-calories desserts. I've never met a recipe I didn't love or find a way to make better. Once you've seen me cook on here, you're going to rush to follow me on TikTok! Now let's get down to cooking!

Chapter Ten

"The time starts…now!" Gideon threw down his hand, and the remaining chefs began gathering ingredients. Soon, the entire room was filled with the heady scents of cumin, garlic, onion, chili powder, and cilantro.

Holly was stunned that she was still in the competition, especially since she considered the others there with her to be the best chefs on the island. Though Walt didn't want Kayla to be included, there was no doubt that her recipes were among the best anywhere. Dawn's grasp of local cuisine was inspiring. Cynthia was young and wild at heart, and it was easy to see why she had such a huge online following. She was fun to watch, and her food was delicious. Lorenzo had generations of cooking expertise to draw on as did Walt. As she looked around at her fellow contestants, Holly marveled at the fact that she was still in the running. Anna's missing Latina flare was the only downside, and they all felt her absence. She would have claimed top chef with an advantage over them all in today's challenge.

The day before had been a complete disaster, but everyone seemed confident today. They were preparing the same dishes they'd planned before Gideon halted filming, which helped immensely, and Holly felt pretty good about her own chances.

Since pastries and homemade breads were her specialty, Holly opted to make her own taco shells, both soft and hard. She knew she couldn't compete with Dawn's shrimp mango tacos, but she had her own favorite taco recipe that her girlfriends loved when it was her turn to host their weekly get-togethers.

For her soft tacos, she was repeating the pitas she made earlier in the week. They were a hit and would be the perfect soft shells for her Greek Goddess taco.

"This looks interesting," Christina said as she came to a check out Holly's cooking.

"It's a specialty of mine," Holly said, explaining the premise behind her taco.

"So, kind of a gyro taco-style?"

"Yes, Chef, and one that doesn't disappoint."

"I like the confidence. But make sure that lamb is fully cooked and properly seasoned."

"Got it, Chef."

"Lorenzo? What have you got cooking for us today?"

"Tacos with an Italian twist, Chef. I'm making meatballs for the protein and filling the tacos with corn, tomatoes, spinach, and chopped pears for some sweetness. I'll top it with a hearty tomato, onion, and pepper salsa and gorgonzola cheese."

"Sounds interesting. Love the pears. Good luck." Christina went to join Gideon at another station.

"Pears in tacos?" Holly asked.

"Pears are used in a lot of Italian dishes. They're not overwhelming but add sweetness and a nice texture. Have you had pasta pockets with pears?"

"I can't say that I have."

"Order it next time. You'll love it."

"I'm looking forward to it." She felt an inner glow at the thought of going back to Lorenzo's restaurant. Unlike the first time, they were now friends, and she trusted him, at least to a point. She was glad he'd opened up to her, and she appreciated that Chad's weakness had been Lorenzo's strength. Still, she wasn't beyond friendship, at least for now.

While her lamb cooked, Holly concentrated on her tzatziki sauce and refrained from taking occasional glances at the boy next door.

***

"A real disappointment," Christina said after tasting the spicy shredded beef tacos with pineapple salsa. "There just isn't enough going on here."

The camera panned to Cynthia who rolled her lips inward and frowned.

"I agree," said José. "The vegetables are really lacking. Sprouts are fine as a lettuce substitute, but the salsa needs more than onion, tomato, and pineapple. There's nothing to really pull this together."

"And no dairy. I'm a sour cream girl. This needs something creamy like that working to break up the acidity."

The camera zoomed in on the next plate.

"Here, we have a true Tex-Mex dish, sloppy Joe tacos." Gideon gestured to the dish.

"I'm first," José said. "I've been smelling this for the past hour, and I'm dying to try it." He picked up a taco and took a large bite. His eyes widened. Even with a mouth full of food, his smile was obvious.

Christina took a bite of hers, and her expression was much the same as José's. "Oh my gosh. Is that zucchini? What a great surprise! I can taste cilantro, just the right amount, and onion and peppers that enhance rather than overwhelm. And wow, don't get me started on the sloppy Joe. Kayla, I can tell you have kids, because mine would love this."

Kayla's smiling face filled the camera's lens, her eyes glowing with excitement.

"Kayla has two kids," Gideon said, "and I'm told this is a family favorite."

"I bet," Christina said. "I could go for another, or three."

"But moving on…" Gideon said as the camera followed him to the next plate on the counter.

"A Greek Goddess taco with lamb, tzatziki sauce, and a tomato and cucumber salsa."

"Mediterranean is my favorite, so this better be good."

Holly looked worried through the lens of the camera. Kayla reached over and took her hand, squeezing it for good luck.

"I love the combination of the soft taco glued to the hard taco with the tzatziki. I would not have done that," José said. "It's a risky move since the crunchy hard taco could be too much for this light Mediterranean dish, but it works."

Christina nodded. "I like the way it holds the whole thing together, cradling the hard taco inside the cushion of the soft one so nothing is lost. It's quite tasty. This way, you get all the flavors in every bite without anything falling off. Nice touch. And it's a pita instead of a flour tortilla, which is perfect for a Greek taco."

"The lamb is cooked flawlessly," said Gideon. "And the tomato cucumber salsa, in my opinion, really makes the dish."

"All the right Greek flavors," Christina said, nodding.

Holly breathed a sigh of relief, and Lorenzo winked at her, a slight gesture not lost on the cameraman. He'd been watching the two closely and thought the rest of America would as well. He was playing up whatever was going on there, though the two contestants seemed to be unaware of the camera's extra attention as well as each other's feelings. He knew that made for good reality TV.

"An Italian meatball taco," said Gideon. "I'm curious about this one."

"Interesting," agreed José as he picked one up and took a bite. "The meatball is kind of bland. I get not wanting to overpower the taco with a big juicy, spiced-up meatball, but I'm not tasting any garlic or oregano or other seasonings."

"I love the vegetables you chose, Lorenzo. And the pears and gorgonzola are perfect here, but he's right about the meatballs. I'm not getting any real taste there," Gideon said.

Holly flashed a sympathetic smile at Lorenzo, but he continued to stare ahead with a stoic look. The camera caught it all.

"Two more to go," Gideon said. The camera followed him to the Mango Tango taco.

After Dawn's dish had been highly praised, and Walt's turkey and black bean soft taco had been deemed, "not bad but not really up to level of the rest," the judges disappeared.

"Well? What do you think?" Holly asked Kayla. "It's going to be a close one."

"It is, between both the top and bottom. They loved three and were not happy with three. I don't know what will happen."

It didn't take long to find out. Cynthia and, once again, Lorenzo found themselves in the elimination round.

***

"You know, I'm good with the outcome," Cynthia said. "I made it farther than a lot of social media chefs do on these shows." Everyone was gathered in the Harbor meeting room recapping the day and sharing their experience with the ousted contestants.

"You made it farther than I did," Jake said.

Holly noticed that they were no longer sneaking off in the evenings or pretending not to be into one another. Jake had his arm around Cynthia on the sofa, and her hand was placed on his thigh.

"And I think I'm going to like hanging around the resort all day," Cynthia said, looking up at Jake, batting long lashes over her big, brown eyes.

"Special delivery." The door opened, and one of the Harbor staff brought in a bottle of champagne in a basket filled with chocolates and fresh fruit.

"It has your name on it, Kayla," Bob said.

Kayla beamed as she reached for the bottle. "And we're going to celebrate, but not for my third win. We're celebrating Jane's good news."

Jane's face began to glow with a pink blush and a look of love. She turned to Bob and shrugged. "I had to tell someone. I can't call my girls."

"Of course, you had to tell. I want to tell the world."

"How about filling in the rest of us?" Jerry said, though his grin conveyed that he knew what was happening.

"Jane and I are getting married, and you're all invited!"

"Invited? They're all catering!" Jane said with a laugh.

Cheers went up around the room. Hugs, high-fives, and congratulatory handshakes were given to the happy couple.

"I think we should," said Dawn as she filled glasses.

"Should what?" Robby asked.

"Cater. One of us can do the engagement party. One of us can do the bridesmaid luncheon, and another can do the bachelor party. Someone can do the bachelorette party, then there's the rehearsal dinner. Oh, and Holly could do the morning of pastries and coffee. Then there's the reception and the next-day brunch."

"Whoa," said Jane. "It's a second marriage for both of us. We don't need all that."

"Sure, you do," Holly said, nodding emphatically. "You're in love. You're starting a new chapter in your lives. Jane, you've been lonely and unhappy for a long time, and Bob, you did so much for your wife, putting your own needs aside. You deserve a giant celebration. I think Dawn's right. We can all take part in some way."

"I'll do a whole series of episodes on my show about wedding prep and what to cook," Cynthia said.

"I'm claiming the rehearsal dinner. Who doesn't love a good barbecue to kick off the weekend?" said Jake.

"I'll do anything you need," Walt said, enveloping Jane in a hug. "We've all been friends for a long time, and I couldn't be happier for you." His words and actions were sincere, but Walt's eyes were clouded, and his mouth was firmly set in a frown.

"Walt," Jane said. "What's wrong?"

"Nothing. It's just…" He glanced at the others and shook his head. "I'm not the best person to give marital advice, so I'll just say, I wish you the best."

Holly felt sorry for Walt. She was beginning to think he was all bluster on the outside and a sentimental dreamer on the inside.

"We all wish you the best," Kayla said.

Jane's eyes sparkled with tears as she looked around the room at the enthusiastic faces of her friends, old and new. "You know, I may have lost on day one of this competition, but in so many ways, I feel like the real winner here."

A flurry of activity, note-taking, and some friendly competition ensued over who would cater which event. Kayla was chosen as the overall coordinator of all the meals and menus, and it was agreed that Dawn would oversee wine pairings for each meal. Though Holly missed her girlfriends enormously, she suddenly realized how much she had come to love this group of people.

"Lots of excitement." Lorenzo whispered into her ear.

"Sure is," Holly agreed. As she looked up into his eyes, she felt her stomach drop, and one kind of exhilaration transformed into another. She swallowed and saw the same feelings reflected in his eyes.

"It's getting a little overwhelming in here. I'm going for a walk. Would you…?"

Holly looked down at his outstretched hand. If she took it, she was giving into something, and she was certain they both knew it. If she declined, she was turning down something she wanted deep down inside. Was she ready?

She felt eyes on her and glanced sideways. Kayla was smiling at her, and her slight nod was all the encouragement Holly needed. She slid her hand into Lorenzo's and let him lead her out into the salty air of the summer evening.

***

"I'm standing in the Robert Reed Waterfront Park where I'm told we're going to see the most amazing sunset." Gideon points toward the horizon. "Chincoteague Island is on the Atlantic, so most people probably think of it as a prime location to watch a sunrise, and it is, but we're about to find out that the sunsets here are just as glorious."

The view expands to show the myriad of colors streaking across the sky as the sun lowers toward the water.

"One of my favorite things to do on vacation is to find the locations of the perfect sunrise and sunset, and this tiny island provides both without having to go far. You can watch from one of the parks that overlook the water on western side of the island, take a sunset cruise and watch from the water, or find your own paradise to watch from a kayak. Whatever way you choose, you'll see a sunset you'll never forget."

Gideon turns and watches the setting sun as the camera follows the sun sinking beneath the waves. Gideon turns back to the camera.

"That's it for tonight. I'll see you back in the kitchen."

***

They paddled around to the other side of the channel, neither speaking other than Holly's quiet commands while steering the boat. When they reached a small beach on the opposite side, Lorenzo suggested they get out and take a break. Holly coached him in being the first out of the kayak, which allowed him to chivalrously take her hand and help her onto the shore. Together, they pulled the kayak up onto a secure location on the beach.

"We should've brought a blanket," Lorenzo said and then regretted it. "To sit on, I mean. You know, instead of the wet sand."

Holly smiled. "I knew what you meant. But I'm okay with sitting on the sand. My shorts are already wet from the kayak.

"Ah, but you don't like sand," Lorenzo said. Holly smiled. He had been listening.

"No, but that's okay."

Lorenzo looked up at the sky and then assessed the small patch of sand that fringed the marsh.

"Over there," he pointed. "That's the best spot."

"For what?"

"For watching the sunset," he said as though it was obvious.

Holly went to where he was pointing and sat down. "Sometimes I forget there are places to see the sunset here. The sunrises are amazing, of course, but you can still see the sunset if you find the right spots."

She sat down, and Lorenzo planted himself next to her.

"I never saw many sunsets when I was growing up, but this one time, we all went to Italy when a relative died. I don't even remember who it was, but I remember the trip. We stayed for almost a month so my grandparents could visit everyone they knew and show us all the most beautiful cities and towns in the country. One night, when we were in Florence, the whole family climbed to the top of Piazzale Michelangelo. You've never been, right?" He looked over at her.

Holly shook her head. "I've never been out of the States. I've lived all along both sides of the coast, but we never went overseas."

"Florence is spectacular. My Aunt Marta lived there most of her adult life, but we didn't know her then. She and Uncle Dom knew each other as kids and just reconnected a few years ago. It's a long story, but a beautiful one. I'll tell you someday."

"I'd like that," Holly said.

"But back to Florence," he continued. "This piazzale is the best place in Florence, some say in all of Italy, to watch the sunset. Everyone goes up there—locals, tourists, newlyweds, everyone. A trip to Florence isn't complete without watching the sun setting over the Arno with the whole skyline of the city as its backdrop. The colors of the horizon change every few minutes, from a bright blue to a deep purple to a majestic orange. Even as a kid, I knew as I watched that I was seeing something only God could create. Even the long, thin clouds that streaked across the sky looked to me like great paintbrushes that added a touch of color here and there. It was like nothing I'd ever seen before. I knew then that I had to return someday and watch the sunset with the woman I loved, or even with our whole family like we did."

He hoped he was painting the picture in her mind, but he knew that it was a sight one had to see with their own eyes.

"It sounds breathtaking," Holly whispered.

"It was," he answered quietly before reaching over and taking her hand in his. She allowed him the pleasure, and the two of them silently watched the sky across the marsh.

The lush green marshlands in front of them darkened into trees at the horizon, but just above them was a streak of lavender that gave way to orange, topped with a wide swath of grey-blue clouds, tinged with a glow at the top, and blanketed by a pale golden sky.

"It's not Florence," Lorenzo said. "But it's almost as beautiful."

He felt her shift and turned his face toward hers.

"It's the most beautiful sunset I've ever seen," she whispered.

And in the shadows of the setting sun, Lorenzo leaned closer and touched his lips to hers. The gentle kiss slowly deepened, and he let go of her hand to brace himself on the sand. His other hand found the back of her head and gently pulled her closer, further intensifying the kiss. His fingers touched the band that secured her hair, and he pulled back to look at her. Holly stared at him as his fingers played with the elastic.

"Can I?" he asked, tugging on her ponytail. "I've wondered…"

He let the sentence trail off as she raised her hands and pulled her hair loose. Her blonde tresses fell to her shoulders, and she shook them loose, showering his hand with her golden hair.

He looked at her for only a moment before he buried his hand into her locks and pulled her toward him again, claiming her lips with his own. As his breathing quickened, he felt her tongue brush his mouth, and he moaned, breaking away.

Lorenzo looked back toward the horizon, his breathing shallow and in perfect rhythm with hers.

"It's going to get dark quickly."

She nodded. "We'd better get going before we can't see to find our way back."

They looked into each other's eyes for several moments more before Lorenzo pushed himself up from the sand and reached for her. Their hands fit perfectly into each other's, and they both held on as they made their way to the kayak. For a brief second, Lorenzo wondered what would happen if they found the beach empty, the kayak washed away with the tide, but their vessel awaited them as they turned and walked across the soft sand.

They returned to the Harbor in silence. Lorenzo wondered if her thoughts were as jumbled as his—a strange mixture of uncertainty and conviction. Whatever the next few days held, this night would live on in his mind and heart forever.

***

There was just one problem. When he first started this whole thing, he didn't want any part of it. He was angry and frustrated and didn't see the point of the show or spending two weeks with the others. Now, he was beginning to understand how this could be good for all of them and for the island in general.

More than that, he was beginning to like everyone, really, truly like them. Now that he'd taken the time, though he truly hadn't had the choice, to interact and talk with them, he found that he was beginning to think of them all as friends. More than friends in some cases.

He paced the room. It was well past midnight, but he couldn't sleep. He'd put this thing in motion, and based on the message he had just gotten, it was getting way out of control. He wanted it to stop, but his pleas were being ignored. If he didn't find a way to make it stop without implicating himself, things were going to be very bad, and he didn't know how he could live with himself.

***

"Are you sure this is a good idea?" Jenny tried to talk quietly into her phone as she watched Speziato through Taylor's binoculars. The grass tickled her arms and legs, and she knew she'd be broken out in an allergic rash by morning. Why had she agreed to this?

"Do you have another idea?" Molly whispered. "I don't have enough money or materials to rig cameras everywhere. I've done the best I can, but I can't watch every restaurant, and we know they're bound to strike again. It's been two days since the last one."

"How are things on your end?"

"All clear right now. I've got an eye on both Dockside and Ropewalk. Anya?"

Molly's best friend answered from her end. "Good so far. All's quiet on the Seaside front." She giggled and Jenny rolled her eyes.

"Smart kid humor," she muttered. "I bet you read the book before you saw the movie."

"There was a movie?" Anya asked.

Molly's voice drowned out Anya's. "How about you, Chloe?"

"I can see Prime Rib and Rockfish and Uno Taco. Avi?"

"I've got JR's covered. No signs of anything here."

"How did I end up lying on the grass, getting eaten alive by mosquitoes, listening to a bunch of kids on a conference call while keeping surveillance over my place of employment?" Jenny asked, slapping another vampire bug from sucking the life out of her.

"You love your boss and everyone you work with. Besides, I know where you keep your diary."

"Nice try, Molly. I'm not fourteen. That threat doesn't really work with me."

"Yeah, but I also know who you were out with last night, and I know you don't want your sister to find out."

Jenny opened her mouth, and a mosquito the size of a fly hurried in like it was a tunnel. She started coughing. Between coughs, she managed to ask, "How do you know that?"

"Surveillance, remember?"

"I'm never babysitting for you again," Jenny said.

"That's fine. I'm intellectually superior to most babysitters anyway, so I really don't need one."

"Shh," came someone from the call. Jenny's heart skipped a beat. "I see someone. They're heading your way, Molly."

She couldn't tell if the shush came from Anya, Molly's sidekick, or Chloe, Molly's genius friend and camp leader from Wallops space camp.

"Someone's trying to get into the back door at Dockside."

That was definitely Molly. Jenny held her breath and listened.

"No, I think he has a key. Maybe. No, wait."

Jenny sighed. *Amateurs,* she thought.

"Never mind, maybe he's just checking things out, you know, like we are." It went silent for a few minutes. "Okay, he's gone."

A few minutes later, Jenny saw headlights approaching and then disappear. That was strange. She could still hear the vehicle coming, but she didn't see any lights.

"Someone's coming," she whispered and waited to see what the approaching truck would do once it turned into the lot. It looked like it might be turning around, like the person was lost.

But then, instead of turning around, it turned the corner of the building and went to the loading dock behind the restaurant. They never got deliveries this time of night. She was sure of that. She always saw the delivery people come when she was on the day shift.

"What's happening?" Molly asked.

"Shh," Jenny hushed her.

The engine went silent, and she heard the door open and close. The driver must have turned off the interior lights because they didn't come on, but she was certain he'd gotten out of the car. Or she. Jenny couldn't see well enough even with the binoculars. It was too dark

"Jenny—"

"Shh…I'm watching."

The person was casing the building but not going in. He or she seemed to be pacing, as if trying to make a decision. He was going back and forth between the restaurant and the giant dumpster at end of the pavement. A strong gust of wind came up, and Jenny caught a whiff of the unmistakable smell of gasoline.

***

"Zach, get to the Italian place, Spezzio, or whatever it's called. Now!"

Nick hung up the phone and raced toward the restaurant. As a civilian, Zach had no right to be at the scene. As a consultant to the department, he had a little bit of credibility. And as someone who had been closely following the case, Nick wanted him there.

"All engines reporting," came the voice on the radio. "Caller says the fire is nearing the building."

Nick pressed the gas and sped up as fast as he could. He didn't know which was racing faster, his cruiser or his heart. What he did know was that Jenny was there, and she could be in danger.

***

"Jenny, what the heck were you thinking?"

Zach stood outside Nick's cruiser with his arm draped over the open door. He looked at Jenny with a look of part disappointment and part amazement.

"You could've been caught. This guy's crazy. You don't know what he might've done to you."

"I'm sorry, but Molly—"

"Molly's a kid! You let a kid talk you into setting up a sting operation in the middle of the night? Your Godfather is going to kill you." Zach shook his head.

"Please, Zach, please don't tell Uncle Trevor."

"I won't have to. This will be the front-page story in tomorrow's paper."

"You called your sister? Now, everyone will know."

"You don't think she knows everything that happens on the island without me having to tell her?" He ran his hand over his face. "But those aren't your biggest problems."

"What do you mean?" Her heartbeat picked up its pace.

"We don't know who this guy is. You didn't see the truck, just the outline. We don't know the make, model, or color. We don't have a description. We don't know anything. But he knows you were out there, and word travels fast around here."

Jenny gasped. She hadn't thought of that. She told Molly to call 911, and Jenny called her brother-in-law, never giving a thought to what would happen when he arrived along with the rest of the department. She should have run. She should've gotten out of there and told Molly not to tell anyone she was ever there. But that might have put Molly in danger, and Zach was right, she was just a kid. Jenny was an adult and should have known better.

"I'm really sorry, Zach. I didn't think anything would happen. I was just going along because Molly convinced me that we needed to keep an eye on the restaurants. She needed one more person, and since I work here, she thought—"

"Save it, Jenny. As soon as Nick comes back, you're going to give us the names of all the kids, everything they were doing, and everything you saw here. Again. And then you're heading out of town until this is solved."

At that, Jenny felt her blood pressure and her ire rise. She stood and looked at Zach. "You can't do that. You can't make that decision. I'm an adult, and you can't tell me what to do."

"Adult or not, I can tell you what to do." At the sound of her mother's voice, Jenny turned.

She should have been angry. She should have argued, or told her mother no, or any number of things, but what she did instead was run into her mother's arms and allow herself to cry.

I can't believe I was top chef three days in a row. How did that happen? I've never worked anywhere as a chef and have no training at all! I went to school for business. I never thought I'd put that together with my passion for cooking. I wonder how many of my Yale classmates are working as caterers now. [Kayla expels a resounding, joyful laugh.] I'd much rather be doing this than working in a stuffy office or living in a big city. I just hope my knowledge of home-cooked comfort food continues to see me through this thing.

Chapter Eleven

Holly loved waking up to the sound of birdsong rather than an alarm clock. She sighed contentedly and rolled over for just a few minutes in the comfortable bed. She smiled as she settled her head deeper into the pillow, but her smile turned to a frown as her sixth sense kicked in, and she knew she was being watched. She tentatively opened one eye and was not surprised to see two very large green eyes staring back at her.

"I should have left you with Taylor," she groaned. "Go away and let me sleep a little longer."

Tang answered her with a low growl and a not-so-gentle pat in the face with his paw.

"Okay, okay, but it's Sunday. Can't you let me have one morning when I don't have to get out of bed before…" She glanced at the clock on her bedside table. "Ugh! Before six-thirty!"

Tang's intense meow was his response. Holly's blissful night of sleep was over.

After feeding Tang and telling him how much she regretted bringing him on this little vacation, she arched her shoulders, pulled back her arms, and stretched her back. She hurt in places she didn't know she could hurt. She was used to being on her feet during the busiest times of the workday, but she had lots of downtime at work throughout the day when she could sit and relax, go over recipes and the accounting, or share a few minutes of chatter over a cup of coffee with whichever friend stopped by the café.

After an entire week of cooking lessons, interviews, recipe planning, and challenges, all on her feet, all she wanted was to soak all day in a very hot bath with lots of scented candles and Taylor Swift's latest album. Since the tub in the cottage was small, and she had no candles or phone, she opted for a long shower and the old-fashioned CD player Molly had found at a thrift shop and gave her along with several CDs she'd put together with music for every mood. Holly had to admit that though the girl drove her crazy sometimes, but she had a heart of gold.

As she washed her hair, Holly smiled at the memory of Lorenzo tugging on her ponytail and the way his eyes lit up when she let down her hair. He looked like a Roman god and cooked like a cross between Italian chef Michael Chiarello and their mentor himself, Chef Randall. He had brains, a sense of humor, and a rare integrity that Holly had seldom encountered. And he'd kissed her like she was the only woman he'd ever wanted.

The only problem was, she couldn't talk to Taylor or Christy or any of her other friends about him. She couldn't call her mother or Diane and ask for advice or tell them what a gentleman he was. And she and Lorenzo couldn't go on a real date or see what it was like to know each other in the real world.

Once out of the shower, Holly ran a large detangling comb through her hair and looked at her image in the mirror. What did he see when he looked at her? Was she as beautiful as Grace, as smart as Antonia, or as talented in the kitchen as his mother? Would the women in his life like her?

She shook her head and got dressed. She was getting way ahead of herself. She needed to get through the next several days, then time would tell if any of her questions mattered at all.

***

Gideon held his head in his hands in the makeshift office he'd set up in his Airbnb.

"What's wrong, sweetheart?" Tara asked. She went to him and began massaging his shoulders.

He closed his eyes and heaved a long, weary sigh. "What is wrong with this place? It's supposed to be a Mid-Atlantic paradise, but nearly every day I get a call that something has happened to the restaurant or home of one of our chefs."

"What happened now?" She deepened the massage, feeling the tension in his muscles.

"Someone tried to burn down Lorenzo's restaurant."

"Oh my. That's terrible. What are you going to do?"

"Nothing. I've been told to do and say nothing."

"By whom?"

"By the police. The fire was started in the dumpster out back, but enough gasoline was poured, with a line running to the restaurant, that everything could've been destroyed. Either the person wanted to make a statement, didn't have the heart to burn down the building, or thought starting the fire in the dumpster would give him time to escape."

"Why don't they want you to tell him?"

"Two reasons. First, his family has it under control. His sister is the manager, and his parents helped finance the place, so they have the authority to make decisions, deal with insurance, and all that. Plus, the fire trucks got there in time to stop the fire from spreading beyond the outer wall of the storage room."

"So, he's still in business."

"Yes, I believe so."

"And second?"

"Second?" He looked up at his wife of almost thirty years.

"You said there were two reasons."

"Oh, yes. They think someone here may be involved."

"Someone here? As in one of your crew?"

"Or our cast."

"They think the chefs are sabotaging their own businesses?"

"Or one of them is sabotaging everyone else. The first one was harmless but costly."

"The café's electricity, right?"

"Yes, which they're going back and looking into. The police weren't involved in that because it didn't seem like any crime had been committed."

"That makes sense, but then there was that poor girl's wine that was destroyed."

"Dawn, yes. And apparently, something at Kayla's home."

"Her home? Oh, wait. Is she the caterer?"

"Yeah, runs her business from her home. The incidents have escalated each time."

"Wow. What else? I think you mentioned someone's gas being left on." She went around and took a seat in a nearby chair where she could face him.

"Yes. And I think there's a pattern."

Tara thought for a moment. "I don't see it."

"You wouldn't. You're not on set and don't know who's in and out."

"Then what's the pattern?"

"The ones targeted are all our top chefs. At least the incidents I know about. There could've been some I haven't been let in on. But here's the thing. It's almost a pattern, but this latest one? He's a stellar chef, a real Michael Chiarello in the making."

"Ooh, nice. I love it when you work with Michael."

"Yes, but this chef, he hasn't won any challenges, yet, but he was still one of the targets."

"So, there may have been other incidents, or the person doing this is branching out and going after everyone, not just the top ones."

"Maybe, here's the thing. This chef hasn't won top chef yet," Gideon said. "But unless he makes some kind of crazy mistake, he's going to win at some point. Soon."

"I know that look, Gideon. You think he's the one."

"Maybe. Two of the women are just as good, but I think he's better. Just unlucky so far."

"Is there a season shocker? Someone you didn't expect to make it this far?"

"Two, actually. One mediocre cook who owns a family restaurant and one young woman who knows almost nothing about cooking."

"Wow. That's surprising. That she's made it this far, I mean."

"Except for one thing."

"What's that?" Tara asked.

"The future Michael Chiarello."

She shook her head. "I don't get it."

"He's coaching her."

Tara raised an eyebrow. "Really? Why's he doing that?"

Gideon rolled his eyes. "Come on, sweetheart, why do you think?"

"Oh! What do the others think about that?"

"They've kept it quiet. They usually do until after the show airs."

She nodded. "Yes, but there's usually some kind of sign."

"I've been watching the footage we have so far. The signs are there but are subtle. I'm not sure they even know what's happening yet."

Tara grinned broadly. "But you do because those of us who know you best, know you're a romantic at heart even though you'd never admit it to a soul."

He cursed. "Not me."

Tara laughed. "I say otherwise." She reached over and took his hand. "Is there anything I can do?"

"No. Well, maybe."

"What's that?" Gideon stood and pulled her to him. "How about keeping up that massage in the bedroom."

Tara laughed a guttural, alluring laugh. "Luckily for you, the girls took Sam to the beach for the day. That means you and I get to do some cooking together."

***

"Whoa! Good shot," Jake called to Lorenzo after the volleyball went right over Cynthia and Dawn's heads.

"Who wants a hot dog?" Jerry called from the grill.

Lorenzo looked down at his watch. "Will you save some for those of us going to Mass? The priest is supposed to be here in twenty minutes."

"Sure. Who else?"

"I'll need one," Kayla said from the lounge chair where she sat reading a book. "And Holly."

"Where is Holly?" Jane asked.

"I haven't seen her in a while," Cynthia said, wiping the sweat from her brow. "I'll take a hot dog, then I'm getting in the pool."

"I think we should head to the lounge and be ready in case Father Darryl is early," Kayla suggested. "I don't want to take him away from any plans he may have for the rest of the day."

Lorenzo followed Kayla and hoped he might have a few minutes with Father Darryl before Mass. He hadn't been practicing lately like he should and had decided he should make a good confession before Mass.

When they reached the meeting room, the door was closed, and they could hear faint voices inside. After a few minutes, Holly opened the door, dressed in a white t-shirt and orange shorts. Her hair was down but pulled back from her face, and she smiled at them and offered an apology.

"Sorry. I needed to see Father Darryl before Mass."

"It's fine," Kayla said.

Lorenzo cleared his throat. "Um, do you think I could have a few minutes with him?"

Always gracious and understanding, Kayla nodded. "Of course, you can. Holly if you need a few minutes alone, I can wait outside."

"No, I think I'll just go to the garden just outside the door for a few minutes. I won't be long." She hurried outside, and Lorenzo thanked Kayla and went inside, closing the door behind him.

"I'm not sure we've met," Father Darryl said, standing and reaching his hand out to Lorenzo.

"No, I'm afraid I haven't been to Mass for a while, since before I moved here."

"I see," the priest said. "Would you like to sit down and make this official?"

"Yes, I'd like that," Lorenzo said, knowing this was a long time coming. He took a seat and blessed himself, saying the words he'd learned in the second grade.

"Bless me, Father, for I have sinned. It's been almost a year since my last confession."

Lorenzo listed a few minor things that had been weighing on his conscience and then got to the main reason for his absence from the sacraments.

"Father, I've been angry with God and with others, but I'm beginning to see that I'm angry with myself."

"Go on."

"There was a woman. We were in love, or I thought we were. It turns out that she loved her career more than she loved me. I felt, well, I felt so many things when she left to pursue her dreams, and somewhere inside I was happy for her even though I hated her at the same time."

"Sometimes, those emotions can feel the same. They have the same root, deep in the heart."

Lorenzo nodded. "I decided I didn't want to love anyone ever again. I did some things I'm not proud of trying to forget her."

"We'll get to that. One thing at a time."

"I just wanted to prove to myself that I didn't need her. I didn't need my family or my friends or God. I was pushing everyone away. But then my dad, God love him, he suggested I come here and make a new start."

"Fathers have a way of knowing what we need even when we don't, especially our Heavenly Father."

Lorenzo looked up at the priest and smiled. "He did. He knew just what I needed. Or should I say both knew."

"And now, how are you feeling about your family, this woman, God?"

Lorenzo took a deep breath. "I feel like she taught me some things I wouldn't have known otherwise. She taught me to love, to really love and give my heart to someone, but at the same time, she taught me to listen to my heart when it tells me that someone isn't right for me and when someone is."

"You now see that it wasn't meant to be."

"We were from two different worlds, different upbringings, different interests, and different focuses in life. It would never have worked even though I romanticized it and convinced myself we could live this life that wouldn't have satisfied either of us."

"And the others?"

"I should have listened to them. My parents knew she wasn't right for me, which made me angrier after we broke up than before. And I couldn't understand why God brought her into my life in the first place if she wasn't going to stay."

"And now, based on what you said a few minutes ago, you know the reason."

"I do, and I'm ready to forgive God if He's willing to forgive me."

"Saint John wrote in his first letter, 'If we acknowledge our sins, he is trustworthy and upright, so that he will forgive our sins and will cleanse us from all evil.' God is always ready to forgive our sins. He just needs us to acknowledge our failures and be ready to repent."

As Lorenzo continued his confession, he felt as though a hundred-pound weight had been lifted from his shoulders. By the time the priest absolved him of his sins, "in the name of the Father, and of the Son, and of the Holy Spirit," Lorenzo felt like a new man.

***

"Kayla, thank you for asking Gideon to have Father Darryl come," Holly said as they left the meeting room and headed out to join the others.

"You're welcome, Holly. I hope we'll see more of you in church after this. I know it would mean a lot to Taylor."

"It would mean a lot to me. More than I ever knew." She'd forgotten the peace that accompanies being at Mass, the beautiful harmony of the readings and prayers, and the intimacy of receiving Christ in the Eucharist. Even if this was a small service with only three people and the priest in the meeting room of a tiny resort, she still felt the long-lost familiarity that was like she'd just returned home after a long, painful journey. She was looking forward to being back in the church building with the glowing candles and the stained-glass windows depicting the wheat and grapes that would become the body and blood of Jesus.

"Hey, is anyone else going to the cooking lesson?" Kayla asked as they exited the building. "It's almost 1:30, and the bus will be here then."

"I signed up," Holly said. "I figured I should take advantage of everything Gideon can teach me while he's here."

"I did, too," Lorenzo said.

"I feel the same," said Kayla. "I know Bob and Jane are both going."

"I heard Jerry and Robby talking about it, too," Lorenzo told them. "I think Walt, Jake, and Cynthia may be the only ones not going."

"Why wouldn't they go?" Holly asked.

Lorenzo shrugged. "Beats me. I think Cynthia said she needed a break, and Jake is following her lead. Not sure about Walt."

"Well, let's get something to eat so we don't scarf down our ingredients," Kayla suggested.

"Yeah, we don't want to be on Chef Randall's bad side," agreed Anna.

They found everyone else by the pool. Jerry, as promised, had saved them hot dogs along with chips and pickles.

"Oh, my gosh, it's so nice to eat junk," Holly said.

"I hear you," Kayla agreed. "I love the gourmet food we all make and get to share with the crew after taping, but there's nothing like a perfectly cooked hot dog from the grill."

"Well, Jerry did a pretty good job making the hot dogs, but when this is over, I'll have you all over for some of my grilling. I wish I'd had more of a chance to show my skills on the show," Jake said.

"Maybe Gideon will do a show someday all about grilling, and you'll get to be on that," Cynthia suggested.

"I'm in!" Jake said, and they all laughed.

After they ate, those going to the cooking lesson headed to the bus. Holly didn't relish spending the day off back at her station, but she was looking forward to a lesson from Gideon without the pressure of being taped or preparing for a challenge.

"Hey," Lorenzo said as he caught up with her on the short walk to the street. "This morning was nice. The Mass, I mean."

"It was. I'm going to make some changes so that going to Mass is a priority from now own. Diane always managed to do that. I don't think I realized how much I missed going until today."

"Once you stop going every week, it becomes easy to stay away."

"But it shouldn't. I'm not going to let that happen again."

"Next Sunday, maybe we could go together?" He looked at her hopefully.

"I think that would be nice. Thanks."

And she meant it, not just because it was Lorenzo, but because she realized she had stopped going because she didn't feel part of the community. That was her own fault. She hadn't really tried. Even though Taylor and Nick went faithfully as did Christy, Jared, and Molly, Holly found too many easy excuses that allowed her not to go. Being with Kayla and Anna all week, she realized she needed more in her life than work, one night out with the girls, and relationships that went nowhere. She'd been chasing love and happiness when she should have been chasing God. It was nice to hear Father Darryl remind them in his homily that God was always waiting just outside, and all they had to do was open the door and let him in.

***

Zach stopped by the rectory later that day and was happy to see that Father was home.

"Hey, Father Darryl, how're you doing?"

"Zach, good to see you. What brings you by this afternoon. Oh, wait, if you're here because—"

"I am. I heard you went out to Chincoteague Harbor this morning."

"Zach, you know how I feel about you and your family. You've all become my family here on the island, but don't ask me any questions. I had to sign a confidentiality statement and had to agree not to talk to any of the contestants about anything having to do with the show."

"I know, Father. I figured that, but it's just that, well, you know how Kayla gets. She looks out for everyone else, including her clients, and she doesn't take care of herself. And right now, I feel like I'm not doing a very good job."

"Well, you can hardly look after Kayla when she's secluded away from you, but Zach, I'm sure you're looking after the boys."

He nodded. "Of course, and I've even taken a couple small orders and delivered the food, hoping of course, that it stands up to Kayla's cooking."

"That was brave," Father chuckled.

"Yeah, I was scared to death I'd poison them."

"Oh, come on. I've tasted your cooking. It's as good as Kayla's. And aren't half the recipes she uses ones that you taught her and make alongside her?"

"Yeah, but that's part of the problem. She's not beside me."

Father Darryl leaned toward his friend. "Zach, is Kayla okay? The cancer isn't—"

"No, no, unless… Did she look okay? Did she look tired? Sick?"

"She looked healthy as a horse. Stop worrying. She'll be home soon."

"Not soon enough," Zach said. "By the way, I've been looking into the stuff that's happened at the restaurants. Have you heard about any of it?"

"Ted told me about the wine, and everyone heard about Anna's stove being left on. What kind of person would do that, knowing her family was upstairs?" The priest shook his head. "I met Lorenzo's sisters today at Mass, and they filled me in about the fire. I'm praying they catch whoever is doing this very soon. Are there any leads?"

Zach shook his head. "None that I can say." He told Father what happened to their pantry. "I'm just so angry that we haven't figured out who it is. I'm worried they might strike the set or the Harbor."

"I never thought of that."

"Yeah, well, you've never thought about most of the scenarios I've had to face. I just hate thinking strategically like that when it comes to my family."

"I can understand. Ask the Lord to protect them, Zach. He's always come through for you. You know that."

"Has he ever," Zach said and repeated, "Has he ever."

***

"This quaint colonial structure you see behind me is the Captain Timothy Hill House, built around 1800, and is the oldest house on the island of Chincoteague. It's listed on The National Register of Historic Places and The Virginia Landmarks Register, and you can tour it on Friday afternoons or by appointment."

Gideon walks through the split-rail fence and the camera follows him up into the house.

"When you visit this house, you feel like you've traveled back in time to an era when life was slower, neighbors were family, and cooking was damn hard!" Gideon laughs. "I mean, look at that wooden chimney! What kind of stove did they have, how did the house not burn down?" The camera pans the tiny two-room house, zeroing in on the modern woodstove. "I can't imagine living here with a family. We have this small living space down here and a tiny bedroom loft upstairs. No counter space at all!" Gideon throws up his hands.

He walks outside and stands in front of the small, wooden house. "It's fascinating to me to think that someone like Mary Randolph or Fannie Farmer, 18th Century American cooks and authors, may have cooked in a kitchen like this. Of course, I could say the same about my great-great-grandmother back in Scotland. We've come a long way in how we cook, and on that note, I'll see you back in the kitchen."

***

Molly needed to talk to Zach. Something had been bothering her ever since the night of the fire, and she needed to see what he thought about it. She tried to talk to Nick, but he was so angry with her, he wouldn't listen. They all thought she was just a kid who put herself, Jenny, and the others in danger, but Molly knew that if they hadn't been surveilling the restaurants, Speziato would have burned to the ground. She thought they deserved some credit.

But no, she was grounded. Her phone had been taken away, she'd lost computer access, and she wasn't allowed to see her friends at all. She wasn't allowed to do anything but go to work. She kept hoping Zach would come by for a donut or cup of coffee, but she hadn't seen him at the café since he was there for lunch with Nick. She was hoping to catch him at church, but he and the boys must have gone the night before. Just her luck.

Molly washed the windows, her least favorite job which she now had to do twice a day instead of just once because, it seemed, Diane was punishing her, too. While she wiped, she continued to think about what she'd seen. A photographic memory had not been one of the prodigious gifts she'd been blessed with, and after all that happened, she was having a hard time conjuring the scene in her mind. But she knew there was something important she wasn't seeing. Something she saw that night that was just beyond her grasp.

There was something hidden in Molly's mind that would unlock this mysterious puzzle they were all trying to solve. She just had to figure out what it was.

***

With everyone was back at the Harbor, and dinner was a festive affair. They were down to three more days of cooking and then a final day to tape extra footage.

Back in his room, he felt out of sorts. He was more than ready to be done, out of this fishbowl, and back in the restaurant where he belonged. He hated not knowing what was going on there even though he trusted his family to keep it going. The one person he'd had contact with was no longer answering his calls.

What he really hated was not knowing what was happening with the police investigation. How long would it take before they zeroed in on him? Even though his own place had been hit, he knew that might not throw them off. Why had he started this whole thing to begin with?

He began pacing. He regretted all that he had done, and he wanted it to stop, but it had taken on a life of its own, one that he no longer had any control over. He felt immensely guilty and had even considered telling the priest about it, confessing what he had done, but he couldn't do it. He couldn't face the repercussions of it all.

Not only would he lose his restaurant if he was caught, he'd lose everything he'd ever wanted. His family would be disgraced, his new friends would hate him, and the person who meant the most in the world to him would never look at him the same again. He had to put a stop to this, but at this point, he didn't know how. And in the end, would it really matter?

"I'm Holly, and I have no idea how I got here. [She laughs nervously]. I went to school for hospitality and worked on a cruise ship and hated it. I then went into waitressing—I worked for Jane at the deli, believe it or not—to make some money while deciding what to do with my life, and I realized I love working in a restaurant. I became a manager at Jerry's restaurant, Ropewalk— hmmm…the irony of all this. [She looks thoughtfully at the camera]. And before I knew it, I was the owner of Sand and Sugar. I have zero cooking experience, so I expect to be out right away, but I like to approach every new thing as a potentially life-changing endeavor. Who knows what this will do for me and my future!"

Chapter Twelve

"For some of you, today will be an easy challenge." Gideon looked at the increasingly smaller group and chuckled. "Easy being a relative term."

Holly glanced at the others before looking back at Gideon.

What does he have up his sleeve today?

"Today, we will be baking. But not just baking, elevated baking! You'll take something ordinary and make it extraordinary. There are no boundaries, but it must be something more than just a two-layer cake or a basic fruit pie. Challenge yourselves. We're down to the final five, so show me you deserve to go on."

When the clock finally started, Holly knew exactly what she would bake. When she first came to the area, she made it a priority to head over to Smith Island, Maryland, not far from Chincoteague, to take a baking class from the famous Mary Ada Marshall, known to many as the Smith Island Cake Lady. Though the ten-layer cake's most famous and most popular flavor was yellow cake with chocolate fudge icing, there was no end to the flavor creations the locals came up with.

Holly rushed to the supply closet and grabbed every single cake pan on the shelf. If anyone else was planning on baking a cake, she was unabashedly depriving them of the pans they would need, but they were nearing the end of the competition, and she needed those pans to show why she deserved to stay on the show. The most important ingredient would be the evaporated milk, which would give the cake it's ultra-moist texture and melt-in-the-mouth decadence. That was the first thing Holly took from the pantry. She checked the fresh food items and grabbed the one thing that would make this her signature cake.

To save time, two-and-a-half ovens would be needed for the ten pans, and since there were now seven vacant stations, that would not be a problem. Without delay, Holly rushed to each of the unoccupied stations and preheated the ovens to 350°. Then she got to work on creating the batter she knew how to make in her sleep.

By the time Gideon and Christina got to Holly's station, her chocolate-strawberry batter was in all three ovens, and she was making the famous chocolate fudge icing.

"I smell chocolate baking. I hope you're not going to try to win over the judges with boring chocolate cake, especially one with chocolate icing. Chocolate on chocolate can be risky."

"No, Chef, this is anything but boring."

"Then what makes it stand out?" Gideon asked.

"First, it's not just any cake. It's a Smith Island Cake."

Christina's jaw dropped, and her eyes widened. Gideon was at a loss for words.

"Second, it's not just chocolate. It's a creamy strawberry infused decadence that, when combined with the traditional fudge icing, will bring an explosion of flavor to the mouths of the judges."

Holly grinned at the judges, quite proud of herself for the buildup she gave her cake. She knew she wasn't wrong. Everyone loved her own Smith Island Cake recipe.

"You're making a Smith Island Cake? All ten layers?" Gideon asked.

"Yes, Chef. It's my own recipe, but the necessary ingredients are there, and I'm making the original icing."

"And you're doing this in ninety minutes?"

"I sure am, Chef," Holly responded, feeling more confident than ever.

"I've got to see this," Christina said before they turned to Lorenzo.

Holly didn't pay any attention to their dialog. She was too busy paying close attention to the baking cakes and making sure the consistency of the fudge icing was perfect. It wasn't until Lorenzo knocked a pan to the floor and uttered a very Gideon Randall-like expletive that she realized he was in trouble.

Holly looked at Lorenzo who looked helplessly at the spinning Kitchen Aid mixer. She thought about all the times he'd given her help and advice over the past week. She looked at the timer for her cakes—one minute left—and then glanced at the competition time clock. The icing was finished, and the cake needed time to cool. She had to slice the berries and tear some mint for garnish, but the biggest feat was the one she had left— frosting the cake—all ten layers and the outside. She took a deep breath and looked at Lorenzo.

"One of the most difficult things to do in a kitchen is get the cream to form peaks. Trust me. It took years for me to get it right. What have you done so far?"

He explained how he had dissolved the sugar into the eggs over a simmering pot of water, then he whisked them in the mixer with the heavy cream and vanilla. No matter how fast he whisked, all he got was liquid.

"You're rushing. Start over."

Lorenzo just stared at her, his mouth agape without uttering words.

"Now, Lorenzo. You have time if you do it now. Don't lose a second."

Without arguing, he ran around the kitchen gathering ingredients. Holly hurriedly removed the pans from the ovens and set them all on cooling racks. She washed the berries and mint leaves while Lorenzo beat his eggs. Holly sliced strawberries while Lorenzo dissolved the sugar into the simmering eggs.

"What happened?" Gideon asked.

"No peaks," Lorenzo said.

Holly kept quiet while Gideon admonished Lorenzo for rushing and warned him that this would probably cost him the competition. Holly looked up in time to see disappointment flash across Gideon's face. Like her, he knew that Lorenzo was one of the best, despite not having won a challenge yet. For the briefest of moments, she considered coaching Lorenzo to victory, but she knew he wouldn't want it that way. She'd worked too hard to get this far even with his help.

"Get those eggs chilled, now. Don't let them sit out. You don't have time." Gideon said.

"What if it congeals?"

"Don't let it chill that long. Just do it. You can't pour a hot or even lukewarm mixture in with the cream and expect it to peak. What's your base?"

"Biscuits soaked in Kahlua and amaretto."

"Are they soaking?" he asked.

"Cooling."

Gideon leaned over and touched one of the biscuits on a cooling rack. "Soak them. They're cool enough." He walked away but yelled back, "Get them soaking, Lorenzo!"

Holly checked her cakes and took a deep breath. She didn't want to make the same mistake Lorenzo had made. If she tried to lift the thin layers from the pans too soon, they would fall apart. If she waited too long, she wouldn't have time to frost them. She'd give them another few minutes.

"When you're done with the biscuits, check the eggs. Stir them if they're still hot. Do not put them in the cream if you feel any warmth at all. They must be completely cooled." She advised Lorenzo.

He nodded, and Holly began preparing her platter for the first layer. She closed her eyes, took a deep breath, and said a prayer that her own layers were completely cooled. She had twenty minutes left to present the best, most perfectly layered and decorated cake of her life. She couldn't help but wonder if God answered the prayers of people who had stopped taking the time to pray.

***

"These jam fritters look amazing," José said. "A Virginia delicacy, I believe."

Dawn nodded.

"They're beautiful in color, fried just right, with the red strawberry jam peeking through."

The camera followed closely as he picked up one of the golden, fried balls with his fork and put it in his mouth. He closed his eyes while he savored it, groaning in ecstasy.

The camera showed Dawn, glowing with pride while the rest of the group nervously looked on.

"I love this," he pronounced. "Delicioso."

"I agree. It's delicious. But shouldn't we be elevating the dish rather than creating a deep-fried carnival concession at this point? I'm not so sure," Christina said.

Gideon agreed with Christina's assessment.

Kayla's chocolate soufflé drizzled with crème anglaise and topped with finely chopped strawberries had the judges going crazy.

"Next to baked Alaska, this is considered the hardest dessert to bake, and you've done it perfectly," Gideon told her.

"I could lick the ramekin clean," Christina said as she scooped another bite from the small white baking cup.

"Here's another real treat," Gideon told them as the camera moved to the three-inch thick, ten-layer masterpiece of rich chocolate topped with sliced strawberries and mint leaves. "A Smith Island Cake."

Christina picked up the slice and turned it from side-to-side before counting the layers. "Something every East Coast chef with a brain travels to experience. I almost took the class once, but I couldn't make it out to the island in time."

"Have you ever been?" Gideon asked.

She nodded. "Once. Getting there was an ordeal, but I talked to the local chefs and Mrs. Marshall herself and left with a whole new appreciation for their way of life and the local foods they not only make but also harvest."

"Eat any crabs when you were there?"

She shook her head and answered with a mouth full of cake. "Too early. We had oysters."

"Even better," Gideon said.

"Mmm. This cake is to die for." She wiped some chocolate icing from her face with a napkin. "Wow. Perfectly moist, and I can taste the strawberries in every bite. Heavenly. And the presentation is just beautiful."

Walt shifted anxiously as the camera panned to his cheesecake.

"Cheesecake?" José asked with a wrinkle in his brow.

"Yes, topped with chocolate sauce and cherries."

José took a bite and frowned. "One of my favorites, and it looks tantalizing, but I'm not impressed. Where's the elevation? It tastes like any cheesecake you can get frozen."

"Truly a disappointment," Christina agreed.

Walt hung his head, and the camera moved on to Lorenzo.

"Now this looks interesting. I love the swirls and the way the sauce—what is this sauce?—lightly sits in the folds. It's a stunning presentation." Christina touched her finger to the translucent brown liquid and licked it. Her eyes lit up. "Mmm. A sweet coffee syrup. Love it."

The camera watched her dig out a scoop of the creamy dessert as Gideon told them about it.

"This is an espresso amaretto tiramisu. A heady version of the classic dessert."

"Heady is right. Amaretto makes everything stand out, and this is sensuous, as tiramisu should be."

"Very nice," José agreed. "I'm tasting everything—espresso, amaretto, Kahlua, and a nice wave of vanilla. What a beautiful blend of flavors."

The camera caught Lorenzo looking at Holly and mouthing, *thank you*. Would that admission make the cut? That was up to Gideon to decide.

"Well," Gideon said. "Shall we go have a chat?"

The judges left the room, and all five contestants breathed a sigh of relief.

"That was the most challenging one yet," Kayla said.

"I think so, too," Holly admitted. "And I bake for a living."

"Well, I don't," said Lorenzo. "I'll be happy to be back in the restaurant with Ben, my own pastry chef."

"Maybe so, but I can't wait to dig into that tiramisu," Dawn said.

They all nodded in agreement and took their seats to wait for the judges to return.

***

"There wasn't a bad dessert served today. Everything was well made, delicious, and beautifully presented," Gideon told them, rubbing his hands together as he spoke. "However, we did have two desserts that just weren't up to the standards we're looking for."

"But before we tell you who's facing elimination, let's congratulate the creator of the best dessert." He paused for dramatic effect, and Lorenzo waited to hear Holly or Kayla's name called. "Today's top chef was the creator of the tiramisu, Lorenzo!"

Lorenzo felt like he needed to shake water from his ears. He couldn't have heard correctly. He glanced at Holly and saw genuine happiness in her wide smile and bright eyes. The others turned to congratulate him, and Lorenzo accepted it gracefully though he didn't feel deserving of the praise.

"Well done, Lorenzo," Christina said. "Beautiful and delicious dessert. The addition of amaretto always elevates."

"Now, for the two who will be going head-to-head this afternoon…Dawn and Walt." Gideon waited for them to take front and center. "Now, for this challenge…"

Lorenzo zoned out, wishing he felt better about being on top. He'd screwed up. He rushed, he got angry and frustrated, and he'd lost his ability to think clearly. He glanced toward Holly, who was listening intently to Chef Randall. If not for her, he'd be out of the competition.

After Gideon finished explaining the challenge and called for a break, he walked over to where Lorenzo stood.

Gideon leaned toward Lorenzo and said in a very low voice, "You owe her one. I mean, you really owe her."

Lorenzo nodded. "Yes, Chef, I sure do."

***

"I like these shorter days," Kayla remarked, dipping her head backwards into the water.

"Me, too, but honestly, I'm stunned," said Holly, clinging to the side of the pool beside the other women. "I can't believe the way today went."

"Same," said Dawn. "I really thought you had top chef. Your cake was amazing. Don't they know how hard a Smith Island Cake is to make? You deserve so much more credit for what you pulled off."

Holly shook her head. "I didn't mean that. I'm not looking for praise, and I'm not upset I didn't get top chef. Lorenzo's dessert was absolutely wonderful. The flavors were heavenly. I meant, I can't believe you're out."

Dawn smiled. 'But I'm okay with it. I knew it would probably come to an end soon."

"But you're an amazing chef, twice the one I am. I'm not even a real chef."

"Don't say that, Holly," Kayla admonished her. "First, this whole competition is designed to do two things: put us all on equal ground and challenge us to dig deeper. You've had challenges that were right up your alley, like they'd been designed just for you, yet still, you've had to reach way past your existing skills and push yourself to go farther and work harder."

Holly scrunched her nose and looked at Kayla. "You think the challenges are fixed so that we all have something that was meant just for us to excel at?"

"Of course, they are," Cynthia said. You and Dawn serve the best breakfast foods on the island. Lorenzo and Anna have international menus. Dawn, Jerry, and Bob all specialize in local seafood. Kayla and Walt make comfort foods. You and I focus on baking. Think about it."

"So, that means we must have something grilled or something that could be grilled coming up. Even though Jake is out, they wouldn't have known that when it was all planned." Holly's head spun as she thought ahead to what else might be coming their way.

"That's probably tomorrow because the final three will have some kind of technical challenge," Jane chimed in.

"Hmm… I hadn't thought about any of this." Holly said.

"That's because your mind has been elsewhere," Cynthia said with a knowing smile.

"What's that supposed to mean?"

"You know what I mean. Gone kayaking lately?"

Holly felt her face grow hot. "Taken a walk on the beach lately?"

Cynthia laughed. "Lots of them. I told you, we're secretly on *Passion Island*."

"Well, back to what I was saying earlier, Dawn, I'm stunned you lost. I can't imagine you not being there tomorrow.

"I'll be there in spirit. Dessert isn't my thing. I knew that going into this. I can't wrap my head around the exact measurements and baking powder versus baking soda or regular flour versus cake flour. I'm just happy I lasted this long."

"Well, *I'm* just happy for the two weeks at the resort," Jane said. "If anyone had told me it would be this nice, I would've planned on losing that first competition instead of just getting eliminated first by chance. I haven't had a vacation in years!"

They all laughed, but Holly looked skyward and frowned.

"Those dark clouds are getting closer. I think we should get out and get dried off."

The other women looked up. "I think you're right," Kayla said. "It looks like it's going to be a nasty one."

"Well, I'm going to go find a nice quiet place to cuddle—I mean relax." Cynthia shot them a wicked grin.

"You go ahead," Jane said before winking at Cynthia. "I'm going to do the same.

They barely had their towels in hand before a streak of lightning crossed the sky, and thunder rolled in the distance.

"Better buckle down," Kayla warned. "I've lived through many summer storms on the island, and I don't like the looks of that sky."

Holly glanced once more at the darkening sky and headed toward her bungalow. As she got closer, she saw a beautiful bouquet of flowers in a tall vase standing outside the door. She reached down and plucked the note from the arrangement.

Meet me in the dining room. 7pm. Please.

Holly smiled as she opened the door, managing to get the flowers inside without letting Tang out.

"Well, Tang, it looks like you're on your own again this evening. If I'm not mistaken, I have a date."

***

"Today, we're doing one of my favorite things: drinking alcohol. We're visiting the Black Narrows Brewing Company, the first craft brewery on Virginia's

Eastern Shore." Gideon strolls around the inside of the building, which has a children's play area in one corner.

"The brewery is located in a converted oyster shucking house and serves a dozen specialty beers, including Cockle Creek, a Scottish ale I'm quite fond of."

He picks up a glass beer stein from the bar and takes a long drink, sighing with satisfaction.

"They have something for everyone, from fruity to sour and everything in between. And of course, no beer is complete without…" he reaches to the counter behind him, "a giant Bavarian soft pretzel."

Gideon takes a bite of the pretzel and another slug of beer. "They also have a huge selection of local seafood. And speaking of local, almost all their ingredients are locally sourced. By the way, I try to locally source as many ingredients as possible for my cooking shows, which reminds me that we need to get back to the kitchen."

Gideon downs the rest of his beer and starts to leave. He stops, turns back to the bar and picks up the pretzel, then walks out the door.

***

The resort didn't have a kitchen. All the cottages had their own kitchenettes, and their food had been provided by the show all week, so Holly had to ask one of the Harbor staff where the dining room was. It was small but quaint and must have been used for private gatherings the same as the meeting room where they all got together after the show each evening.

The lights in the room were turned down low when Holly arrived. She wore the only non-cooking apparel she'd packed: a red, flowered bathing suit cover-up she'd bought when she and her girlfriends went to the Caribbean. It wasn't too sheer and was long enough to pass for a dress. She hoped she wasn't overdressed.

She didn't see any movement in the dimly lit room, and she wondered if she'd misjudged this. Maybe it wasn't a date. Maybe it wasn't even from him. She was about to turn and leave when she heard music begin to play. It was a beautiful orchestral piece, and she was pretty sure that only one person at this resort knew his way around classical music. She looked around but still didn't see anyone, so she followed the sound of the music.

In the back of the empty dining room stood a small, candlelit table. Nearby, a speaker played music, and a bottle of wine stood next to two glasses and a small plate with some kind of appetizer. When she moved closer, she saw an assortment of finger foods—crab balls, shrimp cocktail, clams casino, and beautiful golden rolls that glistened with butter.

"Thank you for coming," said a voice behind her, and Holly turned to see Lorenzo dressed in jeans and a pressed white shirt.

"Thank you for asking," she said, suddenly feeling self-conscious. "This looks nice. How did you—"

"Rachel helped. She knows some people who cook."

Holly laughed, and once she started, she couldn't stop. "I'm sorry," she said. "It's just that we've spent all week cooking all day, but you had to find someone on the set to make a special dinner for us." She covered her mouth to try to stop the laughing, but she couldn't control it. "I'm sorry. I know it's not that funny." Still, she couldn't stop laughing. She realized she was nervous. More nervous than she'd ever been.

Lorenzo took a step closer, and the intensity in his eyes brought her laughter to a sudden halt. Her breath caught in her throat as she gazed up at him. She'd let her hair down and brushed it until it shined, and he slowly lifted his hand and gently ran his fingers through the long strands until they came to rest on her shoulder. Her breathing was shallow, and her heart was beating wildly against her rib cage. A sudden clap of thunder shook the room, and she jumped. His hand closed over her shoulder and steadied her.

"Thank you," he said again, quieter and with meaning.

"You said that already." She swallowed, wanting to close the eight or so inches between them.

"I mean for today. That wasn't my spot at the top. It was yours. You saved me, and it should've been you being recognized by Gideon."

"You're the only one I need to recognize me." She'd never said anything so honest, so deeply personal, to anyone. For a moment, she didn't realize she'd said it out loud.

"I didn't plan on this," he said with just as much honesty and sincerity.

She smiled. "Neither did I. I didn't even like you at first."

He chuckled. "I know."

Someone cleared a throat from behind them, and they turned to see Peter, one of Gideon's sous chefs. "Dinner is almost ready."

"Thank you, Peter." Lorenzo turned back to Holly. "I guess we should eat the appetizers."

"Probably," she said.

She popped a crab ball into her mouth while Lorenzo poured two glasses of wine.

"I had one of the hotel staff pick this up. It's not exactly my aunt's family Amarone, but it will do."

"Well, since I have no idea what Amarone is…" She took the glass he offered. "I'm sure this will be just fine."

"A toast," he said, raising his glass. "To the top chefs of the day."

Holly chuckled. "You're welcome," she said, clinking her glass to his.

They ate the rest of the appetizers and took their seats as one of the other crew members brought them their plates.

"Do I want to know what you're paying them to do this?"

Lorenzo shook his head as he pulled out her chair. "Let's just say, I hope Antonia is doing really well in my absence."

"Then it's my turn to thank you." Holly sat down and looked at their meal. "This looks amazing. Is it ribeye?"

"Gideon's recipe. I would have gone for the beef Wellington, but I only had so much time to work with."

"Did you make it? I thought you said Rachel got you a cook."

Lorenzo looked down with modesty. "Mostly. I had to get myself ready, and Peter did a lot of the prep."

"You cooked for me. After cooking all day and going through all that anxiety when things weren't working right, on top of the most stressful weeks of our lives, you cooked for me." The gravity of his actions hit like an ocean wave, and she felt it difficult not to cry. As it was, her eyes filled with tears, and she hastily wiped them with her napkin. "Nobody has ever done anything like this for me."

"Maybe they should have. Maybe you haven't had somebody who wants to do this for you, who wants to…" He hesitated. "To show you how special you are."

His brown eyes glowed in the flickering candlelight, and she saw in them something she hadn't seen before, not the night he almost kissed her nor the night he did kiss her. She was certain it reflected what he saw in her eyes, in her heart.

Is it possible to fall this hard, this fast?

Lorenzo gestured toward her plate. "Don't let it get cold."

"Always the chef," she said with a laugh.

***

Though thunder shook the building, and torrents of rain beat against the windows, Lorenzo only noticed how the flashes of lightning illuminated Holly's hair. She reminded him of a saint with a halo around her head, and in his mind, he saw that painting of the guardian angel that hung in his sister's childhood bedroom. He remembered how Holly reminded him of an angel that night on the beach earlier in the week, a night that seemed like years ago. After today, he knew that she was most assuredly his guardian angel.

"How did you get this broccoli so crisp and tasty?" she asked, pulling him from his thoughts.

"It's a little secret of mine."

Holly tilted her head and cocked her jaw to the side. "Really? Now I'm even more intrigued."

"Air fryer," he confided.

Her mouth opened wide. "No way. Seriously? Isn't that like, cheating?"

Lorenzo shook his head. "Gideon uses one."

She put her fork down. "He does not."

"He does. I've seen his YouTube videos that give tips on how he uses his at home. Not kidding."

"Wow. You learn something new every day."

"Tell me something new about yourself."

"Something new?"

"Something you haven't already told me."

He reached for the wine he had put on the table and refilled their glasses.

"No more, okay? I have to get up early tomorrow."

Lorenzo laughed. "That makes two of us. So, tell me something I don't know."

Holly took a bite of steak and chewed it purposefully. She washed it down with a sip of wine and tossed her hair over her shoulders.

"I'm afraid of the dark."

"No, seriously."

She leveled her gaze at him. "Seriously. I've always had this fear of the dark, especially of being outside in the dark. I'm petrified to walk outside when I can't see what I might step on."

"So, it's not really the dark as much as what might be out there in the dark."

"Are you trying to analyze me?"

"Maybe, but let's call it getting to know you."

Holly laughed, and the sound of it sent his stomach aflutter.

"Your turn," she said.

Lorenzo hesitated. What did he want her to know? What one thing did he want to share with her?

"I'm afraid of being left behind. No, it's more than that. I'm afraid of losing the person I love. It's kind of a pattern with my family and with me."

"Maybe it's not as much a pattern with you as a sign that you haven't found your true love yet."

Her eyes held his, and he wondered, *is it possible to fall this hard, this fast?*

I was pretty much raised in Terra e Mare, my parents' restaurant in Little Italy, Baltimore. [Old family photographs inside and in front of the restaurant filter on and off the screen.] The name means Land and Sea. My great-grandparents owned a restaurant in Sicily, and though my grandparents never owned one, my father always wanted to. He and Mamma were the perfect match. They brought up five kids who all went into the business in one way or another. I don't have the kind of schooling some of these other chefs have, but I have generations of restaurant blood in my veins. Speziato, Spicy, is our family's first restaurant outside Italy or Little Italy, and I'm working hard to make my parents proud. [Lorenzo smiles at the camera.]

Chapter Thirteen

Holly startled when her alarm went off, but she allowed herself a few precious moments in bed to recall last night's dinner. A large body suddenly thumped on top of her and caused her breath to whoosh from her crushed lungs, reminding her that she hadn't gone to bed alone the night before. Tang meowed loudly from his perch on her chest, and she reached to stroke his fur, hoping to put off his fury at her lack of desire to leap from the bed and feed him.

"Lorenzo was such a gentleman last night. He made me the most amazing meal, and then he surprised me with a truly decadent banana split for dessert." Tang began licking his paws while she spoke, and she took that as a sign he was listening. "He looked so sweet when he told me that Kayla shared with him that it was my favorite guilty pleasure." She smiled at the memory.

"By the time we finished eating, the storm was over, and Lorenzo walked me back here. We had to sidestep puddles and leap over some rushing water, but it added to the fun we were having."

She thought about the awkwardness she felt after he kissed her goodnight in the doorway. Holly said to him, "I'd ask you in, but I'm chaperoned on this little hiatus by a very possessive and protective mini lion named Tang, and he wouldn't approve."

"You know what he said to me, Tang? He said, 'I have no intention of turning this into *Passionate Island*, or whatever that awful show is called. We'll leave all that stuff for later once we see what the real world brings.' I didn't correct him on the name of the show, by the way. I just liked that he was such a gentleman."

When Lorenzo said that, Holly hadn't known how to respond, and it occurred to her that she didn't know any true gentlemen in the real world. Whether they were just living out a fantasy or starting something truly meaningful, she appreciated Lorenzo feeling the same way she did in not wanting to blur the lines.

Tang broke into her thoughts with an angry meow before leaping from the bed and looking up at with her obvious disdain.

"I'm coming, your highness. Give me a few minutes in the bathroom, will you?"

Holly put off her shower until after her personal king of the house had been fed, then she cranked up Molly's CD player before beginning her morning routine. As the water sprayed on her back, she sang along with Harry Styles, aware that she was opening her heart to the possibility of another painful goodbye, yet willing to take the chance.

***

"If there's one thing I can make, it's steak," Walt proudly professed. Lorenzo had been thinking the same thing.

"Good," Gideon said. "Because this is one of the most popular and hardest of all the challenges on my shows. But today, we're not just cooking any steak. Each one of you will be cooking filet mignon, and it had better be the best filet you've ever cooked in your life. Remember, there are no more elimination rounds. We're not weeding people out anymore. We're searching for the best of the best. You're either in, or you're out."

Once the director yelled, "Cut," and they headed to their stations for their daily lesson, Holly leaned over to Lorenzo.

"I've never cooked a filet mignon. I have no idea where to start. And…" She held up her hand. "I'm not asking you to help me. I need to figure this out on my own. I'm just telling you that this will probably be it for me. So, thank you. For everything."

"Don't talk like that. It's not that difficult. Listen to your mentor chef, talk about the recipes, and choose the one you're most comfortable with. It's so much easier than most people think. It's all about the spices and the heat. You've got this." He could tell Holly was still unsure, but he smiled and pushed her toward her station.

They worked with their mentor chefs for a couple hours before taking a break and starting again.

Lorenzo was in his zone. Tuscan filet with a balsamic reduction was one of the most popular dishes at his restaurant. It was a recipe his Aunt Marta introduced him to, based on a dish at one of her favorite restaurants in Florence. He'd made it so many times, the recipe was ingrained in his brain, and each time he made it, it was better than the last. He served it with sautéed spinach and a generous helping of perfectly cooked mushrooms. A nice, crusty slice of bread was a must for soaking up the juices, and he was pleased to find a loaf of Italian bread in the pantry.

He was so absorbed in his own cooking that he'd failed to look Holly's way even once. When he did, he gasped at what he saw.

"Holly," he urgently whispered. "You need to turn that filet. Don't let it sit."

She did as she was told and turned toward him, her face red and tears imminent. "I spent so much time on my mashed potatoes, I forgot to put on the filet. I was hoping to get it to cook faster."

Lorenzo shook his head. "It doesn't work like that. You want it to cook fast but evenly, and the inside must be pink." He looked at her filet. "Did you sear it?"

"Did I sear it?"

"Like your mentor told you to do, with the herb crust and melted butter on a high heat to get the crispy outside?"

Her eyes widened. "Um, no. I marinated it while I prepared the potatoes and broccolini, then I started cooking it. I completely forgot about the searing."

Lorenzo swallowed. "I'm sure it will be fine," he lied. Disappointed and feeling like he let her down, he turned back to his filet. Maybe she'd get lucky, and Kayla or Walt would run into a problem with their meals. Somehow, he didn't think that would be the case.

***

"Our top chef today is…Lorenzo," Gideon smiled, and everyone gave Lorenzo a round of applause. "Lorenzo, earlier in the competition, you had a balsamic glaze that ruined your sandwich. Today, that glaze set your filet apart from the crowd. We all agree that it was outstanding. Great job."

"Thanks, Chef. My Aunt Marta, who introduced this recipe to me, will be really pleased."

"And well she should be," Gideon said. He clapped his hands together and rubbed them in circles. "Unfortunately, we do have to name the worst filet and send someone home."

Lorenzo held his breath. They'd already heard the judges' assessment of the meals. Kayla's filet, cooked in rosemary and brown butter, was deemed "full of flavor with just the right amount of pink inside." Walt's steak, which he seared on a cast iron skillet that then went into the oven, "melted in the mouths" of the judges.

Holly's filet was overcooked and under seasoned. When Gideon asked, "What is this? Did someone go outside and shoot a pony for you to cook?" there was no laughter. Moreover, her mashed potatoes were "boring," and her broccolini was "wilted beyond recognition."

"I'm sorry to say it, but Holly, you will be leaving us."

Holly nodded. "Yes, Chef."

"Did you think you'd make it this far?"

"No, Chef, not in a million years. I was certain I'd be out on day one."

"And you were top chef that day."

"Yes, Chef. I was shocked." She sniffled, and Lorenzo saw a tear slide down her face. He had to fight the instinct to wipe it away. He made himself look away and kept his expression neutral. If he kept watching, he knew he would release a tear or two himself.

"You've done a great job, Holly. You should be proud of yourself. You've been able to keep up with some of the best chefs I've ever worked with."

"Thank you, Chef." Her voice cracked, and Lorenzo knew without looking that she'd let loose the tears. "It's been the best two weeks of my life. Thank you for the opportunity." Her last few words were choked out.

"You're very welcome. Now, say goodbye to your fellow chefs."

Kayla hugged Holly fiercely, and both women wiped numerous tears from their cheeks. Walt gave her a hug and said, "I'm proud of you, kid." Then Holly turned to Lorenzo.

He held out his arms, and she went into them with a sad smile.

Rather than make a big show for the camera, Lorenzo purposely leaned away from the microphone and whispered, "I'll miss you, and the week's not over."

Holly clung onto him for a moment longer and then let go and said goodbye.

As the camera followed Holly out, Lorenzo caught Gideon's eye. The famous chef nodded in an understanding way, and Lorenzo knew then that nothing had gotten past him. Then the man Lorenzo knew as a tower of steel gave him a sad, sympathetic smile.

***

Holly was taken back to hair and makeup where she was redone for her final interview. She made sure she was finished crying before letting the makeup artist refresh her looks.

"It's okay, honey," the woman told her. "Everyone cries when they leave, even the men."

Holly smiled. "Thanks. I knew I wouldn't make it to the end, but it feels strange knowing I won't be coming back tomorrow."

"Aw, but you'll have something special to take with you when you get back."

Startled, Holly looked up at the woman reapplying her toner. "Excuse me?"

"Oh, don't worry. The news won't leave this building before the show airs. I mean, unless you two let people know before then, which I guess you will."

"Us two?"

The woman drew back. "You know that those mics pick up everything, right? Every tiny word you whisper is recorded."

"It is? All of it?" She felt a rush of panic.

"All of it. You and your hunky Italian chef are the talk of the crew. Good for you."

"The crew? Did Peter tell everyone about the dinner?"

"Dinner? Don't know what you're talking about. Peter doesn't gossip about the contestants. Why? What dinner?"

Her eyes were glowing with interest.

"Um, is this a problem? I mean, nobody said anything…"

"Sheesh, don't worry. You're both single and young." She leaned down and whispered conspiratorially, "And honey, I've seen married people hook up off-set. It's not the norm on our shows at all, but it happens."

"Oh, we haven't—"

"Shh, don't ruin the fun of it for the rest of us."

Holly slunk down into the chair. She was already dreading the exit interview. How was she going to face anybody on the crew now?

***

Zach took the boys to Uno Taco Dos Tequilas for dinner. He looked over the menu and let his gaze wander around the room. Everything seemed to be running smoothly, and it was apparent that tourist season was well underway. After a few minutes, their waitress appeared and introduced herself.

"Hey, Maddie," EJ said with an easy smile.

"Hey, EJ. How's your mom doing? Have you heard from her?"

"Nah, we're not allowed to have contact with her."

"I wish I could go for a week without contact with my mom," Maddie said in a disgruntled voice.

Zach almost spit his water back into his glass and tried to hide his surprise. He didn't know whether to laugh or tell the young lady she should show some respect to her mother. But since he didn't know her parents, he did neither.

"We heard about the incident the other night," he said instead.

"Yeah, pretty freaky. Some of us take turns babysitting, and it's really scary to think that something could've happened to one of the kids. Or to Marcos. I can't believe someone did that to us—I mean to them." She furrowed her brow and tightened her lips, and Zach picked up on the anger she was holding back.

"Have they figured out what happened?"

"No, but everyone knows someone broke in. The back door was jimmied. It's weird that a lot of the restaurants have had things happen to them while that show is being filmed. I heard one of the cooks say that

Anna was pretty upset about walking out. She said she made a mistake letting this spook her, but once she left, she wasn't allowed to go back. She can't tell us anything, but if she's that upset about leaving, then she must've been doing okay. In the competition, I mean."

"I'm sure she thought she was doing the right thing at the time. Did any of you see anyone strange hanging around or watching the place? I mean, before that night?"

"Not that I know of. The police talked to everyone, but I don't think it was much help."

"And everyone here gets along with Anna and her husband?"

"Everyone loves Anna. She's awesome. So is Marcos. They're great bosses. Nobody here would have done that if that's what you're asking."

Zach didn't want anyone to know he was asking around, so he decided he'd pushed it as far as he could.

"Oh, no, I was just thinking you all must not be too happy about the whole thing. That's all. What are your specials tonight?" he asked, picking up his menu.

He only half listened and let the boys decide what to order. Unfortunately, it looked like he'd hit another dead end.

***

Holly returned to the Harbor after her interview. She wouldn't see Lorenzo or the others until they returned that evening. She had no idea what they would be doing without an elimination round, but Rachel told her they would be very busy all afternoon.

She avoided running into anyone at the Harbor and busied herself in the guest laundry facilities. She started packing to return home in a few days and began working on some new recipes she wanted to add to her menu. She was inspired by the cooking classes, challenges, and what she'd learned from both the pros and her fellow contestants.

When evening came, Holly went in search of the others and found them in the meeting room as was their usual custom. As soon as Jane saw Holly, she stood and went to her with outstretched arms.

"Why didn't you come find us when you returned?"

"I wasn't ready to talk about it," she said, feeling funny that she'd been so sad when the others had bounced back so easily. She pulled back and looked around the room. "You all seemed just fine with being eliminated, and I...I just wasn't ready."

Kayla looked at her with sympathy. "I understand, honey. You were down to the final four. That's a lot of time, effort, and emotions spent on something, and you feel like you didn't see it through to the end."

Holly nodded. "I feel like I should've held on longer even though I know I don't belong at the top. And I've loved being with everyone. It's just hard saying goodbye." She started to cry, and Kayla hugged her tightly.

"Shh, shh. It's okay. We're all here for each other, and you're going to take a piece of each of us with you.

We're all so blessed to begin with, not because of the show but because we all live here on the island and call it home. We'll still be here for each other. Always."

When Holly looked up, she saw Lorenzo through the hazy lens of teary eyes. She wasn't sure if she was seeing the moisture in her eyes or if his eyes were also filled with tears. He nodded, and she knew that meant he would be there as more than a friend and colleague. That's when she realized she wouldn't just miss being with everyone, she would miss working alongside them. They were no longer separate chefs, cooks, and bakers working in their own bubbles. They were partners with the shared goal of promoting each other's restaurants and helping each other succeed. Mostly, she would miss being with Lorenzo, discussing their recipe plans, and helping one another through each day's challenges.

She thought back to something she learned when she first arrived in Chincoteague. She'd been struggling to find a job, and she'd gone to the newspaper office to see if they had posted any openings. She met Kate Middleton Kelly, now the owner of the Herald, who was just starting as a writer for the paper. Holly overheard Marge, who was the owner, tell Kate, "Don't ever hesitate to ask anyone for help here on the island. We're all family here. We look out for one another."

Looking around the room now, she finally understood what Marge meant when she said those words almost seven years ago. Holly's parents were in California, and her other relatives were scattered around the world, but in this tiny room, on this little barrier island in the immense Atlantic Ocean, Holly was standing with family.

Unfortunately, she knew that family often went its own way, each person finding their own path in life, leaving the others behind. When the show was over and they all returned home and went back to their own lives, Holly would be left alone again. Her parents moved away when she was in college. Her roommate graduated and never looked back. Her college boyfriend broke up with her and moved back home. Her cruise ship friends continued to party and sail around the world without so much as keeping up their Snapchat streaks with her. Chad left her. Molly would quit at the end of the summer and go back to school. Diane would go back to being retired. And Lorenzo? Why would he stick around? Nobody in her life ever did.

***

After their group dinner, Holly and Lorenzo walked down the dock, holding hands. Lorenzo would miss these waterside twilight strolls when they returned to reality. He'd miss everything about this week—well almost everything. He wouldn't miss the ridiculously early mornings, the isolation, getting cursed at several times a day, and the uncertainty that came with each new challenge.

However, he would very much miss the creativity he'd rediscovered, the new friends he'd made he hadn't known he needed, and these evenings spent with Holly.

He wondered if she felt the same as they quietly walked to the end of the dock. They didn't speak as they sat down and took off their shoes, hanging their feet over the side and testing the water. The evening was calm, and the humidity had lessened, a result of the previous night's storms.

Lorenzo leaned back on his hands and stared at Holly's long braid trailing down the back of her yellow t-shirt. Knowing it had been an emotional day for her, he allowed her the silence. She needed to find peace with her elimination, and he needed to not feel guilty that she had left the show and he hadn't. It wasn't something he'd been prepared for, this reality that his winning meant she had to lose. From almost the first day of taping, he'd felt like it was the two of them, a team, working toward a shared goal. He pictured Katniss and Peeta considering whether to share the poisoned berries rather than allowing the other to lose The Hunger Games.

"Everything's going to change now, isn't it?" Holly asked, her voice tinged with sadness.

Lorenzo squeezed her hand and pulled her close, and she rested her head on his shoulder.

"Not if I can help it," he said. "Not this, not us. If you're willing, I'd like us to keep this up for a very long time."

Holly smiled up at him, but her smile didn't reach her eyes. "I'd like that, but—"

He put his finger to her lips. "No buts. If you want this, and I want this, then we're both in."

"It's just that…" She sighed. "Everything is different here. It's not real life. Like Cynthia said, it's *Passion Island,* only there's no winning couple at the end."

"Why not?" he asked. "Why can't there be a winning couple?"

"Because it's not realistic. Everyone leaves at some point. You, of all people, know that."

He felt like she'd kicked him in the gut. Holly was the last person he expected to bring up his biggest heartache and throw it in his face. He pulled back from her.

"That's not fair. I didn't choose that, and neither did you from what you've told me."

"I didn't, but it happened. Grace left you. Chad left me. You left your parents, and my parents left me. It happens all the time. People don't stick around."

"We could change that."

"I don't know if we can. It's the way of the world."

He couldn't understand why she was saying this. Was she angry that he was still on the show? That made no sense, not for Holly. She was kind and generous and supportive of everyone. She wouldn't hold that against him, would she? He decided to try another tack.

"How long have your parents been together?"

"Thirty years," she answered.

"Over thirty-five for mine. They've made it through some tough stuff. They've never thought of giving in or giving up."

"That's how it used to be, but how many people stay together these days?"

He thought of Marissa and her husband, Adrian and his wife, his aunts and uncles, some of his friends who'd gotten married out of college.

"A lot. I know a lot of people who stay together."

"Well, I don't."

He knew she was lying. She'd talked about her best friend, Taylor, and how much in love she and her husband were. She'd told him about Molly and her older sister, Christy, how they'd both fallen in love with Jared, who married Christy and was both a brother and father to Molly. She was close to Kayla, and her entire family was a picture postcard of togetherness. This wasn't about other people staying together; it was about them, Lorenzo and Holly.

Letting anger get the better of him, Lorenzo stood. "Well, then, I guess that's it. We won't stay together, so why try to make it work? In three days, I'll go back to my life, and you'll go back to yours. I hope you enjoy it."

He turned and walked away, but his heart stayed at the end of dock, ripped to pieces in her hands.

***

His anger consumed him. The phone he wasn't supposed to have rang and rang, but nobody answered. After three tries, he flung it across the room. He was furious at the way things had gotten out of control, and there wasn't anything he could do about it. He'd messed up. He'd let jealousy and anger push him to a place he never thought he'd go. He'd put lives in danger.

He was afraid to think about what was going to happen next. When this was over and he was found out—at this point, he was certain he'd be found out—he'd be alone. He'd have nobody to turn to, to explain himself to, nobody to count on or understand his side of things.

For years, he thought he wasn't good enough, couldn't be the person others thought he was. He'd lost the love of his life and didn't even try to win her back. He'd let his own pride and arrogance get in the way of every relationship he'd had, personal and professional. He was a jerk to his employees and ungrateful to his family.

Now, he was perched to have it all: fame, glory, respect, and a title to hide the fact that he had been pretending all these years. Yet he had nobody to share it with, and once word got out about what he'd done, he'd lose everything he'd gained.

***

Molly awoke in the middle of the night. She'd been dreaming, but it wasn't a dream. She knew for certain that it was a memory, the elusive memory she'd been searching for in her mind for days.

She jerked back the covers and ran to her dresser. She yanked it open and pulled out a pair of shorts, switching them with her pajama boxers. She pulled off her oversized sleep shirt and grabbed a t-shirt from her drawer.

Molly wasn't going to waste time waking up Christy. She'd never listen anyway. She knew who she needed to tell, and she couldn't wait.

She quietly led her bike out of the shed and jumped on, pedaling as quickly as she could. Without looking back to see if her sister or Jared heard her, she rounded the corner and headed toward the row of houses that lined the beach in one of the somewhat newer parts of the island. She knew which house it was. She'd babysat next door for his sister.

As the two houses came into view, she put her head down and pedaled faster. She felt like one of the kids in the movie, *The Goonies*, that she and Jared liked to watch together on rainy days. Jared said the kids in the movie were just like them—super smart outcasts who used their brains to save their town. It was up to her to save the island, and she wasn't going to let anyone stop her. That guy could be out there right now, and only Molly knew how to find him.

Molly threw her bike down on the lawn and ran up the steps that led to the front door. Almost all the newer houses were built on stilts to keep them from flooding, and Molly stumbled on the last step, barely able to see in the dark. She slammed her fists against the door, pounding with all her might.

"Hey, what are you doing here?" A sleepy teenaged boy asked, rubbing his eyes with his knuckles after opening the door.

"I need to see your dad. Right now."

"EJ, who's there?"

Zach opened the door wider and looked at Molly in surprise. He looked past her to the driveway.

"Molly, what are you doing here? How'd you get here? It's the middle of the night."

"I rode my bike," she said, trying to catch her breath.

"In the dark? Where's your sister? Is there an emergency?"

"Yes, no, I mean. I know who did it. I know who tried to burn down the restaurant and all the other stuff."

Zach looked around again, took Molly by the arm, and pulled her inside before closing the door behind her.

"What are you talking about?"

"I saw him, the night of the fire. Officer Nick kept asking me all those questions, and I told him everything I could remember, but there was something I couldn't remember. It was there, but it wasn't coming to me. I kept trying to remember, to picture what I saw, but the harder I tried, the more it faded. The picture, I mean. In my head. Not like eidetic imagery, though. I don't have that. I mean, I remember a lot, but not in that kind of way."

"Dad," EJ said. "What's she talking about? Is she crazy?"

"I don't know, EJ. I, um… Molly, get to the point."

Molly took a deep breath, let it out, and said slowly, "I remember. I saw him at the restaurant with a gas can. I saw him get the gas can and put it in his truck."

"You saw who? Someone at Speziato?"

"No, at Dockside. I saw him at Dockside take the can from behind the restaurant and put it in his truck. Before the fire."

"You saw someone trying to start a fire at Dockside? When? Just now?"

"No!" Molly shouted. "I saw the owner of Dockside, not the older guy, his son, put a gas can in his truck about ten minutes before Jenny saw him light the fire at Speziato."

Zach stared at Molly for several moments before he turned to his son.

"EJ, go call Uncle Nick. Tell him to get here. Fast."

I felt terrible for Holly. [Walt looked genuinely sad.] She was doing such a great job. But here we are, the final three, and I'm just honored to be here. I never thought I'd have this kind of opportunity, and all I care about now is making my family proud of me. [He looked down at his hands and back up at the camera.] And I want the others to know that I have great respect for all of them. Whatever happens after this, I hope they all know that I wish them the best. And Sherry, baby, I love you. No matter what I ever said or did, I have always loved you. If I could do it again, I'd choose you.

Chapter Fourteen

"Today is the dreaded technical challenge," Gideon told the three remaining contestants. "It's going to combine all the skills of a good chef from beginning to end and will require you to step out of your role of chef and into the role of seafood distributor."

Lorenzo blinked his eyes a few times and leaned closer, wondering that could mean. He noticed Walt and Kayla exchange looks before zeroing back in on Gideon, and he wondered if they had an inkling about the challenge.

"I know the island holds the hugely popular annual Chincoteague Oyster Festival every fall, so I assume you've all cooked with oysters." He tilted his head and raised a brow as he waited for them to respond.

Walt and Kayla both nodded. Lorenzo hesitated but then nodded as well. Oysters were a luxury item on Italian menus, and though his mother had an oyster dish on her menu during the winter, Lorenzo had only observed her making it one time. His restaurant was too young to have any oyster dishes yet. He swallowed and tried to go over his mother's recipe in his head.

"Okay, so far, all the food you've used in your recipes has been prepared for your use ahead of time. Not so this time." Gideon paused and nodded toward the door opening behind them. They turned to look.

Three carts were wheeled in, each containing a classic, Chesapeake Bay bushel basket. Each basket was piled high with grey and white shells that Lorenzo recognized as the mollusk shells of oysters. He felt an inward groan as he realized what they were about to do.

"Each of you will receive a bushel of oysters. You will have twenty minutes to shuck as many oysters as possible. Whatever you end up with will be what you have to cook with. Try to have more than you will need. Head to your stations, and we'll start the clock."

"Cut!" The familiar call rang out, and Lorenzo tried to wrap his head around what he knew about shucking oysters. It wasn't much.

"Okay," Gideon said. "We had these brought up for the show. It's not oyster season here yet, but they're the same type of oyster you'd find here. The bad news is, there is a fair amount of skill involved in properly shucking oysters. The good news is, that's why we have assembled a team of experts for this morning's lesson."

Lorenzo breathed a sigh of relief as three people walked in wearing heavy aprons and gloves that looked like they belonged to a suit of armor.

"At your stations, you will find your own aprons and chainmail gloves along with a couple oyster knives. Put on your apron and gloves and just practice holding the knives to start."

They followed Gideon's orders, went to their stations, and donned their aprons and gloves. Lorenzo didn't feel natural holding the bulb-shaped handle of the knife and shifted it back and forth a few times trying to get the feel of it.

"Let me show you how to hold that. I'm Sam," said Lorenzo's oyster mentor.

"Hi, Sam."

"Ever shucked an oyster before?"

Lorenzo shook his head. "I grew up in Baltimore, so I'm no stranger to it. I've watched the guys on the docks, and occasionally, my parents or their staff shucked them at the restaurant, but I've never done it myself."

"Okay, then let's go over your basic knife skills first."

Lorenzo took a quick glance around. Walt looked ready to tackle his basket without any reservations. Lorenzo figured he'd shucked his share of oysters over his lifetime. Kayla looked confident as she listened to the instructions of her mentor.

After watching Sam's technique on several oysters, Lorenzo felt ready to give it a try himself. For the next hour, he learned how to properly grip the oyster knife and the shell and how to find the right place on the shell to insert the knife. He mastered how to flip open the shell with a properly inserted knife and the flick of his wrist. He had a couple close calls with the knife slipping, but he got the hang of it. He was taught to dip his hand and the knife into a very cold bucket of ice water to keep grit from getting into the jelly-like oyster liquor, and he learned to keep a close eye on each oyster to make sure no pieces of shell clung to it. He wasn't going to win any timed contests with bountiful bowls of oysters, but he felt confident he could shuck what he needed with a few extras.

By the time Gideon called for a break, Lorenzo's hands were freezing cold, and his fingers felt tight and in need of some stretching exercises. He peeled off his stainless-steel gloves and flexed his fingers and wrists until the cramps eased. After using the bathroom, he began jotting down what he remembered about his mother's recipe. Whatever he couldn't remember, he'd have to use his skills as a chef to compensate. Those old doubts began to creep in, and he worried his skills weren't good enough to fill in the gaps. He reminded himself that he'd come a long way in the past week, and he was in the top three for a reason.

***

Holly couldn't believe she'd slept until after nine o'clock. Then again, she shouldn't have been surprised since she'd laid in bed half the night thinking about her argument with Lorenzo.

Had they broken up? Were they ever official? Lorenzo's last words echoed in her mind. *In three days, I'll go back to my life, and you'll go back to yours. I hope you enjoy it.* They stung more than she wanted to admit.

Tang pounced on her. Holly was surprised he'd let her sleep this long. Did he have some kind of sense that she'd had a rough night? Had she kept him up with her tossing and turning? She reached out and stroked his soft fur as tears stung her eyes.

"I messed up, Tang," she said. "I'm so confused. For the first time, I felt completely accepted by my community, by more than just the girls. I felt like I'd become one of the family, a real islander. But then, I remembered the other times I felt that way, and that reminded me of the painful times. Saying goodbye to my parents when they moved across the country without me, never really feeling like I fit in at college because I didn't party or sleep around, never having a close relationship with my roommate. And then there are all the guys who broke my heart. Why did I always think every boy was 'the one'? Why do I always let myself believe that this one will be different, this one will stick around, this one will love me enough to want to stay?"

Tang started to purr.

"I know you're still here. I appreciate that. But it would be nice to have a guy love me for reasons other than food and litter box cleanup."

Tang opened one eye and gave her that look that often made her think he understood her words.

"I guess you're hungry," she said, and he immediately leaped to the floor and stretched. "How much do you understand?" she asked with narrowed eyes. "I swear, you become more human every day."

She sat on the side of the bed and stretched. She had no idea what to do with her day. What did the others do all day? She thought about how cozy Cynthia and Jake had gotten and scrunched her nose.

"Never mind," she said out loud. "I don't want to know."

Tang led the way down the hall to the little kitchenette, and Holly fed him as she weighed her options. She could lounge by the pool, read one of the many books she brought with her on the assumption she'd be here all day for the whole twelve days, or she could just stay in bed and watch Netflix all day. That was the only choice they'd been given as far as programming because it guaranteed they didn't see any news.

She wondered what was going on out there on the island. How was the café doing? How was Diane holding up? Was Anna okay? She hadn't had time to think about any of those things when her days were occupied with nonstop cooking lessons, and interviews.

After a long shower, she emerged from her cottage in search of life. She still didn't know what to do about Lorenzo, or if there even was anything she could do. She'd blown it, and she didn't know if things could be repaired. Did she even wanted them to be?

***

"Molly, are you sure about what you saw?" Sargent Paul Parker asked after Molly had taken a seat in the conference room at the station. Zach had taken Molly home and given her strict orders not to tell anyone else what she had seen. He talked to Christy and Jared, who were shocked when they'd been awakened at three in the morning, and told them to have Molly at the station no later than ten.

"I'm sure. It took me a while to remember, but I know what I saw."

"And you're confident about who it was you saw?"

"Yes, I'm confident."

Paul laid out six photographs in front of Molly on the conference table. "Do you recognize any of these as the man you saw? Not the man you think it was, but the man you saw. Do you understand the difference?"

Molly narrowed her eyes and gave Paul a look that was meant to remind him that she was a twelve-year-old about to go to Harvard and not a middle school child.

"Molly, this is important. I need to know that you're going to identify the man you actually saw that night."

"Molly," Christy said in their mother's tone that she had perfected to a T. "Sargent Parker needs you to take this seriously."

Molly huffed out a breath and rolled her eyes. She knew it was him, but how could she admit that she didn't know *how* she knew? She just did. She had to make them believe her, but looking at the photos wasn't going to help. If she told them that, she would be letting them down.

"I know. I get it. If I don't have the right person, the whole case goes out the window. I'm the star witness, and I've got to be right and believable. I know.

The police can't go to the DA with my testimony unless I'm a solid witness. 'In the criminal justice system, the people are represented by two separate yet equally important groups. The police who investigate crime and the district attorneys who prosecute the offenders. These are their stories.' Blah, blah, blah."

Paul threw up his hands and cursed.

Molly looked out the window and a sudden sense of shock caused the sensation of a spider crawling up her back. She shivered.

"Molly," Christy said in astonishment. "What is wrong with you? Don't you understand how important this is?"

With equal parts fear and excitement, Molly turned to her sister. "Don't you understand that I know what I saw? I can't look at these stupid pictures and say, 'oh, it's this guy for sure because I saw his face' because I didn't see his face. But I know it was him."

"How do you know that?" The Sargent asked, his frustration causing spittle to form in the corners of his mouth.

"Because I also saw his license plate in the parking lot light when he pulled away," Molly shouted. She looked toward the door and said in a quieter voice, "It said 'DOCSID'."

Paul froze. "Why didn't you tell us that before?"

Molly hunched her shoulders and said in a small voice, "I just remembered when I saw it pull up over there." She pointed out the window to the truck that sat in front of the hardware store across the street.

***

"We have three amazing dishes in front of us," Gideon said to Christina and José. "We have an oyster and ham soufflé, oysters marsala au gratin, and classic oyster stew. Now, it might sound like these are three different levels of cooking oysters, but let me tell you that each of these dishes takes time and talent to pull off. So, with that said, let's see who was able to do that."

The camera zeroed in on the soufflé.

"I love the golden sheen on this pastry," Christina said, lightly tapping the top of the pastry shell with her fork. "The key to a good soufflé, though, is to be able to taste all the ingredients, especially the oysters."

She put a bite in her mouth and chewed for a moment before wincing.

"And it's important to get the grit out of the oyster liquor before you begin cooking."

"The flavors are all there," José said. "This chef got that right. I love the way the bits of ham and the oyster work together to give that surf and turf flavor without overdoing the saltiness. And nothing says Virginia better than the combination of oysters and ham. Nice oyster taste, too. Just the right consistency with the sauce."

"Let's move on to the oysters marsala," Gideon told them.

"Beautiful presentation," José commented. "Look at those colors. The green parsley, red speck, purple onion, and golden eggs with a hint of white oyster peeking through. I love it."

"And I love the shells that were chosen to serve them in, not the most perfectly shaped ones, but ones with some personality."

"Ah, but it's what's in the shells that counts," Gideon reminded them.

José tried the first bite. "I will say, it's missing something." He took another bite and moved it around in his mouth. "I'm not sure what. There's a lack of something…"

"Not onion," Christina said and continued to chew. A light went on in her eyes. "Chives. I would've done chives in addition to, or even instead of, the parsley. That would give this a real kick. Other than that, I like it. I'd order it again if I was at a restaurant."

"And finally, the oyster stew."

"You know," Christina said. "there's a fine line between cooking the oysters and overcooking the oysters. You should know exactly when to add them to the stew. It's not a given that it will be good just because you drop them in."

"And I like a creamy oyster stew. None of that watered down, over-liquored soup," said José as he took a spoonful to his mouth.

"Agreed," said Christina. "It must be thick. A stew isn't meant to be watery." She took a spoonful and swirled it around her mouth.

"Nice," said Gideon. "Creamy and tasty. Not too much onion or spices."

"And just the right consistency. Lots of oysters in every bite, and not little pieces, but big, juicy oysters. You know how to shuck and got a nice, hearty number of oysters." José said to the chef.

"Okay," Gideon clapped his hands together. "Ready to go chat?"

They followed him out of the room, and the contestants breathed a sigh of relief that it was over. They'd all done well, but nobody stood out. Who would be going home today?

***

"It's a beautiful afternoon, isn't it?" Dawn said as she dropped onto the lounge chair next to Holly.

Holly laid her book face down on her lap. "It is. I can't believe I've spent my entire day going between reading, swimming laps, and taking naps."

Dawn laughed. "Welcome to the way the other half lives."

"You mean the half that don't have to work all day?"

"Exactly. This is what I want to do in retirement. Sleep in, read lots of books, lay by the pool, and not worry about a thousand things."

"Retirement. That's eons away."

"Yes, but it will get here someday." Dawn took a sip of water. "I wonder what's going on at the community center. What do you think today's challenge was?"

"I could only guess. And I can't decide who I think will win."

"Lorenzo has a good shot. You should be proud of him. I know he's very new to being his own chef."

"Yeah, well Kayla's pretty good, too, and Walt has been running a restaurant and cooking for years."

Dawn turned her head to the side and squinted at Holly. "You don't want Lorenzo to win?"

"I didn't say that," Holly said defensively.

"Your tone implied it. What's going on? You two seemed to be heading in a certain direction."

"Well, it may have seemed that way, but let's face it. This isn't real." She spread her hands out and gestured to their surroundings. "It's easy to pretend that this is the way things are, the way things are supposed to be, but in two more days, we'll all be saying goodbye and going our separate ways."

"Do you really believe that?"

"Don't you?" Holly looked at her with a set jaw and steely eyes.

"You know, I love what I do. I'm blessed to have a successful restaurant and a wonderful husband. I have a great life. But sometimes, I'm not so happy. We all feel that way sometimes. In fact, Anna told me, before she left, there have been times when she was working, running around, waiting on customers, and she would see this group of girls come in, all her age, but single or newly married, out for a girls' night of fun. And she said that she would think to herself, why can I not be with them? Why can I not have friends like that?

"She told me she left her friends back in Miami, and all she has now are customers and people she sees at work or at church. Being here all these days, she said she felt like she was making friends and building relationships that would last past this competition. Do you think what she felt was just pretend?"

Holly looked down and blinked. She remembered going to Anna's place a couple times, laughing with her friends, and not paying any attention to Anna except to say hello. She'd forgotten what it was like to come from somewhere else, to not have a built-in group of friends. It was pure luck that she'd met Taylor right away and that Taylor, Dina, and Tori had grown up on the island. Not only did Anna not have that, she had the added stigma of dark skin and a thick accent.

"Oh, gosh. She meant me, us, our friend group," Holly said quietly. "And she's right. We completely ignored her, and now that I know her, I truly enjoy spending time with her." She looked at Dawn. "I love being friends with all of you."

"So, you think we will all stay friends when we leave? Will you include Anna in the group of friends you go out with?"

Holly smiled. "I'd like that. A lot. And I'd love to introduce all of you to my friends."

Dawn smiled back. "I'd like that, too." She took another sip of water. "Now, about Lorenzo…"

Holly shook her head. "Not the same thing."

"Of course not. I only look at Ted the way Lorenzo looks at you."

Holly opened her mouth to say something but closed it. Lorenzo didn't look at her in any special way, did he? The image of him gazing at her through the flickering candlelight entered her mind. And the way he looked at her just before he kissed her. And how he stared longingly into her eyes when they stood on her doorstep in the rain.

"Ah, now you see it, don't you?" Dawn said.

"I don't know," Holly said. "I mean, don't you think this is kind of other-worldly? Being shut off from civilization, no interference from jobs or other obligations, with nothing to do but sit by the pool or the water and talk about our silly hopes and dreams?"

"Dreams are only silly dreams if you don't make them into reality."

"But isn't it telling that six of the twelve of us paired off, the only six who are single? Doesn't that mean we were just lonely and looking to fill some kind of void?"

"Maybe in one case, it does. I think Cynthia is having fun pretending she's on *Passion Island*. This is her chance to find her Ricky."

"Ricky? Wait, you watch it, too?"

"Don't you?"

"Of course, but…" Holly laughed. "Never mind. So, you agree they won't last? Cynthia and Jake?"

"I'm not going to judge their relationship, but I have my doubts."

"But Bob and Jane, they're for real, right?"

"As real as it gets. They had history before they came here," Dawn said.

"True," Holly agreed. "They're so happy together, and they've been around the block. They know what they're getting into."

"Is that what scares you? That you haven't known Lorenzo for very long?"

Holly shrugged. "I don't know. I just, well, I've never had anyone stick around long enough to get to know them."

"I don't think Lorenzo is going anywhere, Holly. I think you need to give him a chance."

"What if he breaks my heart?"

"You know what my favorite movie is?"

Holly shook her head, unsure where this was going.

"*The Sound of Music.* You've seen it, right?"

"Yeah, when I was young. What does that have to do with this?"

"It's about a woman who thinks she wants to be a nun. She's ready to spend her life in a convent after losing both her parents. Her mother died of pneumonia when Maria was only two, and her father left her with family and traveled the world without her. That's not in the movie, but I read her biography, and I always wondered if she was drawn to the nuns because she was alone, and they were as close to a family as anything she'd ever seen."

"Okay," Holly said, waiting for more.

"The Mother Abbess knew Maria wasn't cut out to be a nun, but Maria wanted it so badly, I think because she didn't know how to do anything except be alone, and she was afraid that if she loved someone, they would leave her."

Holly pressed her lips together and looked down at her hands.

"And then there was the captain. His wife died, leaving him with seven children. He was a horrible father, refusing to give them love because they reminded him of his wife. He didn't even allow music in the house because she had loved it so. After Maria went to become their nanny, she and the captain both learned something about each other and themselves."

"That they loved each other?"

"More than that. They learned that they could love even after having lost someone. They learned that life goes on, and that love, though it can hurt, can also heal. You're lucky to be here on an island where everyone looks out for one another, and you're lucky to have found Lorenzo. I don't think he will break your heart, but I do know that hearts can heal and love again."

Holly thought about Chad and how she had thought he was the one, how she had thought every man she dated was the one.

"And how do I know if this is real? How do I let myself believe that he won't break my heart?"

"By trusting him and yourself. See the good in him, but see the good in yourself as well. Take what he has to offer, and offer to him what you have to give. Be open to love while being open to heartbreak because heartbreak happens in love, too. My heart breaks every time Ted hurts, every time we lose a loved one, every time one of my grown girls reminds me she doesn't need me anymore. But those heartbreaks are what make me human and what make me love even more. Without feeling heartbreak, we can never feel joy. It's through pain, loss, and yes, heartbreak, that we truly learn to live and love. If you had never suffered from losing those people in your past, you wouldn't know the importance of holding on to true love now and in the future."

Holly let Dawn's words settle in her soul, and as she thought about what her new friend said, she recalled the prayer card she kept tucked into the frame of her dresser mirror. It was a quote from the Gospel of John that was read at her grandmother's funeral. She had read it so many times, the words had lost their meaning. Until now.

So you have pain now; but I will see you again, and your hearts will rejoice, and no one will take your joy from you.

***

"Today, my kids and I are visiting Beebe Ranch." The camera shows Gideon's kids petting ponies. "This is the ranch where the real Misty of Chincoteague lived and where the fictionalized book was based. It's a working ranch, owned by the Chincoteague Island Museum, where families can enjoy a tour and hear the history of the ranch and its famous inhabitants."

Gideon walks into the gift shop.

"You can even buy some of the books in the Misty series and have them stamped with Grandpa Beebe's branding iron. For fans of the book, that's a cool thing."

He holds up a copy of *Stormy* and opens to show the brand before he heads back outside.

"After touring the ranch, you can take the family to the Chincoteague Island Museum to see the real Misty, stuffed and on display. Enjoy your visit, and I'll see you back in the kitchen."

***

Lorenzo was physically and emotionally exhausted when he stepped off the bus at the Harbor. The fight with Holly the night before combined with the ups and downs and frenetic pace of the day weighed on him. He hadn't thought he'd make it this far, that he was good enough to stay the course, and he was amazed every day when he walked back onto the set to face another challenge.

Tomorrow, things would be different.

"I'm kind of in a state of disbelief," Kayla said as they walked toward the cottages. "A total state of shock, to be honest."

"Me, too," Walt said. "It's been a good run and a great experience. No matter what happens when this is all over, I hope everyone knows how much you all have come to mean to me."

"Of course, we do, Walt," Kayla said. "We've all bonded over the past several days. Tomorrow won't change that."

"We'll see," Walt said. He walked ahead, leaving Lorenzo and Kayla to wonder about his words.

"I guess he's just sad about it ending," Kayla said.

"Probably," Lorenzo agreed. "But he's right that things are going to change."

"They don't have to," she said grabbing his arm and pulling him to a stop. "Look, I don't know what happened last night, but I saw Holly come back from the dock alone, and she was crying. I didn't want to embarrass her or make her feel worse, so I didn't go to her, but let me say this. I've gotten to know her over the past couple years because her best friend, Taylor, is my father's goddaughter and the wife of Zach's best friend. They're ten years younger than we are, but Zach and Nick were in the military together, and that bonds people. Now, we haven't been at war, and I will never diminish what those guys went through, but we've been through a similar situation these past couple weeks. We've been put through the ringer emotionally with long days, short nights, high stress, battling it out, and suffering wins and losses. Why do you think we had to undergo psychological testing? That kind of thing can change a person.

"I don't know what kind of person you were going into this, but I know what kind of person Holly was. Though she always has a smile on her face and acts supremely confident, she is as insecure as they come. She grew up in a military house like I did, but she moved a lot more than my family did, and she didn't have a brother or a close relationship with her parents. When she opens her heart to love, she opens it all the way, and that means that when it gets broken, it gets all the way broken. Now, maybe you pushed her away, or maybe she pushed you; I don't know. What I do know is that I've never seen the glow in her eyes that has been there for the past few days, and it has nothing to do with being on TV."

Kayla took a deep breath. "Look, you may not know this, but my husband was shot and killed a long time ago, almost ten years now, and it nearly broke me. I didn't trust anyone, especially myself, because I didn't ever want to be hurt like that again. I've seen that look in Holly's eyes, but when she looks at you, I see pure happiness. If that doesn't mean anything to you, then you can go back to your normal life at the end of the week, and she can go back to hers, and everyone will survive. But if you think there's something there worth taking a chance on, then fight for her. I had cancer and almost died, and I still didn't know if I was willing to fight for love. Luckily, Zach decided that fighting for love and fighting for life were one in the same. So, think about that, okay?"

Lorenzo was overcome by her words. He couldn't speak, so he only nodded. Kayla turned to go, but before she got far, she turned back with a smile.

"And as far as tomorrow goes," she told him, "I'm going to kick your butt."

***

"I just watched the security footage from the library," Nick told Paul. "I didn't even know that existed."

"Neither did I. That article Kate wrote about the incidents brought in lots of tips, most were worthless, but if you can see Uno Taco from the library cam, and we get a hit, it will be worth the hours spent watching the footage."

"Then this will make you very happy."

"You found something?"

"Yep, the camera had a straight shot of Uno Taco across the parking lot."

"And?"

Nick smiled. "We got him," Nick said. "License plate and all. Do you want me to go get him?"

"No, not tonight. I don't think he has a clue we're on to him, and what we have is pretty thin. Let's keep an eye on him tonight and tomorrow night and see if he decides to go out again. This time, we'll be ready."

***

Lorenzo stopped before he got to his cottage and turned abruptly, heading for the dock. His slow walk became a jog which, by the time he reached the dock, was a full-out run. He was panting by the time he dropped to his knees by her side.

"I hoped I'd find you here."

He couldn't tell by the startled look on her face what she was thinking, but as the pink reflection of the setting sun settled over the channel, Holly smiled.

"I was hoping you'd come look for me."

"Holly, listen, I was—"

She put a finger to his lips the same way he'd done to her what seemed like years prior but had only been that very week.

"Don't. It was me. I was wrong. Look, I'm not very good at trusting others or myself, but if you'll give me a chance, I'd like to try."

"You'll give me a chance?" he asked. "At learning to trust alongside you?"

"I'd like that," Holly said. "But first, what happened today?"

Lorenzo couldn't hold back his joy, and his expression must have made that apparent.

"You made it? You did! You made it!"

Holly threw her arms around him. Lorenzo hugged her back. When she pulled away, her smile was as big as his.

"I knew you would. Congratulations. Who else? Was it Kayla? Please say it was Kayla."

Lorenzo laughed and bobbed his head. "It was Kayla, but neither of us was a shoe-in. It was pretty close."

"I want to hear about it, but first, I have a really important question for you that could change everything between us."

He braced himself and drew out his response. "Okay."

She reached over and picked up a decades old CD player from the dock next to where she was sitting. She asked, "Do you like dancing to Taylor Swift?"

He laughed. "Press play, and you'll see that I can dance along with the best of them."

As they swayed to *Begin Again*, he gazed into her eyes and heard the words to the song echoing in his heart.

I had to completely guess at the ingredients of my mom's recipe. I knew it looked right, but when Christina pointed out that I'd used parsley when I should've used chives, I thought that was it. I was done. The competition was so tight. A screw-up like that could've cost me everything, but it didn't. I messed up, but I'm still here giving it my all. [Lorenzo smiles.] I never really thought I had what it takes to be as good a chef as my parents, but I guess I do. I guess I just needed to trust myself, let go of my fears, and just go for it. Either that, or I've got a guardian angel watching over me. [He winks at the camera.]

Chapter Fifteen

Holly was up early, showered, dressed, and on her way out the door as Tang ate his breakfast. She could see the sun beginning to rise over the channel. The bright blue sky was on fire just above the horizon. A kaleidoscope of reds, oranges, yellows, and pinks radiated out like flames amidst the puffy clouds. The sight took Holly's breath away, and for perhaps the first time in her life, she felt like she was seeing the hand of God at work.

"Hey, what are you doing up?"

Holly turned and smiled at Lorenzo, who had joined her where she stood. She was unable to move as the day revealed itself in all its splendor.

"I came to see you and Kayla off and to wish you both luck."

Lorenzo's smile told her he was happy to see her, but he shook his head. "Both of us?"

Holly laughed. "Yes, both of you." She gave him a light punch on the arm.

They looked up in time to see the yellow sun rising steadily above the water.

"It's so beautiful," Holly breathed, and she felt him take her hand.

"I wish there was time for this every day. As much as I'm looking forward to getting back to my routine, there's so much I'm going to miss."

Holly squeezed his hand. "I know exactly what you mean." She sighed with contentment but wondered how much was going to change when they were ensconced in their daily lives once again. Their evenings would be busy—his occupied with cooking for the dinner crowd and hers spent prepping for the next morning's breakfast crowd. They wouldn't be working alongside each other, sharing tips and tricks or providing encouragement when they needed it. There would be no more kayaking trips to watch the sunset and no more sitting lazily on the dock learning about each other's lives.

"What's wrong?" Lorenzo asked.

"Who said anything was wrong?" She kept her eyes focused on the sky.

"I felt the shift. You were happy, and then…"

She turned toward him in amazement. "How did you know?"

"Lorenzo, the bus is here."

They turned toward Kayla who was heading in their direction.

"It's all going to be okay," Lorenzo told Holly before bending down and kissing her cheek. "We'll work it out."

How did he know exactly what she'd been thinking?

"Good luck," she said with a smile. She went up on tiptoes and kissed his cheek in return. "You're going to do great today." She looked at Kayla. "You, too. I know you're both going to do an amazing job."

Holly gave Kayla a hug, and Kayla thanked her. "I'm a jumble of nerves," she admitted.

"You've got this. You've both got this." Holly looked from one to the other. "Go give those judges the hardest challenge of the whole competition—deciding who to choose."

She watched as Lorenzo and Kayla climbed aboard the bus and waved as they drove away. It was going to be a long day.

***

"You know," Kayla said to Abby, the hairdresser. "I love not having to deal with my hair every day, but I'm really looking forward to not wearing all this makeup."

Lorenzo grinned. "I was thinking the same thing, except for the part about the hair. Mine is easy, but I've never worn makeup in my life and look forward to never wearing it again."

Kayla laughed. "You do have great hair, though. You and Zach got lucky in that department. My brother, Aaron, is losing his, much to the dismay of my boys."

"I've heard a lot about Zach this week between you and Holly. What's Aaron like?"

"A lot like Zach but with a much better sense of humor. Zach is serious all the time, but Aaron's a light-hearted guy. He had his military traumas, like Zach and the rest, but he never lets them detract from his happy-go-lucky demeanor."

"Older or younger?"

"Twins."

Lorenzo's mouth dropped open. "Really?"

"Yep. And nothing alike, but he's my brother and my hero, as much as Zach is. I've been blessed. And you?"

"Two sisters and two brothers. One set of twins."

"No kidding."

"Yep, my younger brother and sister. I'm the proverbial middle child."

"Nice. I bet you had a great childhood."

Lorenzo didn't hesitate when he answered. "You know, I did. I really did."

"That's good. Holly needs that, a big family. I get the impression she feels like she missed something as an only child."

Lorenzo hadn't thought about that. If he and Holly were together, his family would pounce like lions, herding her into their pride, and he liked the thought of that. It was never like that with Grace. Antonia and Antony were too young to care, but Marissa and Adrian always thought she was pretentious. Boy, had they fought over that. Looking back, maybe he hadn't given them enough credit for their insight.

"I'm sorry if I said something wrong," Kayla said when Lorenzo didn't answer.

"No, it's okay. Better than okay. You made me realize how much my family is going to love Holly. I just hope she isn't overwhelmed by them all."

"I get it. There's only Aaron and me, and my family can be overwhelming."

"Let's go. Gideon is on the set," Rachel called into the dressing room.

"The master chef awaits," Kayla said, getting up from her chair.

Lorenzo stood and waited for the makeup artist to remove his smock. He hadn't thought about how Holly would react to his big, boisterous family. Now, he pictured how the scene might go, and he found himself smiling all the way to the set.

***

Holly was separating her personal clothes from the clothes she'd been given by the wardrobe department. They'd each been given a list of what clothing to pack, but they often ended up being given something different to wear once they arrived on set. Lighting, makeup, how they looked on film, and what they were cooking all dictated what was worn. She was allowed to keep the clothes she'd been given, but did she want to?

She held up the cute yellow shirt with a top designer label that she'd worn on day three. Yep, that was a keeper. The purple t-shirt she'd worn on day five, not so much. Holly wrinkled her nose and tossed that into the pile to share with her friends.

She stopped and thought about her friends. What had they all been up to? How was Dina getting on at the bank? Had Tori applied to PA school? Had Christy decided on a nursing program? Was Taylor already running herself ragged with her landscaping business?

And how was the café doing? Was Diane holding up okay? Was Molly driving them all crazy with her incessant talking and non-stop intellect? Was Freddy still enjoying the job? She'd been gone just less than two weeks, yet it felt like years.

She sat down on the bed and let out a long breath. When she returned home, nothing would be the same. She had learned so much, and there were changes she wanted to make at the café, foods she wanted to add to her menu, tasks she wanted done differently. At home, there would also be changes. She thought of Chad's sweatshirt that was neatly folded in her dresser drawer, his t-shirt she sometimes slept in. She felt like she'd matured a lifetime in the past several days, and she no longer wanted or needed those things to help her remember the good times. They were good, but they were over, and she was moving on.

The things she'd done with Chad and her friends—charter boat fishing and deep-sea diving—they were fun, but she decided she'd rather kayak in the channel and hike the trails on Assateague she'd never taken the time to explore. Yes, she was definitely going to buy a kayak. And hiking shoes. And make the time to use them. She was going to close the café on Sundays except mid-June to mid-August, and on those days, she'd open at ten instead of eight. Eight weeks. That's all she needed to be open seven days a week. The rest of the year, she'd get up and go to Mass and spend the day doing the things that mattered—enjoying the life which she'd been gifted. She would explore the area, take day trips, and if she wanted, just sit in a kayak and watch the sunset.

And she wanted to do all those things with Lorenzo. Would he be willing to take off on Sundays? Willing to let his staff run the restaurant while he enjoyed life? Would this time away allow him to see that he didn't need to work fourteen-hour days, seven days a week? That was the life he described to her, and she could see that's who he was. Could he change? Would he try? Did he want to?

And that's when the realization hit Holly, hit her hard. She was in love with Lorenzo. All the things she saw herself doing from now on, she pictured doing with him. Along with everything else she wanted them to do together, she envisioned a drive to Baltimore and a flight to California. She knew her parents would love him as much as she did, and she already knew that she would love the big, rapturous family he'd described.

She closed her eyes and said a silent prayer that Lorenzo felt the same.

***

"So, here we are on our last day of our competition with only two chefs left. Kayla, Lorenzo, how are you both feeling?"

"Pretty good, Chef," Lorenzo told Gideon.

"Ready to cook, Chef," Kayla answered.

"Good. Today won't be easy. You're each going to prepare a full three-course meal. I want appetizers that really raise the stakes. I want a main course with a protein, a carb, and a nice side of vegetables that is worthy of being served in any of my restaurants. Then, I want to end the meal with a show-stopping dessert."

Lorenzo and Kayla both nodded and answered, "Yes, Chef."

"You'll be creating your own menus, but remember, this isn't something you'd eat at home on any given weeknight. These meals need to show off all the skills you've learned throughout your time here. I want a high level of technique and no mistakes on the cooking. This must be the best meal of your lives. The winner's meal must be perfect."

Lorenzo thought back to his best and worst dishes of the competition. What had he learned? What could he improve? How far did he want to push himself? He looked over at Kayla, a woman he'd come to admire, respect, and even love, and he knew would be an insult to her if he didn't push himself to the limit.

***

Walt paced the tiny cottage wondering why his son wasn't answering his calls. What was happening on the outside? He wasn't confident Danny had stopped when Walt asked him to. The boy had a habit of taking things too far, and it often got him into trouble.

When Danny had devised the plan to buy the burner phone and sneak it into Walt's bag, Walt didn't think any harm could come from their actions. He wanted Danny to make it hard for the other chefs—the ones who were winning—to stay in the competition. Walt had the idea of shutting off Holly's electricity and smashing some of Dawn's wine. He didn't know Danny would ruin her entire collection, nor did he expect his son to turn on the gas at Anna's, nearly killing her family. After Walt argued with Danny about crossing the line, Walt hadn't heard back from him. What else had his son done?

Of course, when Walt first agreed to Danny's plan, he wasn't thinking of his fellow contestants as friends and neighbors. They were simply the competition, and the things Danny was doing were mere means to an end. That had all changed, though, over the course of two weeks. Walt liked these people, and he saw how they could work together for the mutual benefit of them all. Talking about Bob and Jane's wedding made him see them in a new light. . They now shared a bond, and Walt thought of them as family.

He tried calling Danny again, but his call went straight to voicemail, and Walt began to panic.

Danny always took things a step too far. That was something Walt didn't like to admit and refused to consider when they talked about what he would do to the other businesses. Danny had always had a propensity toward—toward what? Evil? No, that wasn't it. But maybe that was it. Walt's third wife, Sherry, hadn't left because he spent too much time at work. Oh, that's what he wanted people to think and what he told himself. The truth was, she was afraid of Danny. She always thought he was looking at her strangely, mocking her, trying to make her feel unwelcome, even threatened. Walt hadn't wanted to see it. He defended his son. What else could he do? Danny was his kid.

But the day Sherry left, she told him, "You'd better open your eyes, Walt. There's something in him that you're not seeing, or not admitting is there. He's going to go too far one of these days, and I'm not going to be here when he does."

Had Walt given Danny the perfect opportunity to fulfil Sherry's prophecy?

Was it too late to stop this? To make things right?

The more he thought about it, the more agitated Walt became. He felt like he couldn't get any air. He pulled at the collar of his shirt, but his breathing just became more labored. The room was getting hotter. Was the air conditioning broken? Why couldn't he take a deep breath? Why was sweat suddenly pouring down his face, his back?

Still gripping the burner phone, Walt fell to his knees. When a sharp pain ripped through his chest, he fell forward. His last thought before losing consciousness was of Sherry. He should have listened to her. He should've paid more attention to Danny and given more credence to the trouble he'd gotten into growing up, the things he did that just weren't right. He should have chosen Sherry and gotten help for his son.

"Sherry," he gasped. "There's no help for any of us now."

***

The background blurs as the camera focuses on the dishes set before the three judges. Christina's eyes widen. José licks his lips.

"The smell in this studio right now is enough to make me feel like I've died and gone to Heaven," Christina says. "I cannot wait to try these, but everything is so beautiful, I almost don't want to cut into them!"

"Look at the dark, rich coloring on that Cornish game hen," Gideon remarks. "I don't know that I've ever seen better. It looks like the cover of a magazine. I just hope it's juicy inside. With such perfectly cooked, aesthetically amazing skin, I can't help but worry that the meat will be dry and overcooked."

The camera pans to Kayla, whose expression gives nothing away.

"Better than undercooked," says José. "But not by much."

"Okay, well, we've got lots to judge here, so let's get started," Gideon reminds them. "For the appetizer, we have mac and cheese bites, not something I normally see in a gourmet, restaurant-quality meal. If these are dry, they'll be inedible. If they're too rich, they'll upset the balance between appetizer and main course."

"They're just beautiful, though," Christina says. "So much color. And look at this crispy outer layer topped with cheesy shells. I can't wait to try one."

The camera shows all three chefs each picking up a mac and cheese bite and popping it into his or her mouth.

"Mmm… These taste even better than they look," Christina says, as the camera zooms to show her rolling the appetizer around in her mouth. "Creamy and cheesy, but with a wonderful savory flavor."

"I can taste the paprika, chives, and garlic. Amazing," Gideon says. "And the crispy outside and creamy inside are absolutely perfect."

"I agree," says José "Delicious."

"Moving on to the main course," Gideon says as the camera focuses on the shiny dark-skinned game hen garnished with rosemary sprigs and surrounded by carrots, red potatoes, and slices of apple. Gideon slices open the chicken, and clear juices run out onto the plate. "Beautiful. Look at those glistening juices. My mouth is watering."

The camera focuses on a pair of hands carefully slicing the meat, placing it delicately on a plate with a slice of skin, and then adding several vegetables.

José takes the first bite, going for the vegetables before the poultry. "This is a sumptuous honey mustard glaze." he says. "Genius. Not simply vegetables cooked with chicken, these glazed beauties add a whole new dimension to the meal."

"I taste ginger," remarks Christina. "Along with red pepper and curry. What a nice combination with the honey mustard."

"And look at this," Gideon says as the camera focuses on the apple slice he moves across the plate. "She's added apples to the vegetables for the fiber instead of a green." He stabs it with his fork and lifts it to his mouth. "Wonderful. Just wonderful."

"And the meat is so juicy and tender and full of flavor," Christina adds. "The rosemary, and oh, the balsamic vinegar. Who thinks to add that to baked or roasted poultry? Just magnificent."

"Kayla," Gideon says. "You have outdone yourself."

"Thank you, Chef."

"What gave you the idea to add the apples?" José asks.

"Well, Chef, I have boys, and when they were younger, it was impossible to get them to eat green vegetables, but they loved apples. I found all kinds of ways to incorporate apples, so they were getting that infusion of fiber they needed."

"Love it," says Christina.

"Brilliant," agrees Gideon. "Now, on to dessert. We have a homemade peach pie with French vanilla ice cream a la mode and a sweet bourbon sauce."

"You had me at peach pie," José says, putting a large bite into his mouth.

"Oh, this is county fair blue ribbon quality pie," Christina says. "And I judged a lot of county fairs in my early years."

"I was surprised you went with store-bought ice cream over making your own whipping cream," Gideon says. "But this bourbon sauce takes it to the next level. Well done."

"Thank you, Chef." Kayla beams into the camera.

Gideon huffs out a breath. "And now, we move on to something completely different. Rather than a hearty dinner that satisfies on a cold winter evening, we have a light and tangy shrimp pasta primavera, perfect for a summer evening."

Lorenzo stands stoic as always. The only sign he might be nervous is a quick inward roll of his lips.

"Look at those shrimp," Christina says as the camera moves in to showcase the plate. "Such beautiful coloring, bright orange with lots of picture-perfect white flesh. They look to be cooked just perfectly."

"And the golden-brown mushrooms, bright green asparagus, and beautiful diced tomatoes blended with angel hair pasta," José says. "It's a cookbook picture for sure. All the right colors with a sprinkling of parmesan cheese."

"Pecorino Romano," Lorenzo says, then clears his throat.

"He knows his Italian cheeses," Gideon says with a chuckle.

"Even better." José nods to Lorenzo.

"First," Gideon says. "We have caponata with homemade crostini."

The camera pans to the appetizer and holds while three hands pick up crostini and dig into the bowl.

"Oh, super tasty," Christina says. "Eggplant, capers, olives, celery, bell pepper, and, wait. Do I taste raisins? Mmm, wonderful. I love it."

"The combination of olive oil, red wine vinegar, and honey give this an amazing flavor," Gideon says.

"And the homemade crostini is perfect," José adds.

Lorenzo cracks a quick smile then returns to his poker face demeanor, revealing nothing about the state of his nerves.

"I can't wait to dig into this pasta," Christina says, twirling the angel hair on her fork, ensuring she has some of each ingredient in the bite. She chews and nods emphatically, swallowing before she speaks. "So flavorful, just an explosion on my palate."

"Very little seasoning," Gideon says. "And it doesn't need more. The flavors of the shrimp, asparagus, and mushrooms blend perfectly. Just a hint of red pepper, basil, oregano, thyme, and parsley really add to the overall essence of the dish."

"And what do we have for dessert?" José asks.

"We have a freshly made granita with ice, lemon, and sugar," Gideon tells them. "Simple yet elegant."

"And the perfect dessert for a garlicky seafood pasta," Christina says. "A good palate cleanser with a tangy, refreshing taste." She takes a spoonful. "And this does not disappoint."

"Lorenzo, you really stuck to your roots throughout this competition," Gideon remarks. "No taking chances, going out on a limb?"

"No, Chef. I decided early in the competition that this is really about the menus we prepare and serve in our businesses and what we want the public to see. I tried to experiment a little here and there, but it was the customer favorites that really served me well throughout this whole thing."

"Wise choice," Gideon says. "You'll have people flocking to your restaurant. Speziato, which means spicy, right?"

"Yes, Chef."

"I know you just opened this year. From what I've seen, you'll be very successful. Good luck."

"Thank you, chef."

Gideon turns to Kayla. "Kayla, you never failed to impress us. I can see why your catering business serving comfort food is so popular. You never participated in even one elimination round. Amazing."

Kayla flashes a radiant smile. "Thank you, Chef. I missed having my husband here as my cooking partner, but I know that I'm leaving with an even bigger family than I had before." She sniffs and blinks, and a tear flows down her cheek. She laughs and wipes it away.

"Okay, then," Gideon says. "It's time for us to deliberate. It's not going to be an easy decision. Hold tight."

Kayla and Lorenzo hug and wish each other good luck as the camera pans from them to the exiting judges.

***

Holly watched Jerry bang on the door over and over.

"I told you," she said. "He's not answering. I've been banging on it for five minutes. He's going to miss the finale."

"Walt, open up," Jerry yelled. "The bus is here. We've got to go."

"Should I get someone from the office?" Holly asked.

Jerry tried to peer through the window. "Are you sure you haven't seen him today?"

"Not since breakfast. You?"

Jerry shook his head. "I don't think so. He wasn't at lunch." He banged on the door again. "Yeah, go see if you can find someone to let us in."

Holly ran as quickly as she could to the office. "Help!" she called as she entered. "We need help. We can't find Walt, and he's not answering his door. We were supposed to be on the bus five minutes ago. We're going to hold up the final taping."

"Oh my. I'm coming." Peg, the woman who owned the Harbor, grabbed a set of keys and followed Holly to Walt's bungalow. She inserted the key into the lock and pushed open the door.

Holly gasped, and Jerry shoved his way inside. He felt Walt's pulse before yelling for someone to call 911 and beginning CPR.

"Walt, Walt, can you hear me?" Jerry tapped Walt's arm, but Walt remained unresponsive. Jerry tilted back his head, checked his airway, and began breathing into his mouth.

Holly dropped beside Jerry. Peg stood in the doorway talking to the 911 operator. When Jerry finished administering rescue breaths into Walt's lungs, Holly took over, giving chest compressions. All her years of training as a Girl Scout and a summer camp counselor came back to her as she tried to pump air in and out of his lungs. She and Jerry continued their back-and-forth rhythm until the EMTs arrived.

Holly looked up and gave her friend, Tori, a grateful look. "You've got to help him."

"How long has he been like this?"

"We don't know," Holly told her. "We just found him."

Bob appeared in the door as Holly and Jerry backed up, and Tori and Jimmy went to work on Walt.

"Holly?"

"Bob, is the bus still here? What should we do?" She looked from him to Jerry.

"Go," Peg said. "Walt would want you all to go."

"She's right," Jerry said. "We can't do anything for him now. He's in good hands."

"I'll let Peg know what happens," Tori told them as she took a break from using the manual pulmonary resuscitator so that Jimmy could do compressions. "She can get word to you."

Holly nodded then stood. The three of them joined the others on the bus and let them know what was going on. The short ride to the community center was completely silent.

*****

Angela rushed into the clinic after receiving the call about her father. She hadn't been able to locate Danny, and she had no idea where he could be if he wasn't at the restaurant. When she arrived, she found Nick and Paul waiting outside her father's door.

"What's going on?" She asked. "Why are you here?"

"Angela," Paul spoke. "We're sorry about your father. We're trying to find Danny. Have you seen him?"

A cold chill made its way down her back. How many years had she dreaded this? How long had she known this day would come? Perhaps since the day Danny threatened to kill her dog if she told on him for stealing from their first stepmother's wallet. Angela always knew she should have told her father what Danny was really like, but truthfully, she was afraid of him.

"What's he done?" she asked.

"We just need to talk to him," Paul said. "Do you know where he is?"

Angela shook her head. "I've been trying to reach him myself. Now, if you'll excuse me, I'd like to talk to the doctor."

"Just one more question," Paul asked. "Do you recognize this?" He held out a small flip phone, the kind she rarely saw anyone use anymore.

"I'm sorry," she said, shaking her head. "I don't. Why?"

"Your father had it with him when he was found."

"No, that can't be. They weren't allowed to have phones." A sick feeling came over her.

Oh, Daddy, what have you done? What did Danny talk you into doing?

"I…I have to go. My dad…"

"Of course," Paul said, backing away from the door. "Again, we're very sorry."

"Angela!" A voice rang out in the hallway, and Angela turned to see Sherry, her father's third wife.

Relief washed over her. She knew Sherry would come. Sherry was the one Angela had felt closest to of either of her stepmothers, and with Angela's mother gone, Sherry remained the only woman Walt loved as much as his daughter.

Chapter Sixteen

Lorenzo knew something was wrong as soon as the doors opened, and the others came in. They shouted and cheered and made all the appropriate gestures, but something was off. One look at Holly, and he knew he wasn't wrong. Her eyes held a sadness he couldn't understand. He was certain it had nothing to do with him or the show, and he wished he could talk to her before the taping resumed.

It was after several more moments that Lorenzo realized someone was missing. He scanned the faces, naming each person in is mind. Where was Walt? Was he the reason Holly looked sad, Jerry looked distracted, and both Bob and Jane kept looking at each other with worry in their eyes?

"Your friends and colleagues, now former competitors, are here to witness the naming of the first winner of *Neighbor vs. Neighbor*." Even Gideon seemed off, his voice not quite normal. Lorenzo couldn't decipher exactly what was wrong, but Gideon seemed either irritated or upset. He kept clenching his jaw, and his eyes were intense. His hands balled into fists repetitively, and he kept rubbing his temple.

"So, uh, are you ready for the big reveal?"

Everyone cheered, but when Lorenzo and Kayla looked at each other, he saw the question in her eyes. Herr body was rigid, and her brown eyes flashed with an acknowledgment that she felt it, too. He swallowed and focused on Kayla.

"It wasn't easy, coming up with a winner. You were both fantastic throughout the competition. Lorenzo, I look forward to eating at Speziato and taking my whole crew for dinner. Kayla, we'll have to talk about a catered party I may be having later this summer." Everyone laughed, and that seemed to break the tension. Gideon smiled. "I think you're both incredible chefs with impeccable understanding of what makes a meal outstanding. Unfortunately, only one of you will be receiving $300,000 and a year's worth of advertising during all my shows."

Gideon looked at Christina to his right and José to his left. "We're all in agreement, right?"

"We are, Gideon," Christina said. "And as difficult as it was, I'm really excited about the show's first winner."

"The winner of the first season of *Neighbor vs. Neighbor* is…"

Gideon looked back and forth between Lorenzo and Kayla, and Lorenzo held his breath in anticipation. No matter the outcome, this had been a life-changing experience for him in so many ways. He felt like he'd already won.

"Kayla Middleton!"

The entire room broke out in applause, and Kayla slapped her hands over her face, her whole body shaking as her tears poured. When she took her hands away, she looked at Lorenzo with such admiration, he couldn't help but reach for her and wrap his arms around her.

"Congratulations, Kayla. You deserve it."

"Thank you. I can't believe it. This is like a dream come true." She sniffed and wiped her cheeks before turning toward the judges. "Thank you. You have no idea what this means to me."

"I think we do," Christina laughed. "I think we all do."

Lorenzo watched as Kayla hugged the three judges, and then the others were urged to join in the celebration. Lorenzo shook hands with Jerry and Bob. Jake pulled him into a huge hug as did Jane and Dawn. Robby gave him a manly hug and pat on the back before Cynthia hugged him and planted a big kiss on his lips. When she pulled back, he met Holly's eyes, which were dancing with amusement. He opened his arms, and she walked into them.

"I'm so happy for Kayla, but I'm happy for you, too. You made it to the final show, and I'm so proud of you."

The merriment continued for a good ten minutes before Gideon raised his hand and gestured for them all to quiet down. At some point, filming had stopped, but Lorenzo didn't know when.

"Okay, well, I hate to end these festivities on a down note, but I guess it must be done."

Lorenzo felt Holly's hand slip into his and give it a squeeze. He looked down at her, and her eyes, so bright and happy a few minutes before, clouded with sadness.

"I've got to be honest. I've never had this many things go wrong while filming a show. If it didn't mean I would be unable to showcase some amazing chefs on this beautiful island, I would cancel the series altogether." Gideon shook his head and looked down at the floor for several moments before looking up and continuing.

"There are a few things you all know about and several things you don't. That wasn't an easy decision, but it was made by me and by your loved ones with your best interests in mind."

Lorenzo and Holly exchanged worried looks, and he felt her hand tighten in his.

"Holly," Gideon looked at her, and Lorenzo felt her stiffen. "At the beginning of the competition, the electricity was turned off at your café. You lost everything in the walk-in and freezer, but your staff rallied, and the café never closed. After some investigating, following other incidents over the last two weeks, the police don't think it was turned off by accident."

"What? I mean, how? What happened?"

"They believe your restaurant was sabotaged."

Holly gasped. "What? Why? By whom?"

"Dawn," Gideon said without answering Holly's questions.

"My restaurant, too?"

Gideon nodded. "Yes. All your wine bottles were smashed, all the wine, gone."

"What?"

"And Anna's?" Jerry asked.

"Anna's place was part of it. A gas burner was left on overnight that could have killed her family while they slept."

Several gasps rang out.

"That's why she left. We had to tell her. Her husband insisted. And at Kayla's house—"

"My house?" Kayla asked, panic in her voice. "My boys? Zach?"

Gideon held out his hands. "Everyone is okay. Someone thought it would be a good idea to release bugs into your food storage area. Luckily, your husband heard them and was able to salvage most of it."

"Did he catch them?"

"No, I'm afraid not. Which is how they got away with all this and more."

Everyone waited for Gideon to explain.

"Lorenzo, yours was the tipping point, the one that made the police begin putting things together."

Lorenzo stood up straighter. "My place?"

"Someone tried to burn it down, but some local kids had decided to stake out the restaurants and witnessed it. They called it in, and nothing was damaged other than a dumpster and the outer brick wall. Everything inside remained untouched."

Lorenzo cursed under his breath.

"Local kids?" Kayla asked.

"I don't know any more than that," Gideon said. "Except they were pretty brave and apparently more intelligent than the police."

Lorenzo saw Holly and Kayla look at each other and grin. "Molly," Holly said, and Kayla nodded. "Probably."

"What else?" Bob asked.

"There was one other place that was hit," Gideon said. "At first, it was thought to be another target, but apparently, it was a ruse meant to throw off suspicion."

"Where?" Jerry asked, his voice tinged with anger.

"Well, that's where it gets complicated."

"It was someone here, wasn't it?" Jerry asked, his voice rising. "One of us was in on this, maybe planning it. Am I right? Someone who had a phone this whole time? Someone who had a phone in his hand this morning. Sheesh. I didn't even think about it at the time."

Lorenzo felt Holly pull away, and he looked at her as she spun around to face Jerry. She had gone white. "No, no it can't be. He—he…"

"Yes," said Gideon. "That's the assumption. Now, there isn't a lot of solid proof, but someone did have a phone."

"That son of a…" Jerry pounded his fist onto a counter. "He played us. He acted like he was our friend."

"I can't believe this. It can't be true," Holly said.

"Could someone please fill the rest of us in?" Jake asked.

"Walt," Holly said quietly. "I didn't see it, but I was so concerned with doing chest compressions, I wasn't paying attention to anything else."

Kayla looked from one to the other. "What about Walt? Where is he?"

"Walt had a heart attack this morning," Gideon said with a sigh.

"No!" Kayla said, her voice cracking. "But what is this about a phone?"

"I saw it," Jerry said. "He was clutching it when Holly and I tried to revive him."

"The only number he called was his son, um—"

"Danny," Bob said. "That's his name."

"Right," Gideon said, running his hand through his thick hair.

"And where's Danny now?" Jane asked.

"Nobody knows," Gideon told them. "The police can't find him."

"And how's Walt?" Holly asked.

"I'm sorry, folks. He's dead," Gideon told them. "He was dead before he got to the hospital."

Lorenzo saw Holly begin to crumple, and he caught her before she hit the floor. She folded herself into his arms and wept.

***

Rather than being taken home by the bus, they were all allowed to call someone to pick them up from the Harbor. They were supposed to be there for two more days, but they took out a challenge when Anna left, and Gideon's crew said they had enough film and didn't need any more. They had pre-taped both Lorenzo and Kayla being interviewed as the winner while the judges were deliberating. By that time, the judges knew about Walt, and it was decided they would not keep the actual winner for interviews after the results were announced.

Holly gathered her bags and left her key inside the room as instructed. She began walking, weighed down by the bags as well as Tang in his carrier, toward the entrance to the Harbor. Her head was full of so many revelations. She'd met Danny. He had gone to school with Taylor and was part of the local bar crowd. He'd said hi to Taylor, Dina, and Tori a few times when they'd been out.

"You okay?" Lorenzo asked, appearing by her side with his own bags in hand.

"Yeah. It's all just shocking."

"I know. I'm not sure what to do with all that we learned, and I'm equally not sure I'm ready to go back." He smiled at Holly. "At first, I really didn't want to do this, but I'm actually gonna miss it."

Holly smiled up at him. "Me, too." She thought back to earlier that morning. Was it only this morning? It seemed so long ago. "I'm going to be making some changes to my personal and professional lives."

"May I make a suggestion?" he asked.

"Okay," Holly said.

"I suggest you make some changes that involve dating a local chef. Someone tall, dark-haired, from a big family."

"You know, I was thinking the same thing. I thought I'd see what Jake has going on this weekend."

"Ha! I knew it. He has all the girls wrapped around his finger."

Holly laughed and shifted her heavy bags. "Only one, and it's not me. So, um, what are you doing this weekend? When you're not working, I mean."

"This weekend might be hard. I'll be trying to figure things out. But we're closed on Monday evenings."

"And I close at three on Mondays, so maybe we could think of something to do together?"

"Holly!"

Holly dropped her bags, set Tang's carrier beside them, and ran to her best friend. They hugged like they hadn't seen each other in years. Holly let go and looked over Taylor's shoulder.

"You have a lot to fill me in on," she said to Nick, who was leaning against his truck.

Taylor nudged Holly and nodded toward Lorenzo. "And I think you have a lot to fill me in on."

"That I do," Holly said with a wide grin. "I really do."

Nick walked over to Holly's bags and picked them up, looking up at Lorenzo as he did so.

"We'll talk," he said in his big brother-police officer warning voice, and Holly saw Lorenzo smile.

She went back to him and stood on tiptoe to give him a kiss on the cheek.

"We'll talk later?"

Lorenzo nodded but didn't have a chance to answer before his own name was called.

"Enzo!"

They both turned toward the woman getting out of a blue SUV. Not Antonia, Holly thought, remembering the youngest sibling from the restaurant. Marissa? She looked older than Holly thought she would.

"Mamma," Lorenzo said with a smile.

His mother hurried to him and pulled him into a hug. Lorenzo hugged her back.

"I didn't expect to see you."

"Your father and I wanted to be here when you came home." She turned to Holly. "And you are?" she asked with a smile.

"Mamma, this is Holly. She owns the Sand and Sugar Café. I think you'll be seeing a lot of her." Lorenzo smiled broadly at Holly.

The woman took Holly's hands into hers "It's so nice to meet you. I'm Maria, and I look forward to getting to know you."

Holly liked her instantly and smiled at her and then at Lorenzo. "Me, too," Holly said.

"I'll call you," Lorenzo told her, and gave her a hug and chaste kiss before loading his things into the car.

Holly climbed into the back of Nick's truck, closed the door, and looked at Nick in the rearview mirror.

"Start talking. What's going on with Walt's son? What happened while I was here? It sounds like everything went crazy."

Taylor turned around in her seat and looked at Holly. "Oh no, you go first. I want to know everything."

Holly grinned like the Cheshire cat. "What's everyone else doing tonight? I have a feeling you've already texted the group, and I have a lot to tell them."

***

Tara wrapped her arms around Gideon from behind as he zippered his suitcase.

"Can I make a suggestion?"

Gideon sighed. "Go ahead," he said, turning around in her arms so he faced her.

"No more coming up with business ideas when we're supposed to be on vacation."

Gideon smiled. "It's a promise."

She'd heard it before, and it was a promise she didn't expect him to keep, but for now, it was enough.

Epilogue

October

An eighties classic, Loverboy's *Heaven in Your Eyes*, played as the bride and groom swayed together on the dance floor. He stared down into her eyes, and she gazed up into his. Their road to happiness hadn't been paved with roses, yet here they were. Heartache and loss had, for a time, rendered them immune to love's bidding, but in the end, they couldn't resist its pull. He didn't think he could risk saying goodbye again, and she didn't think she could handle another person leaving her, but life put them in just the right place at just the right time, and that place and time led them to each other.

Holly smiled up at Lorenzo, and just then, her stomach growled. She laughed.

"I haven't eaten anything since this morning, and even then, it was only a pastry and a cup of coffee. The wedding party devoured everything in a matter of minutes."

"Come on," Lorenzo said, taking her hand and leading her to the appetizer spread. "Everything looks great," he said to Dawn.

"Thank you. I'm just so happy to be here and be able to contribute. I'm really happy with the appetizers. I just wish…"

Holly reached for her hand. "I know. Me, too. He wasn't all that bad. I think he really came to regret what he did."

"I think so, too. It's that son of his who was really at fault. I'm glad they caught him."

"And with his confession that it was all his idea and that his father asked him not to continue, Walt gets a pass from me," Lorenzo said, reaching for a crab-stuffed mushroom.

The crowd began to clap. Lorenzo, Holly, and Dawn turned toward the dance floor.

"Could we have everyone in the bridal party join us on the dance floor?" the DJ said into the microphone.

"I guess that's us," Lorenzo said. Holly scooped up a crab ball and popped it into her mouth, followed by another, before taking his hand and letting him lead her to the dance floor.

Dawn followed and was met on the floor by Jerry, who left the rest of the dinner preparations to his sous chef. Jake, host of the rehearsal dinner the night before, and Cynthia, whose new videographer followed closely, left their respective dates to take their place with the others. Anna, who had hosted the bachelorette party, and Robby, who was hosting the day-after brunch, joined them along with Kayla, wedding coordinator, and Jane's son, Ted. Bob's daughter and her husband were the last to make it to the floor. They were all handed glasses of champagne and raised them together.

"A toast to Bob and Jane," the DJ said.

Everyone downed their champagne and handed off their glasses as the music began to play for their dance.

"Are the desserts ready?" Holly asked Lorenzo.

"They're ready and being chilled," he assured her.

"This has been the best day ever," Holly said, looking back at Bob and Jane.

"They look really happy."

"They are really happy," Holly said wistfully. She turned back to Lorenzo. "So am I."

When the song stopped, Lorenzo took her hand and led her away from the crowd.

"Where are we going?" Holly asked.

"You'll see, but don't worry. We'll be back in time for dinner."

He led her down a path to a small dock that extended out onto the water. Holly gasped as she gazed across the channel.

The sky was a pallet of color—dark blue, light blue, white, and the palest of yellows. Just above the water, the horizon was deep red topped by a slash of orange that faded into a golden yellow. There wasn't the slightest breeze to cause a ripple, and the smooth plate-glass water mirrored a perfect image of the sky.

"It's breathtaking," Holly whispered.

"I agree," Lorenzo said. "Breathtaking."

She turned toward him, and the light of the sunset shined in his eyes.

"I don't want to take away from Bob and Jane," he said, "so I'd like to keep this quiet for tonight."

"Keep what quiet?" she asked.

Lorenzo genuflected in front of her and held out a small, black box.

"Holly, I know it's only been four months since we met, but I firmly believe that God put you in my life for this moment and forever. If you'll take me, I'd like to bring you into my crazy, mixed-up family and make you the promise that you'll never be left alone ever again."

Holly wiped away a tear, and in front of God's masterpiece painting of a magnificent Chincoteague sunset, she said, "Yes."

Chincoteague Sunsets Books Three,
Coming Soon…

Acknowledgements

I can't do what I do without the help of so many. We always hear that authors are solitary creatures, but I don't believe that is true at all. Yes, I sit alone in my office all day as I write, but I am in touch constantly with a whole team of people. They are as much a part of this work as I am, and they contribute to every step of the writing process.

Anne and Mom, thank you for reading all my books, chapter by chapter, throughout the whole writing process, and letting me know what works and what doesn't. Rebecca, thank you for lending me your reality cooking show expertise every time I texted or called and asked my many questions! Jeanne, thank you for pre-reading my book and helping make it better!

Cayley, thank you for signing on as my editor. I see a prosperous career in editing and writing in your future! Pat, you are the absolute best cover creator ever! I love seeing how you take those incoherent thoughts in my mind and turn them into a stunning representation of my work. Thank you both!

Katie Ann, thank you for your willingness to help me with my online presence even when I come up with crazy ideas that may not work. You always find a way to make my vision possible. Morgan, thank you for attending shows with me, for sharing my books with everyone you meet, and for sharing with me, in such a special way, a deep and beautifully inspiring love for our faith.

Ken, thank you for your never-ending support, encouragement, and love. You are my rock.

About the Author

Amy began writing as a child and never stopped. She wrote articles for magazines and newspapers before writing children's books and adult fiction. A graduate of the University of Maryland with a Master of Library and Information Science, Amy worked as a librarian for fifteen years and, in 2010, began writing full time.

Amy Schisler writes inspirational women's fiction for people of all ages. She has published two children's books and numerous novels, including the award-winning Picture Me, Whispering Vines, and the Chincoteague Island Trilogy. A former librarian, Amy enjoys a busy life on the Eastern Shore of Maryland.

The recipient of numerous national literary awards, including the Illumination Award, LYRA award, Independent Publisher Book Award, International Digital Award, and the Golden Quill Award as well as honors from the Catholic Press Association and the Eric Hoffer Book Award, Amy's writing has been hailed "a verbal masterpiece of art" (author Alexa Jacobs) and "Everything you want in a book" (Amazon reviewer). Amy's books are available internationally, wherever books are sold, in print and eBook formats.

Follow Amy at:
http://amyschislerauthor.com
http://facebook.com/amyschislerauthor
https://twitter.com/AmySchislerAuth
https://www.goodreads.com/amyschisler

Book Club Discussion Questions

1. Are you a cooking show fanatic? What did you think of the premise of Gideon's new show? Did you know any of the insider secrets revealed in the book?

2. Small towns can be known for being both close-knit and back-stabbing. If a show like this were to take place in a small town with which you are familiar, how do you think it would turn out? Would the contestants end up best friends or bitter enemies?

3. Lorenzo and Walt both had something in common. Both men believed they were imposters in their field and in their family. We often see families like theirs—a family of doctors, a family of teachers, a family of chefs. Do you think there is often someone in the family who doesn't feel he or she is living up to the family name and reputation? How do you think that plays out in their personal and professional lives?

4. Holly and Lorenzo each suffered broken hearts which affected their outlooks and behaviors and helped them grow as persons. Did a broken heart change the way you see yourself or the world? How did it help you grow as a person? Would you go back and change that time if you could?

5. Many of the single participants paired off during their isolation. Do you think this is normal human behavior?

What do you think their odds of staying together are? Why or why now?

6. Though Holly has a close group of girlfriends on the island, she discovers the joy and importance of connecting with women outside of her regular group of friends. Do you have real friends, not just acquaintances, of different ages and backgrounds? Why do you think this is important?

7. Belonging is one of the five essential needs as taught by psychologist Abraham Maslow. According to his Hierarchy of Needs, friendship, intimacy, family, and a sense of connection are some of the central prerequisites for happiness and are necessary components of life which must be obtained before we can reach our full potential as human beings. How are Holly and Lorenzo, as individuals and not a couple, examples of this teaching?

8. What is your specialty in the kitchen? Did it come from someone or something special to you? Tell us about it!

9. What do you think prompted both Holly and Lorenzo to reassess their spirituality and not only return to the Church but to begin with a good confession? How do you think being in the competition, staying in isolation, and connecting with their peers contributed to this?

10. In their time at the resort, Holly and Lorenzo realize they don't leave time in their busy lives to enjoy the activities they love. After the competition, they vow to change that. When was the last time you reassessed your life to ensure you are doing the things you love. What would you make room for in your schedule?

Just for fun: Molly—who first appeared in *Seeking Tranquility*—has become my readers most beloved character in all my books. She's still too young for romance, but what kind of man do you think would sweep her off her feet and be able to keep up with her intellect?